DISNEY

A WHOLE NEW WORLD

LIZ BRASWELL

D1514013

AUTUMN
PUBLISHING

AUTUMN
PUBLISHING

Published in 2020
First published in the UK by Autumn Publishing
An imprint of Igloo Books Ltd
Cottage Farm, NN6 0BJ, UK
Owned by Bonnier Books
Sveavägen 56, Stockholm, Sweden
www.igloobooks.com

Autumn is an imprint of Bonnier Books UK

0920 001
2 4 6 8 10 9 7 5 3 1
ISBN 978-1-80022-086-7

Printed and manufactured in Italy

Photo credit: Alice Licht

After the sort of introverted childhood you would expect from a writer, Liz Braswell earned a degree in Egyptology at Brown University and then promptly spent the next ten years producing video games. Finally, she caved in to fate and wrote Snow and Rx under the name Tracy Lynn, followed by the Nine Lives of Chloe King series under her real name, because by then the assassins hunting her were all dead. Liz is also the author of Once Upon a Dream: A Twisted Tale. She lives in Brooklyn with a husband, two children, a cat, a part-time dog, three fish and five coffee trees she insists will start producing beans any day. You can e-mail her at me@lizbraswell.com or tweet @LizBraswell.

For my son Alex — who is not, technically, a scamp and is now old enough to read the books I write. Enjoy!

Additional thanks to David Kazemi for details that helped bring ancient Agrabah to life, even if we can't agree on what makes a good baklava.
— L.B.

Prologue

A HIGH WHITE MOON cast its light on the city below as brightly as the sun was said to shine in northern countries. White mud-brick buildings gleamed like pebbles from a faraway beach. The golden onion domes of the capital glittered like a dream against the pale dunes and the dark, starry void.

The heat of the day had long since retreated into the desert, and the city, which had drowsed through the hot afternoon, was finally coming alive. The streets filled with people drinking tea and gossiping, laughing and visiting friends. Old men played *chatrang* on boards set up outside cafés; children stayed up long past their bedtimes playing their own games on the pavements. Men and women bought rose-flavoured ices and trinkets from night-time vendors. Life was noisy and exuberant in moonlit Agrabah.

Well, not everywhere in Agrabah.

In another part of town, the streets were silent as shadow and black as death. It was not safe for any of the gaily dressed people to be there. Even the locals tended to stay indoors or stick to the unseen alleyways and secret passages that riddled the area out of view from the streets. Here the white walls of the buildings were faded and pitted, mud peeling away from their brick underlayers in great swathes. Half-built timber structures were the only evidence of an ancient sultan's dream to improve the district, to widen the roads, to bring in water. After he was poisoned, the whole project was dropped. Now the skeletal remains of his grand plan whistled in the desert wind.

This was the quarter of the Street Rats.

This was where thieves, beggars, murderers and the poorest of the poor lived. The children no one wanted, the adults no one would hire for any kind of honest work; all of them made their homes there. The orphaned, the unlucky, the sick and the discarded. It was a whole other Agrabah.

Among the huts and hovels, the falling-down public buildings, and the decaying houses of worship was one tiny home that was in slightly better repair than the others. Its mud walls looked like they had been whitewashed at least once in the past decade. A broken urn outside the door contained a clutch of desert blooms, kept alive by someone's regular application of precious water. A proper rug, albeit in tatters, lay in front for visitors to leave their sandals on in the unlikely event they owned a pair.

Through a keyhole-shaped window, passers-by could hear the soft sounds of a woman humming. If they peeked through the wooden screen, they would see her: a kind-eyed woman who wore her rags with the grace of a queen. Her clothes were clean, as was the pair of trousers she was carefully mending in the shaft of moonlight that came through the window.

A loud knocking sounded on her door. Three strikes, and very powerful. No one in the Street Rat district knocked like that. It was always furtive, and often in code.

The lady looked surprised but carefully set down her work and adjusted her headscarf before approaching the door.

"Who is it?" she called, fingers on the handle.

"It's me, Mum," said a voice.

The woman smiled with pleasure and unhooked the latch.

"But, Aladdin," she admonished laughingly, opening the door, "you know better than to…"

She stopped when she realised *four* people were standing in the doorway.

One was her son, Aladdin. He was scrawny, like all the children of Street Rats. Barefoot, with dark skin and thick raven-black hair like his father's, which was covered in the dust of the street. He held himself as his mother had taught him: head high, chest up. Street Rat in name only.

His friends, *if* she could use that word, stood a little to the side, giggling and looking ready to bolt. If there was trouble, of *course* Morgiana and Duban would be involved. Aladdin's mother clenched her teeth at their sly eyes and obvious zeal to get away.

Behind Aladdin stood a tall, skinny man in a long blue robe and matching turban. Akram, the dried-fruit and nut seller. He had her son's shoulder in a bony grip that threatened to tighten if the boy so much as thought about escaping.

"Your son," Akram said politely but angrily, "and his… compatriots. Once again they were at the market, stealing. Empty your pockets, Street Rat."

Aladdin shrugged endearingly. As he did, he pulled the insides of his pockets out, revealing dried figs and dates. He was not so careless as to let them fall to the floor, however.

"Aladdin!" his mother said sharply. "You wicked boy! I'm so sorry, good sir. Tomorrow Aladdin will run errands for you all day. Whatever you want. He will fetch you water."

Aladdin started to protest, but a look from his mother silenced him. Duban and Morgiana laughed at him.

"And you two should, as well," she added.

"You're not my mother," Morgiana said insolently. "You can't tell me what to do. No one can."

"It's unfortunate you *don't* have a mother like this poor woman," Akram said sternly. "You will wind up with your head on a spike before you're 16, girl."

Morgiana stuck out her tongue at him.

"Come on," Duban said, a little nervous. "Let's get out of here."

The two scampered off into the night. Aladdin looked after them dolefully, abandoned by his friends to punishments they all deserved.

"You would do well to avoid their company, I think," Akram said thoughtfully. "But all *three* of you are lucky it was I who caught you, and not another. There are *some* vendors who would demand your hand in payment for the fruit you stole."

"Here, let me wrap up your goods to take back with you," Aladdin's mother said, taking the fruit from her son and looking around for a suitable cloth to hold it.

"That's all right," Akram said uncomfortably. His eyes darted around the tiny, dark hovel. "I have already packed up for the day. And a hardworking woman who is so... *alone* shouldn't be punished for the sins of another. Consider it a gift."

Aladdin's mother's eyes flashed.

"I do not need your charity. My husband will return any day now," she said. "Cassim will have made his fortune and will take us to a place more fitting for his family. I'm just ashamed of what he has to come back to in the meantime."

"Of course, of course," Akram said soothingly. "I... eagerly await seeing him again. He loved my cashews."

Aladdin's mother basked in the glow of someone else's memory of her husband.

Aladdin slumped. Akram's hand returned to his shoulder, but instead of the hard pinch of an angry captor, it gave the nervous pat of someone who felt sorry for the boy.

This only made Aladdin feel worse.

"*Here now*, is everything all right?"

A market guard, one of the younger ones, strode out of the night. He held a cudgel in his hand and had a serious look in his eye. "I heard there was a disturbance at your tent, Akram."

"It is nothing, Rasoul," the merchant said, just as soothingly as he had talked to Aladdin's mother. "A misunderstanding. It is all sorted now. Thank you for your concern."

The guard, whose only sin seemed to be indulging in a little too much pastry, did not press the matter as other guards might have. He saw the quietly determined woman, the dejected-looking Aladdin, the poverty of the house.

"All right, then. Akram, I will walk you back to your tent. This is not a safe place for respectable people like yourself to be at night."

"A thousand thanks, Rasoul." Akram gave Aladdin's mother a bow. "Peace be upon you."

"And to you," she said, nodding her head. "And... thanks."

When the merchant and the guard left, she closed the door wearily and ran a hand through her son's hair.

"Aladdin, what are we to do with you?"

"What?" he demanded, no longer slumped but grinning like a thief and jumping up and down with excitement. "Everything worked out! And look! We have a feast tonight!"

He excitedly pulled more figs and dates out of his pockets and put them in a chipped bowl. And then, from the sash that held up his trousers, he pulled fresh almonds and smoked pistachios... and from somewhere under his scrap of a shirt, cashews.

"Aladdin!" His mother admonished him, but she was trying not to chuckle.

"I did it for *you*, Mum. You deserve a treat. You never get anything for yourself."

"Oh, Aladdin, I don't need anything. Except you," she said, taking him in her arms and holding him tightly against her.

"Mum," Aladdin whispered into her robes. "I've *seen* you give me the biggest part of whatever we have to eat. It's not fair. I just want to take care of you."

"There are a lot of things that aren't fair, Aladdin."

She drew back from him, still holding his hands, and looked into his eyes.

"That's just the way life is which is why it's so important for Street Rats to take care of each other. That's a good instinct you have. You should always look out for your friends and your family. Because no one is looking out for us.

"But that doesn't mean you should become a *thief*."

Aladdin looked at the ground, chagrined.

She put her hand under his chin to make him look up at her.

"Don't let life's unfairness, don't let how *poor* you are decide *who* you are. *You* choose who you will be, Aladdin. Will you be a hero who looks after the weak and powerless? Will you be a thief? Will you be a beggar or worse? It's up to *you*, not the things or people around you. You can choose to be something more."

He nodded, lip trembling. He was too old to cry. He *was*.

His mother kissed him again and sighed, then moved past him to examine the fruit.

"Maybe it's because you're just alone here with your

mother all the time," she said, partly to herself. "You don't have any playmates except for those good-for-nothings Duban and Morgiana. You need a real friend, or maybe a pet, or something. Yes, a pet…"

But Aladdin wasn't listening.

He moved to the window and pushed aside the screen. This was the best, the only good thing about their house: due to a trick in the zigzag streets, they had a perfect view of the castle.

He looked at the white towers, even whiter under the moonlight, the glittering onion domes, the colourful flags flying from spires so pointy and perfect they looked like they could pierce the sky itself.

You can choose to be something more…

All This for a Loaf of Bread

PERHAPS THERE WAS a moon in the sky somewhere, but her brother the sun ruled now, and everything faded into the whiteness of the hot day which was even hotter on a glaringly bright sun-bleached roof.

"Safe!" Aladdin said with a big grin, clutching his dearly gotten treasure. He took a quick look over the edge of the building to make sure no one saw him up there, his dark arms flexing with easy strength as he held his chest off the rough bricks. Then he sat down, relaxed, getting ready to break his precious prize in half. His large, clear brown eyes twinkled in happy expectation. "One loaf of bread. More valuable than all the cold, glittering gems at the bazaar."

The little monkey next to him chattered in anticipation.

Abu had been a last gift from his mother. Aladdin's father, of course, had never come back from 'seeking his fortune abroad'. Aladdin had never believed in that fairy tale anyway, so it was no great loss. But his mother had been afraid of his becoming too wild, too much of a loner without a real family. She'd thought a pet would tame him.

And perhaps it had…

…except that he stole for *both* of them now.

"And lunch is finally served," Aladdin said, gesturing at his friend with the bread.

"Stop, thief!"

Abu fled. Aladdin leaped up.

Somehow the market guards had actually managed to clamber up the ladder onto the roof behind him. Two had made it up already, with an enraged Rasoul following close behind. These days he wore the striped turban crowned with a black onyx that marked him as a captain of the guard. Despite their run-ins, even Aladdin had to admit that the man had risen honestly through the ranks.

But that didn't mean Aladdin *liked* him.

"I'll have your hands for a trophy, Street Rat!" Rasoul bellowed. He puffed as he dragged himself up the ladder.

He must have been doubly annoyed by the effort

he had to expend to get up there.

"All this for a loaf of bread?" Aladdin asked, exasperated. He had specifically chosen to lift it from one of the carts loaded up for a royal outing, a picnic for the sultan, for one of his desert kite-flying romps or something equally ridiculous. As fat as he was, one tiny sultan couldn't possibly have missed one little loaf of bread.

But apparently the guards could. And under the law, if an accuser chose to, he could have a thief's hand chopped off in punishment.

And Rasoul's scimitar was looking particularly shiny and pointy in the sunlight at the moment.

So Aladdin leaped off the side of the building.

Aladdin was many things: quick, strong, clever, agile, fast-thinking, nimble.

He was *not* rash.

So while the guards stopped short, shocked at what seemed like a deadly, incredibly insane act, an only mildly nervous Aladdin plummeted down towards the street, grabbing at the clotheslines he knew would be there.

There was, of course, always the chance that the ropes wouldn't hold.

But Aladdin had luck on his side; throwing his hands out resulted in being hit in the head by clean laundry and getting rope burns as he slowed his descent. When it grew too painful to bear, he let go and landed with a bruising, bony crash on the dusty street.

There was no time to reflect on his safety, his luck or any injuries that would have to be looked at later. He had to plan his next move immediately, to stay one step ahead of the guards who would be hurrying back down to see what had happened to him.

The Widow Gulbahar's robes were tangled around him. It occurred to Aladdin that if no one saw, he could easily wrap himself up in them and disguise himself as a pious albeit ugly girl and sneak out through one of the harems.

He paused as loud feminine laughter erupted above him.

He looked up to see the widow herself leaning out of a window and smiling not unkindly at him. Two other women stood nearby, where they'd been enjoying a good gossip before his exciting arrival. That would be their only pleasure today before the task of finding food, and work, began.

"Isn't it a little early for you to be in trouble already, Aladdin?" Gulbahar teased.

"You're... ouch... only in trouble... ouch... if you get *caught*," Aladdin protested, trying not to show pain as he rose and joined them. He hoped they'd taken the hint as he swirled a cloth around his head and neck. He leaned on the wall in what he hoped was a feminine way, throwing his hips out and keeping his back to the end of the alley where the guards would enter.

Gulbahar rolled her eyes and shook her head.

"Aladdin, you've got to settle down," she sighed. "Get a nice girl. She'll sort you out."

The other women nodded in agreement. They knew about nice girls though they could not have passed as 'nice' themselves. But they had to eat, and often in Agrabah nice girls didn't.

"*There he is!*" Rasoul suddenly called out. He and a whole squad of guards stomped down the alley, closing off Aladdin's exit.

"*Now* I'm in trouble," Aladdin said.

He turned to go, but Rasoul must have put all his remaining anger and energy into one furious lunge. He managed to grab Aladdin's arm and spun him round.

"*This* time, Street Rat, I'll—"

But before he could finish his threat, a screaming little monkey leaped onto his head and tore at his eyes with sharp claws.

"Perfect timing, Abu," Aladdin said dramatically for the benefit of the women watching.

Then he ran.

He scooted round Rasoul and managed to duck past the rest of the guards as they grabbed at him ineptly. Ten of them weren't worth one Rasoul thank goodness. *He* was the only one Aladdin needed to worry about and he knew the streets almost as well as the boy did.

Aladdin ducked into what looked like a crack in the city itself, where two buildings crumbled and tilted, leaning on each other like old men. He ran under them and ended up in a badly kept courtyard. A dry and useless fountain stood in the centre. Once, long ago, it had worked maybe, when some sultan cared about things being nice for the poorer residents of Agrabah.

Rasoul appeared at the opposite side of the courtyard, scimitar raised.

"Do *not* think you can escape back to the maze of the Eastern Streets, Aladdin," he said sternly. He *almost* smiled when he saw the surprised look on Aladdin's face. "Oh yes, I know your plan. But you have broken the law. You must accept your punishment."

"You're *really* going to chop my hand off for stealing one… loaf… of… bread," Aladdin said, trying to buy time as he bounced lightly on his toes, circling around, keeping the fountain between them.

"The law is the law."

Aladdin feinted to the left and then tried to lunge to the right. Rasoul wasn't fooled at all; his scimitar sliced across Aladdin's path. Aladdin ducked, sucking his stomach in.

But he didn't come away unscathed: a tiny ribbon of scarlet unfurled across his skin. Aladdin hissed at the pain.

Rasoul paused.

"Perhaps, if you explain to the judge, he will be lenient. He will... weigh your circumstances. But that is his job. Mine is to bring you in."

"Really? I thought your job was to eat baklava. You're slowing down, old man," Aladdin taunted. With a howl of rage Rasoul brought his scimitar down as hard as he could.

Aladdin dropped into a ball and rolled out of the way. Sparks flew when the scimitar hit the cobbled pavement.

He scrambled up rickety old scaffolding that barely held his weight. It certainly wouldn't support Rasoul's. The guard swore in frustration and Aladdin ran as fast as he could, leaping from rooftop to rooftop in a random pattern. Without a clear thought or plan, he concentrated on just putting as much distance between himself and the market as he could before descending into the quieter, darker Quarter of the Street Rats.

A chittering scream announced that Abu had caught up. He leaped onto Aladdin's shoulder and clung there while the boy, still being cautious, kept to the shadows and ducked into empty houses: in through their glass-less windows, out of their gaping doors.

Finally he felt they could stop when they came to a cul-de-sac so decrepit and useless that it acted as a makeshift rubbish dump for the slums. No city workers came to take the refuse away, and it grew in piles that the poorest of the poor picked through, hoping for an overlooked scrap. It was smelly, but it was safe.

"Whew, the old man's getting slower, but he's getting *smarter*," Aladdin admitted grudgingly, clapping the dust off his trousers and vest. "And now, esteemed effendi, we feast."

He settled down at the base of the wall and finally broke his bread, giving half to Abu, who grabbed it excitedly.

But just as Aladdin was about to take a big, welcoming bite, the clatter of something hitting the pavement stopped him.

He expected guards.

He expected to run again.

He *didn't* expect to see two of the smallest, scrawniest children in Agrabah. They jumped, scared by the noise they had made themselves while picking through the rubbish, looking for something to eat. When they spotted Aladdin, they didn't quite *cling* to each other but moved closer for safety. Their eyes were huge. Their bellies were shrunken. Only on closer inspection could he tell one was a girl; their rags were shapeless and they were very, very skinny.

"I'm not gonna hurt you. You look familiar. Have we met before?"

The children said nothing and hid whatever they had, bones, melon rinds behind their backs.

Street Rats take care of each other. The words of his mother travelled across the years to him.

"Here," he said, getting up slowly without making any sudden movements. He knew what it was like being afraid that anyone bigger, healthier or older than you would hurt you and steal whatever you had. He held his hands out: one empty, in peace, the other with the bread.

The two children couldn't help staring at the bread.

"Take it," he urged softly.

They didn't need much compelling. The girl, bolder, reached out and took it, trying not to grab. She murmured, "Thank you," before immediately tearing it *almost* in half. She gave the larger piece to her skinnier, tinier brother.

Abu watched this interestedly, chewing on his piece.

Aladdin felt a lump of anger form in his throat.

When was the last time those two kids had a full meal or a good, long drink of *clean* water? This was the way *he* had been as a child. Nothing had changed. The sultan still sat in his beautiful golden-domed palace, playing with his toys while people starved on the streets. Nothing would *ever* change until the sultan or *someone* woke up and saw how his people were suffering.

Aladdin sighed and lifted Abu onto his shoulder. He walked home slowly, belly empty of bread but full of anger and despair.

... But for an Apple

EVENING CAME: the sun began its downward journey, the moon prepared to rise and Aladdin woke from his afternoon nap eager for the promise of a fresh start. And this, perhaps more than his fleet-as-the-wind feet, his quick mind, and his quicker tongue, was what had kept him alive and healthy all those years growing up in the slums: endless optimism. If he just kept his eyes and mind open, anything was possible.

Even dinner.

He travelled out of the Quarter of the Street Rats to prey on merchants who were perhaps a little less familiar with him and his techniques. Monkeys weren't *that* unusual in Agrabah; monkeys who hung out at the market a lot and continually stole things were.

"I feel like it's a melon day," Aladdin said, scoping out a potential mark from the shadows of a camel wagon. His stomach growled in agreement at the thought of a ripe, juicy piece of fruit. The events of the morning were still fresh in his mind, however, and they weighed in on his decision. The melon merchant in question was *screaming* at a woman and refusing to haggle.

"I would be *starving myself* if I lowered my prices for you. Everybody would demand it. And where is your headscarf, you insolent woman? Go back to the harem, where you belong!"

The woman sadly turned to leave. She had long black hair pulled back into a braid that was streaked with grey. Her robes hung on her loosely. Aladdin couldn't help noticing how much she looked like his mother. A scrawny girl child or grandchild tagged behind her.

"Yeah. Definitely melon," he muttered to himself. He picked up Abu and pointed him towards the stall. "You're up, little buddy."

It didn't take much to encourage the monkey to go towards the giant piles of dark green fruit.

Aladdin leaped up to the balcony above and dropped lightly onto the beam that supported the melon tent. He leaned over and listened carefully. The moment he heard the merchant screaming and chasing Abu around, he stretched down like a sinuous snake and scooped up the closest ripe melon.

Once safely back out of sight, he whistled a short call that could have been mistaken for the song of a dove.

Instantly, the monkey's chittering ceased.

"Yes, be off, you thief!" Aladdin heard the merchant snarl.

A moment later Abu popped up on the beam next to Aladdin. They both squatted in comically similar positions, while Aladdin broke the melon on a pointy piece of wood and served it up.

"This makes it all worthwhile. *This* is the life," Aladdin said, relishing his first big, juicy bite.

He rested comfortably, eating his dinner, feeling the sun warm his skin and muscles. The morning's bruises were already fading from his arms and legs. The crowds were just beginning to throng the marketplace as the last heat of the day began to wane. Colourful tents and awnings clung to every structure as far as the eye could see, like newly hatched butterflies sunning their wings. The late orange light made the white arches, towers and balconies gleam like ancient gold.

Local men in tunics and turbans and vests and trousers, women in long colourful robes, sometimes silk, sometimes cotton, sometimes with matching headscarves, sometimes not, inspected the produce and goods with keen eyes. Among them wandered foreigners, strange-eyed men in dark robes and women with equally dark makeup. Occasionally there was the flash of gold around a wrist, the spark of bright green gems on a neck.

Aladdin sighed in contentment. Could there truly be any more marvellous place in the world than the bustling, cosmopolitan Agrabah?

But in the shadows stood gaunt old men, mostly naked, waiting to be summoned to clean up the camel dung. Hoping for a tip. This is how they would spend the last years of their lives. After a lifetime of taking care of their families, wasn't it *their* turn to be taken care of? To drink tea and play chess and smoke hookahs and enjoy their grandchildren?

"Come on, Abu, let's—"

And then he stopped.

Aladdin felt a shift in the market crowd's mood. People were turning their heads and watching a girl as she walked through. She wore a tan robe and headscarf, the clothes of a local... but didn't *feel* like a market regular. She moved slowly and gazed at everything with a child's wonder. Her eyes were large and clear, her hair as black as midnight. She had a warm smile on her pretty lips and was obviously murmuring *hello*s and *excuse me*s to people who really didn't care or want to talk. She walked with the grace of a cloud in the wind, as if her body weighed nothing at all, and held her head high with easy dignity. *Easy.*

Aladdin felt his heart contract. He had never seen her or anyone *like* her before.

When the girl adjusted her scarf, she revealed an intricate tiara in her hair that had a gigantic emerald in it.

Ah, a rich girl, out for a day of shopping in the market without her servants. Living dangerously, playing truant.

And then, of course, Aladdin saw the other people watching her.

Feral eyes and shifty grins. His stomach sank. *He* only stole food for himself and Abu. And for the occasional hungry child. Other Street Rats were not so discriminating. The way she was walking around, not paying attention, she would be relieved of all her jewellery and worldly goods before she reached the other end of the square. Why, if Duban and Morgiana were here, they would have pickpocketed or tricked her out of her things in less time than it took to eat a melon.

Unless they were too distracted by her dazzling almond-shaped eyes...

A Street Rat 'accidentally' got in her path. Aladdin knew this one: he was small for his age, slender and slight, with a large head and equally large eyes. He always passed for a child years younger than he was, and he was making himself look very, very young and very, very hungry right then. And *somehow* he ended up right in front of the girl.

Aladdin couldn't hear what she was saying, but it was obvious from the pitying look on her face what the tone was. She was a *perfect* mark.

Abu chattered at him. If the human wasn't going to finish his melon like a smart person, the monkey would very much like to eat it.

"Shhh!" Aladdin ordered.

What happened next was nothing he or any Street Rat could possibly have foreseen.

The beautiful girl took an apple from the closest stall and gave it to the boy.

And then walked away.

The boy looked from the apple to the girl's retreating form, confused.

The fruit merchant grabbed her and demanded his money.

She shrugged and shook her head as if he was insane.

The Street Rat and everyone else watched her like *she* was insane. Which she must have been. She had just planned to take that apple? And give it away? Without paying for it?

The merchant also stared at her for a long, silent moment, uncomprehending. Then he grabbed her and threw her against the stall. A crowd gathered to watch. Some men mumbled and protested into their own scarves, but no one moved to help her. The merchant pulled out an extremely sharp dagger and raised it above her wrist.

By the time she started shrieking, Aladdin was already in the air and halfway to the stall.

"Nobody steals from my cart!" the merchant bellowed. The point of his blade gleamed red in the afternoon light.

"No!" the girl screamed.

The knife descended quickly, whistling through the air. The crowd gasped.

"Thank you, kind sir," Aladdin said, suddenly between the merchant and the girl.

Before anyone had a chance to even register this newcomer's presence, he gently pushed the man's arm away with one hand and grabbed the girl with his other.

"A *thousand* blessings to you for finding my sister."

"What?" the man asked, confused. "You know this girl?"

"I've been looking all over for you," Aladdin said, admonishing the girl and waggling a finger in her face.

The girl was more than a little confused herself.

"What are you—?" she began to ask.

"Sssht!" Aladdin mouthed. *"Just play along!"*

"Explain yourself! She was stealing from my cart!" the merchant yelled.

"My apologies, good sir. My sister sometimes causes

trouble. She wandered off from home again," Aladdin said sorrowfully. He tapped the side of his head. "Sadly, she is a little crazy."

The girl seemed furious at those words. Aladdin gave her a desperate look.

Finally she got it.

She nodded her head slightly.

"She said she knew the *sultan*," the merchant spat. He made a show of letting his eyes travel up and down Aladdin. With her large golden earrings, perfect health and glowing skin, the girl seemed like someone who *might* know the sultan. And Aladdin, with his threadbare trousers, was definitely *not*.

Aladdin's mind raced.

Abu chattered inquisitively from the ground. The monkey obviously sensed the general trouble in the air.

That was it.

"She thinks the *monkey* is the sultan," Aladdin whispered loudly into the merchant's ear. Loudly enough for the crowd and the girl to hear.

"Oh, uh, wise, great Sultan," the girl began uncertainly, taking his cue.

She looked at the muck-covered ground and then the sharp khanjar the merchant still had, which was aimed at Aladdin now.

She threw herself into the dirt, prostrating herself in front of Abu.

"How may I serve you?"

The men and women in the crowd made tutting noises and sounds of general sympathy; they began to disperse from the embarrassing scene.

The merchant watched the pretty girl in the street dust and began to look convinced.

This was where Aladdin had to finish up quickly and get out, before anything went south. He palmed another apple off the cart.

"Tragic, isn't it?" he sighed regretfully. He handed the merchant the apple. "Well, no harm done. Come on, Sis, we should get you back home to Aunt Idina now."

The girl stood up and tried to make her eyes look all goofy and crazy. It was a bit much, Aladdin thought, but not half bad for a naive rich girl. He put his hands on her shoulders and steered her through the crowd. She let herself be guided, walking stiffly more like a ghoul than a crazy person, but whatever. It was good enough.

She stopped in front of a camel.

"Hello, Auntie Idina!" she said with a wide, dumb smile.

"*That's* not Auntie," he said through gritted teeth, and pushed her to go faster. He called to Abu. "C'mon, *Sultan*."

Unfortunately, that brought attention back to Abu. The tiny monkey was grabbing as many small apples as he could from the stall, even holding one in his teeth.

The merchant, who had finally lost interest in the proceedings and had just turned round to rearrange his fruit, saw this.

If he had been angry before, it was nothing like what he was experiencing now. His face turned purple and red with rage. For a moment, Aladdin *almost* worried the merchant would drop dead right there on the spot.

"Stop, thief!"

Aladdin grabbed the girl's hand and ran.

Abu skittered after them, desperately trying to hold on to at least one apple.

The Cost of Knowledge

FAR BENEATH THE DEEPEST rooms of the palace, a secret workshop glowed red and orange from liquid fire that flowed in pits around it. Despite the seething, bloody glow, the room was cool, almost cold. Jafar moved around carefully in his enveloping layers of robes, fingers tapping impatiently on the shiny ebony surface of his staff.

He was the sultan's grand vizier, closest adviser and only friend since the sultana had died. If the public gossiped openly about the royal princess, they confined their talk about Jafar to the night-time hours. It was said that he meddled in dark magic. That his cobra-headed staff gave him power over others. That the sultan was so completely within his control that nothing was out of Jafar's reach.

Gossip aside, there were also solid facts about the man: he was the second most powerful person in the kingdom;

he seemed to know everything that happened everywhere in Agrabah; and he had more than a few times taken people and disappeared them into the dungeons or worse.

This workshop was part of that 'worse'.

Strange, terrible equipment covered the table over which Jafar was leaning. Rust-coloured wood was carved into cogs and painted all over with ugly runes that seemed to whisper when he leaned in close. Black metal that wasn't iron twisted and spiked in unsettling shapes like a cage around the wood. Scraps of torn cloth, spider silk and bloody feathers were caught on its thorns and waved in an unseen breeze like hair underwater.

The air in the middle of it all shuddered and ripped like the world itself was being torn apart. In the bleeding, black hole, a wavering shape appeared.

Jafar leaned closer, trying to make out the image. This was the most forbidden magic known to people of his ilk: *Rizar Hadinok*, the Seeing Beyond.

Just then a puffy, sweaty form bounded down the final set of stone steps that led to Jafar's secret room. Rasoul was obviously trying not to appear nervous, and saluted as properly as he could manage.

"You summoned me, Grand Vizier?"

"I need you to find and bring me this man. It is of utmost importance to… the sultan."

Jafar indicated the blurry shape in the air with the tick of a long, pointed finger. The captain of the guard moved close in small, shuffling steps, trying to keep as much of his body as he could away from the evil-looking equipment. When he focused on the picture in the air, he lost his nervousness to surprise.

"*That* one, Vizier? He's but a boy. A Street Rat. A petty thief in the markets, nothing more. He could not possibly cause harm to the sultan."

Jafar raised a sharp eyebrow at the guard's presumption.

"My magic has foretold of his role in certain events involving the fate of Agrabah. It is imperative you fetch him at once," he snarled.

"Yes, of course, Grand Vizier," Rasoul apologised quickly, sweeping down in a low bow.

When he rose, he saluted to go, chancing one last look around the forbidden workshop.

"Where's Iago?" he asked before he could stop himself.

"Hmmm?" Jafar asked distractedly, already turning his attention back to his device.

"The... your... parrot," Rasoul stammered. "You always have him on your shoulder. Or nearby."

Jafar looked out the corner of his eye at the guard for one frightening moment.

"Eating crackers somewhere, I should assume."

"Ye-es. Of course. Grand Vizier," Rasoul said with another low bow. Then he hurried out of the room as fast as he could without making it look like it.

Jafar slowly tapped his fingers on the table, one after another, contemplating the image.

"So," he said slowly to the picture of the boy. "*You* are the only one the ancient powers say can enter the cave and live. Much good it may do you, my '*diamond in the rough*'…"

The Agrabah No One Sees

WHEN THEY WERE what he thought was a safe distance from the market, Aladdin finally collapsed against an old broken water trough.

"Did you see his *face*?" he said, cracking up. "Boy, was he mad. He must feel so stupid now. He bought *everything*! Until you completely ruined it, Abu."

Abu seemed to sense he was being criticised. He jumped off Aladdin's shoulder and chattered sulkily.

The girl was bent over, hand to her side, panting. After her breaths had slowed to mere wheezes, she pressed the palms of her hands together and closed her eyes. Then she did a series of stretches that were graceful and seemed well practised.

"Sorry," Aladdin said. "Guess you're not used to running much, huh?"

"Yes, you should be completely sorry for saving me from having my *hand* cut off. And no, I'm not used to running *from* people. I do race with Rajah, my..." she paused, as if thinking of an appropriate word for "*dog*".

She was being purposefully vague. Not that it took a genius to figure out that she had probably spent her whole life in the women's quarters of some mansion or estate.

"Where are we, anyway?" she asked, changing the subject and looking around.

They were resting in the wide intersection between three broken-down buildings with no particular purpose. There was no one in sight, and the desert breeze blew mournfully through the few dry grasses and weeds that tried to grow in the verges of the hard-packed roads.

The only other noise was from a fight somewhere nearby: shouting punctuated by terrible, wet-sounding blows.

Aladdin suddenly realised what this must be like for the girl. Alone with a stranger, in the middle of nowhere, no idea how to get back to wherever she was from. If he had been the *wrong* sort of person, the more dangerous kind of Street Rat, that was exactly the kind of place he would have taken her before stealing her of all her valuables. A place no one would hear her scream.

"Well, I could tell you, but it probably won't mean much," he said, trying to sound friendly. He stood up and whirled his hands as he talked, a perfect tour guide. "We have officially entered the quaint, *residential* section of the poorest part of Agrabah. A lot of these streets don't even have names. We just call them 'the eastern way by Hakim's', or 'the stinky alley near the rat catcher'. The closest major landmark is the old Ottoman mosque, over there... hasn't been used in centuries, except by pigeons and the homeless when sandstorms come in off the desert."

The girl was frowning. Not angrily, more like she was desperately trying to understand something. Something Aladdin was saying so very simply was eluding her.

"Uh, where'd I lose you?" Aladdin asked. "Was it 'pigeon', or 'sandstorm'? Or 'stinky'?"

"Actually, it was 'homeless'," the girl said slowly. "People *live* in the old mosque?"

"Not all the time. It's a little creepy. Some say it's haunted. Hey, speaking of homes, is there somewhere I can take you?"

It was the right thing to do, of course. Save the pretty girl, take the pretty girl home. Refuse the reward. All right, maybe take the reward. If there *was* a reward. Wasn't there usually a reward? Probably in reality they would take one look at him, grab the girl and order him off at the point of a very pointy scimitar.

He hoped she lived really far away so it would take a long time to get her home.

Like in an oasis, out in the desert. That would be *perfect*.

He was pleasantly surprised when she shook her head. "Show me *your* home. I want to see where you live."

Aladdin found himself blushing, a very unusual condition for him. He tossed his dark hair so she couldn't see. "Oh, you don't want to see that. It's nothing special."

It was, in fact, really *nothing* at all if by *home* one generally meant four walls, a roof and some sort of door.

"Come on!" the girl begged, having recovered her breath and her enthusiasm. "I threw myself down in *camel dung* while playing along with you. Do you think I care what your house looks like?"

Aladdin realised he was grinning.

"All right, but remember, you asked for it!"

He took a quick look around, evaluating the best route. Then he led her around to the back of one of the ancient, crumbling houses and began to scurry up a rickety old ladder.

"Um…" she asked sceptically, wincing with each rung she stepped on as if she feared the whole thing would break. "What are we doing?"

Aladdin hopped onto a balcony and offered his hand. She pretended it wasn't there, nimbly leaping once she saw what she was to do.

"Remember the bit about 'poor' and 'stinky'? Uh, I mean, I'm not stinky, but I don't live in exactly the *safest* part of Agrabah. It's better to get off the streets, where we might be seen."

"What's wrong with being seen?" she asked.

"I don't know. What's wrong with not paying for a piece of fruit and then giving it away?"

"I didn't know…" Her voice trailed off.

"That you have to pay for things?" Aladdin finished, smiling gently.

"All right, it was my first time in a market," she admitted. "I've never actually *bought* anything before. I never thought about how it was all worked out, prices and money and things. You caught me."

He couldn't help looking smug. He had been so right when he'd pegged her as a rich girl in disguise.

But the girl narrowed her eyes and gave him the sort of look he usually expected from the Widow Gulbahar.

"I don't see a purse of gold coins on *you*, smart guy. How do *you* pay for things?"

Aladdin found himself quite possibly for the first time ever speechless.

"That's… clever of you," he finally said. "But that's totally different! I only steal because otherwise I'd starve!"

"So it's all right for you to steal because you need food.

But it's not all right for me, who didn't know any better? And was just trying to help a little child?"

Aladdin crossed his arms.

"All right, yes, you are totally and completely clever. Let's just say that the reason we're going up here on the roofs is because apparently you don't *know* what stealing is, and I do, and I'm used to… that sort of life. Look there."

He crouched down on the balcony and pulled her next to him. In the shadow of a crooked tower, a small group of children and a couple of teenagers were sprawled. They wore rags and had shadows under their eyes. Two of the youngest tried to play a game with a pebble, tossing it back and forth. The older kids were dusting their arms with ashes. Making themselves look sicker than they were.

"The moment anyone, and I mean *anyone,* except for another Street Rat comes through here, these guys will leap up and surround him. Or *her*. Begging.

"And if he or she doesn't give them something, a crust of bread, a coin… or sometimes even if he does, while one child is crying about her hunger, another will be picking that person's pocket."

The girl looked horrified.

"They're all just *pretending* to be poor?"

Aladdin chuckled wryly. "No, they're not pretending. They're not pretending to be poor, or shoeless, or homeless or *starving.* All of that is very, very real. But sometimes it takes costumes and makeup and playacting for people to see the truth that is right under their noses."

She watched the children and he watched her face as she tried to process everything she had just learned. She was innocent; that was true. But there was intelligence in those large eyes. She picked up things very, *very* quickly. It was more than Aladdin could usually say about those who weren't Street Rats. What a waste, for some father to trap such a smart, interesting girl behind a garden gate, like a prized animal.

"Where are their parents?" she asked.

"Dead. Or sick. Or out trying to find work. Or food."

"Where do they…? Why can't they…?"

Aladdin watched as she tried to find words for ideas she had never experienced before.

"Why isn't anything being done about this?" she finally asked, anger in her voice.

"Oh, come on, who cares about us Street Rats?" Aladdin asked, a little more sadly than he meant to. "The sultan stays locked up in his palace, playing with his golden toys all day. He only comes out to observe an eclipse or fly his kites. Who knows if he's even aware that half his city is starving?"

The girl's eyes narrowed at his mention of the sultan. He couldn't tell if she was angry at the sultan as well, or, well, technically, it was worth your head to say anything bad about the sultan or his household. That never stopped anyone in the Quarter of the Street Rats. There might not have been meat, bread or water but there was an endless supply of insults.

He thought she was about to say something, but the girl pressed her lips together with thoughtful finality.

"Come on," Aladdin said, jumping up and giving her his hand, trying to lighten the mood. "It's not all bad. We've got complete freedom of the streets and trust me, if you grew up here, you'd never have to worry about walking by yourself anywhere. People would be afraid of *you*."

This time she accepted his hand, maybe because her thoughts were elsewhere. Her skin was soft and her nails short but perfect. Aladdin gave her hand a little squeeze before regretfully letting it go and helping her up the next ladder.

"You said 'we'," she said slowly. "So, you consider yourself one of these… Street Rats?"

"Everyone else does," he said, a little darkly. "But… yeah. I mean, I'm poor, I grew up here, they were my friends and family… but I'm not really part of them. Not anymore. Like I said, I just steal to eat. When they can, they steal for profit. I want something better out of my life. That *is* their life. Not that they have a choice," he added quickly.

"It's not like anyone is handing out bread or work."

"It sounds very complicated," the girl said. It didn't sound like a platitude.

"I didn't think it was," Aladdin said, pausing to reflect. "*I'm* not. I'm… just me. Part-time thief and bane of the fruit market."

"I think maybe there's more to you than meets the eye."

She had a tiny wicked smile on her face and had obviously been watching the way he climbed. A strange warmth rushed through him; it was like he couldn't decide whether to blush or show off. He chose neither, turning round to quickly throw himself up and over the edge of the roof. Then he reached down and helped her up.

She tripped over her robe as she came over the side, a strange thing from a girl who seemed otherwise so utterly graceful. Aladdin caught her before she hit the ground or, in this case, the roof. She fell into him, pressing her torso against his as she grabbed around his shoulders for support.

The heat of her skin burned through her robes and he felt the softness of her body. She smelled better than anything in the Quarter of the Street Rats, better than anything Aladdin could remember ever having smelled. Better even than the tiny vial of rose oil he'd once stolen for his mother which she'd made him return.

When she stood up, she didn't stand away from him. Instead, she kept close and looked up into his face, apparently just as entranced as he was.

Aladdin felt like falling to the ground himself.

"I..." the girl said.

He made himself focus on how they would get to the next rooftop; the poles that were usually up there to support clay urns drying in the sun were right where he had left them. Of course. He busied himself with reaching for one.

"I never thanked you for saving me from that man," the girl finished weakly, managing not to sound too flustered.

"Oh, forget about it," Aladdin said, meaning it. "You looked like someone who needed help as soon as you entered the market."

With the skill of someone who had long lived on his toes, Aladdin ran to the edge of the building and pole-vaulted to the next one.

"Was I that obvious?" the girl asked ironically.

Aladdin grinned. There was something wonderful about a girl who didn't take herself too seriously.

"You do sort of stand out," he admitted.

She brightened at his unintentional compliment, eyes glowing prettily.

"Uh, I mean, you don't seem to understand how dangerous Agrabah can be," Aladdin corrected himself, running a hand through his hair self-consciously. He looked around for a plank he could lay down between the rooftops for her to walk across.

But before he could think of some way of changing the subject or staying on this one the girl had found a pole of her own and leaped nimbly across to him. Far, *far* more gracefully than he had. Her robes swirled round her as she landed like a queen of the *djinn* alighting on the golden sands of the desert.

"I learn pretty quickly," she said with mock haughtiness.

Aladdin was once again speechless. What sort of rich girl was this? One who could leap like a mountain goat and play crazy at a moment's notice? Who had never seen poverty before and now, confronted with it, thought about it quietly rather than making rash statements? Who didn't care that Aladdin was a thief, except when he applied different standards to her?

He was a loner, not a hermit; he had known other girls. Morgiana the Shadow, Abanbanu the tailor's daughter, Nefret with the strange green eyes, who came from the desert when the moon was new to trade trinkets from faraway lands.

None of them was like this girl.

"Come on," he said, holding out his hand. She took it, as he somehow knew she would. "It's this way."

The girl grinned in delight as he took her over boards brittle with dry rot and loose stones worn down in the middle by countless feet centuries earlier. They entered a tower through a keyhole-shaped window that must have had bright mosaics around it at one time; everything shiny or worth anything at all had been scavenged decades before. Not even rats lived in this high, desolate place anymore.

Well, two did. Two *Street* Rats, if one counted Abu.

"Watch your head," Aladdin said, making sure she ducked under a gigantic timber that slanted crazily from the centre of the tower to the side.

"You… live… *here?*"

She didn't say it with disgust. She was… surprised? Impressed?

Aladdin had never thought he would be bringing a girl back to his place who would actually like it.

They reached the landing he had chosen to call home. His mother had tried to keep their little hut as welcoming and homely as possible; he honoured her memory by trying to do the same now. There were a few threadbare old rugs, some once-colourful cloths he had draped over the uglier, broken bits of stonework and used as curtains. There were even a few pillows for sleeping on and a couple of urns for water and, well, just decoration.

"Yup! Just me and Abu. We come and go as we please."

"That sounds *wonderful*," the girl said with a sigh.

"Well, it's not much, but it's got a great view."

With a dramatic flourish of his arm, he swept back the curtain, knowing how impressed she would be.

Directly in front of them was the palace, a mile away but looming so large it seemed like they could reach out and touch it. At least a dozen of its golden onion-shaped domes were visible, glowing like suns. The giant formal gates and portcullis glowed royal blue, like the sky. The road seemed to lead right from Aladdin's tower through the city to the palace, pushing pesky houses and buildings to either side. Nobody obstructed the road. It had to be kept clear for caravans and deliveries and parades and the horses, litters and wagons of visiting royalty.

There had been a lot of that lately, what with the princess having to marry soon.

"The palace looks pretty amazing, huh?" Aladdin sighed.

"Oh, it's wonderful," the girl said. But she didn't walk over to look with him. Instead, she collapsed on the steps that led up to his sleeping pad, wearily resting her head on her hands.

"I wonder what it would be like to live there. Or in *any* mansion. I'm not picky," Aladdin mused, trying to conceal his disappointment at her reaction. Well, maybe at least he could get her to finally open up about where she was from.

"All those servants… and valets…"

"Oh, sure, people to tell you where to go and how to dress," the girl said, rolling her eyes.

"It's better than here, where you're always scraping for food and dodging the guards," he pointed out.

"You just said you and Abu come and go as you please. If you were born into a royal family, you'd have to do whatever they told you to. Whatever you're *expected* to do. And you can't go *anywhere*."

"Yeah, well, you can't go anywhere *socially* when you're a Street Rat. Our upward mobility is strictly limited. Even if I wanted honest work, no one would hire me. For any job. Not even for a *servant* at an estate. And there's nowhere else to go. Once you're born in the Quarter of the Street Rats, you're—"

"Trapped," the girl finished.

Aladdin looked up at her, surprised. It was like she actually understood, like she felt the same way.

He went over and sat down next to her. She didn't move to give him more room. Their legs touched.

He took a couple of apples out of his sash, handing one to her and the other to Abu. Abu rewarded him with happy, raucous chittering and then did exactly as Aladdin had hoped: he scampered up into the roof of the tower to enjoy the whole thing by himself.

The girl pulled a tiny silver dagger out of her clothes and neatly cut her apple into two halves, handing one to him. He grinned at her and toasted her with his half.

"So where are you from, anyway?" he finally dared to ask.

"What does it matter?" she growled. "I ran away and I am *not* going back."

"Really? How come? What could be so awful that you never want to see your mother or your father again? Or sister, or whatever?"

The girl seemed to soften a little at that.

"I would *love* a sister. Or a brother. And my mother died when I was very young."

Aladdin felt something in his heart break a little. What a truly terrible thing to have in common with a beautiful girl.

"And my father... is forcing me to get married." Her eyes grew hard again. "How would *you* like it if someone told you that you have no choice about who you're going to spend the rest of your life with?"

She balled her fists in anger. Aladdin found himself stepping back.

"He could be 30 years older than me. *But rich*," she snapped at Aladdin, as if it was his idea. He pulled back in fear. "He could be *dumb*. But rich! He could be arrogant.

He could treat me like just another possession. I mean, that's how my father is treating me, handing me over like that. He could be cruel. He could be..." She stopped herself from saying whatever was next, looking at Aladdin with a little embarrassment, like it was something too horrible to mention aloud. "He could force me to give him a large family, one baby every year. Not that there's anything wrong with babies. Like, one or two. Eventually.

"All I know is that I haven't even reached 20 years yet and my father has decided that my life, what little I have to choose of it, is over."

Aladdin gulped. For some reason the Widow Gulbahar appeared in his head: she wasn't bad at all, but if he was told he had to marry her? And spend the rest of his life with her? He also thought about Morgiana. She had a tiny dagger hidden on her, too, but it wasn't silver, and it wasn't for fruit. If anyone even tried to *suggest* her marrying anyone against her will, well, it would go badly for everyone involved. She would never let that happen.

"That's awful," he said with feeling. "I... I'm sorry I..."

Just then Abu leaped down from the ceiling. Aladdin watched with concern as the little monkey made a beeline for the girl's half of the apple. Aladdin grabbed the little monkey out of the air and put him on his shoulder.

"What's wrong? What was he doing?" the girl asked.

She began to relax again at Abu's antics.

"Nothing," Aladdin said, stroking the little monkey's back.

The girl leaned over and tickled Abu's chin.

"Abu was just… ah… just outraged at what a terrible thing your dad is doing to you."

"Oh really?" the girl asked with a knowing smile. She pursed her lips in an expression of disbelief. Aladdin felt his chest go weak and his brain go stupid.

"Oh, yeah. He was just saying how outraged he was that men still control the lives of young women even in this modern, enlightened age," Aladdin said. He was petting Abu, but looking at the girl. He wasn't sure what he was saying, really. He would say anything, keep talking forever, if it kept her looking at him like that.

"Interesting. And does *Abu* have anything else to say?" she asked, leaning closer.

Cinnamon. Her breath smelled of cinnamon. He could even smell her skin at that distance. Though he wasn't one normally prone to poetry, he could only think of a fresh desert breeze that carried a whisper of cypress and sandalwood.

"He wishes there was something he could do to help." That at least was honest. He wasn't *exactly* sure how kissing would help her. He just knew it was going to happen or he was going to die.

"Tell him I just might take him up on that," the girl said, closing her eyes and tilting her head.

Aladdin put his arm around her back and prepared for the best thing that had ever happened to him.

Which was, of course, when the guards showed up.

Rasoul wasn't with them; his second-in-command led the attack. And how a man even larger than Rasoul, with five large guards, had managed to sneak up the stairway without Aladdin hearing was a mystery he would have to solve another day.

A better question, he realised instantly, was how they had known where he was.

"Finally, I've found you!" Rasoul's second shouted.

"And again, *really?*" Aladdin said, leaping up. "All this for *one loaf of bread?*"

"How did you find me?" the girl shouted at the same time.

The two turned to look at each other.

"They're after *you?*" he asked.

"What about bread?" she asked.

Rasoul's second-in-command wasn't the sort of person who would let confusion interrupt his orders.

"You cannot escape. Come now, lest it be worse for you!"

Aladdin leaped up onto the edge of the narrow stone balustrade that separated his sleeping nook from the city below. He held his hand out to the girl.

"Do you trust me?" he asked.

The girl looked confused for a moment.

"Ye-es?" she said uncertainly.

That was enough for Aladdin.

"Then jump!"

He grabbed her too-slow-moving hand and yanked her up next to him. Then he leaped into the air, pulling her along.

She did scream; who could blame her? They were plummeting from rosy twilight into deep midnight as they shot several storeys down through a crack in the ceiling of a building below them.

Their speed was broken by two *very* carefully tied tarps that Aladdin had installed in case of just such an emergency. Their landing, while jarring and painful, was made softer on the piles of sand that had been gathered there by centuries of neglect and wind.

Aladdin leaped up immediately, the girl's hand still in his. She was right by his side, also too smart to take a moment to recover. But the door was suddenly filled by an unfortunately familiar silhouette.

He appeared too quickly for them to change direction.

Aladdin and the girl slammed into Rasoul's chest.

"We just keep running into each other, don't we,

Street Rat?" he said with a tired sneer. He grabbed Aladdin by his vest, shoving him off to the second squad of guards behind him.

Aladdin cursed. He should have realised something was up when the captain of the guard wasn't in the tower with the rest. Rasoul had already reconnoitred his hideout and planted himself by the escape route. Irritatingly intelligent.

"It's the dungeon for you this time, boy. No escape."

The girl, somewhat incredibly, began to attack the giant captain. Aladdin and the guards watched with similar surprise as she hit Rasoul uselessly in the chest again and again with her small fists.

"Let him go!" she shouted.

"Well, look at that," Rasoul said, tossing her aside as easily as he had the monkey. "A Street *Mouse.*"

Aladdin felt his blood boil as the girl tumbled to the floor.

The guards began to laugh; even Rasoul chuckled as he turned to go.

"Unhand him."

The girl stood up and swept off her robe. *"By order of the royal princess!"*

Rasoul stopped chuckling and the guards gasped.

Aladdin felt his stomach flip.

That girl, the girl he had spent the afternoon with,

the girl who had leaped off the sides of buildings and pole-vaulted off others, who had charmed Abu and shared an apple with him, was not some rich girl off for a jaunt or running away from home. She was a princess. *The* royal princess.

Jasmine.

Her eyes were black and hard. Her back was straight; her arms hung gracefully at her sides as if she had too much power even to need to put them on her hips or cross them in anger. Her diadem sparkled.

"The princess…?" Aladdin said faintly.

It was said that Jasmine was beautiful; it was said she was quick-witted. Both of these were without question true.

It was also said that she was a witch with a tiger for a familiar. It was said she tore her suitors to shreds verbally and, by way of the tiger, occasionally literally.

"Princess Jasmine," Rasoul said immediately, lowering his eyes and bowing. "What are you doing outside the palace? And with this… Street Rat?"

"That is none of your concern," Jasmine said. She put her hands on her hips and marched right up into the captain's space as if he was no more to her than an irritating camel. "Do as I command. Release him."

"I would, Princess," Rasoul said. He did seem genuinely regretful. He flicked a look back at Aladdin.

Maybe *he* thought it was all a bit much for a loaf of bread, as well? "Except my orders come from Jafar. You'll have to take it up with him."

Aladdin's heart froze.

Why would the grand vizier care about Aladdin?

"*Jafar?*" Princess Jasmine was apparently thinking the same thing. But she managed to control her surprise, turning the question into a sneer of disgust.

The last thing Aladdin saw before the guards hauled him off was her concerned eyes hardening.

"Believe me," she growled, "I will be paying him a visit."

The Cave of Wonders

IF THERE WAS a moon or sun in the sky, it didn't matter at all.

Underneath the tallest tower in the palace was the deepest pit in Agrabah, the bottom of which was lit by a single torch. No sunlight, moonlight or starlight had ever touched its depths. The bottom-most chamber had been excavated in the dead of a black night by workers who were then murdered and buried under the very stone steps they helped lay to preserve the secrets of the palace dungeons.

There was only one door that led in: it was windowless and triple-barred. Beyond it were a dozen skeletons still shackled to the wall, left there even after they had decomposed like a forgotten detail in a fairy tale. Scurrying around these were rats that had never seen the light of the sun and probably had something to do with the creation of the skeletons.

Aladdin had only been there for a few hours and hadn't quite let the obvious *finality* of the place get to him yet. He was still shocked by the events that had led up to his being there.

"The *princess*," he muttered to himself for the 40th time. "I can't believe she was the *princess*. I must have sounded so *stupid* to her."

But... maybe... just maybe, she liked *him*? A little?

And for a moment, in the chilly, foul-smelling dungeon where he was chained, Aladdin let himself dream of the life he would have if *he* was a prince. Then they could be together. He would have the girl of his dreams and they would all live happily ever after.

Of course, the fact that she was a princess was the reason he was in a dungeon.

It was obvious: his imprisonment had nothing to do with the bread he had stolen. Somehow Jafar had seen them, had *known* a Street Rat was coming close to desecrating the royal daughter, leading her into a life of poverty, crime and villainy... and had stopped it.

"Aww, she was worth it, though," Aladdin sighed, thinking about her eyes, remembering the soft warmth of her hand. For a moment he had touched greatness.

The tiny echoes of chittering interrupted his thoughts.

"Abu?" he asked incredulously, looking up.

Very faintly he could see a tiny shadow of a monkey as it hopped from beam to beam, from stone to stone while he made his way down to the bottom, where Aladdin was.

"Down here!" Aladdin called excitedly.

Abu dropped onto his shoulder. The boy petted him as best he could by rubbing his head into Abu's furry belly. "Hey, boy, am I glad to see you! Turn round!"

After enjoying a few more moments of their cuddly reunion, Abu did as directed. Using his teeth, Aladdin carefully extracted a needle he had pinned into Abu's little vest for an occasion such as this. The little monkey wasn't just a distraction while Aladdin swiped things; the two had many, many other routines they had worked out over the years for getting out of and into trouble.

Aladdin turned his head and strained his neck as far as he could, working the needle into the keyhole of his right-hand manacle with his teeth and lips. It was a simple, crude lock; obviously if you were thrown to the bottom of the deepest dungeon in the palace, extreme measures weren't needed to keep you there.

Which was rapidly bringing Aladdin to the next part of his problem. Once his right hand was free, he easily undid his left, but where was he going to go from there?

Abu chittered angrily. Monkeys obviously did not like being underground or in dungeons. It sounded like he was saying *he* had done *his* part; now it was his human friend's turn to figure out the rest. Fast.

"Yeah, yeah, we're going. Let's get away from the palace as fast as we can. I'll never see her again…" he said wistfully, more concerned with that than their immediate escape. He thought about how she had looked standing on the rooftop, pole in her hand, the wind blowing tendrils of her hair out of her eyes. "She can only marry a prince. I'm a fool."

"You're only a fool if you give up, boy."

Aladdin spun round.

There was nothing but shadows and rats. But the voice was creaky, weak and *human*, not ghostly. One of the other prisoners must still have had a little life left in him.

"Who are you?" Aladdin called out to the shadows. "Show yourself!"

There was the rattle of chains and the light scuffling sound of something bony and hard against the floor. An ancient man hobbled out of the dark. He seemed barely to have the strength to stand, much less move. There were no manacles binding him. There *was* a light left in his eyes, a crazy one.

Aladdin found himself a little afraid of the strange spectre.

"I'm merely a lowly prisoner like yourself," the old man continued, revealing that he still had most of his teeth but they pointed in every direction, thin and yellow with age, like toothpicks. He used an ugly old piece of firewood as a cane and forced himself sideways with the shuffling motion of a crab. "But together, maybe we can be more."

He rubbed his fingers together suggestively, as if he were counting gold coins. Aladdin found himself relaxing. A man with the craze of *greed* in his eyes was something Aladdin was used to.

"I'm listening," he said.

"There is a cave. A cave of *wonders*, boy, filled with treasures beyond your wildest dreams!" He stuck a gnarled hand into his threadbare robe. When he pulled out his closed fist, shoved it into Aladdin's face and opened it, the boy fell back in surprise.

Rubies.

Three of them. Huge. Dusty and old, with the facets of one chipped and in need of a skilled jeweller. But rubies nonetheless. Those three would have bought most of the Quarter of the Street Rats and the people who lived there, too.

"Treasure enough to impress even your 'princess', I would wager," the old man said with a crafty smile, taking them back and hiding them again.

Aladdin felt a blush wash over his face quickly before disappearing.

The rubies...

He started to smile. That was more wealth than he had ever seen up close. Enough to buy horses, fancy clothes, servants...

...and then his smile faded. Until that moment Aladdin never would have imagined that *limitless treasure* wouldn't be enough for him.

"It doesn't matter how much gold or jewels I get," he said morosely. "She has to marry a *prince.* I have to come from a noble family, a line of princes. Or be granted the title and lands, which I can't really see the sultan doing anytime in the near future."

The old man struggled for a moment, frowning and wheezing as some undefined pain bothered him. Then he took a deep breath and stuck his face into Aladdin's.

"You've heard of the Golden Rule, haven't you? *Whoever has the gold makes the rules!*" The man laughed perhaps insanely; perhaps he genuinely thought himself funny. Aladdin noticed as the old man's lips were spread wide with mirth that his only healthy-looking tooth was gold.

"All right," Aladdin said cautiously. It was true: money bought almost anything. All the guards could be bribed to look the other way with enough gold or gifts. All the guards except for Rasoul, of course. He was like a big, stupid rock of morality. Maybe sultans and kings could be bribed, too … or haggled with. Maybe with enough gold, the title of *prince* could be bought.

"But why would you share all of this *wonderful treasure* with me?"

Catches like perfect girls turning out to be unattainable princesses Aladdin was used to. Free treasure, he was not used to and highly suspicious of.

"I need a young pair of legs and a strong back," the old man said, tapping Aladdin's legs as solicitously as a camel buyer. Aladdin suppressed a shiver of fear. Was the man a sorcerer who meant to literally *take* Aladdin's back and legs?

No, that was foolish, Aladdin told himself, shaking his head.

Right?

"Because the treasure is in a *cave*. In the *desert*," the old man spat. "I'm not quite as nimble as I used to be. I need you to go get it for me and bring it out. Now, do we have a deal?"

"Oh, sure," Aladdin laughed. If it wasn't for the existence of the rubies, he would have thought the old man was completely mad. "Except for one thing. The cave is *out there* and we're *in here*."

The old man cackled.

"Things aren't always what they seem!"

He tapped a stone in the wall several times with his cane. It slid aside, slowly, grindingly, but somehow under its own power.

"So, I repeat," the old man said as if enjoying the taste of every word. He put his hand out. "Do we have a deal?"

Aladdin hesitated. Perhaps the old man really was a sorcerer after all. Or an ancient, angry djinn.

But then again, *treasure...*

Aladdin squared his shoulders, set his jaw and shook the old man's hand.

After he crawled through the narrow space, Aladdin found himself in a pitch-black cave. Strange subterranean winds blew frigid one moment and searingly hot the next. The walls suddenly flickered with an evil red light, and a gust of hot air burned the side of Aladdin's face.

Abu screamed and clutched Aladdin's neck.

"The very blood of the earth comes up through here," the old man explained, leading the way with his crabby shuffle. As they rounded a corner, they came upon the source of the flickering red light: a slowly bubbling pool of molten rock that burned hotter than the inside of a smithy's kiln. "We are deep beneath the palace now, in the living stone upon which it was built."

"I had no idea anything like this existed," Aladdin said, full of wonder. And also full of ideas. Caves that led under the city and into the palace? That sounded like a *very bad* security risk. He wondered if they were anywhere near the vaults that were filled with royal gold.

"Nobody does. Nobody *living*, that is," the old man cackled.

Aladdin again felt the stirrings of fright. But then, what would a ghoul want with treasure? This man was surely alive. And secretive. And insane. Perhaps it was all an act to protect his secrets. They went on.

The old man occasionally mumbled and muttered to himself and made squawking noises like a bird. Having conversations with the long dead, probably. Aladdin noted with interest how very few splits and turnoffs there were, and how smooth the corridors were. Now and then he flicked out his knife to scratch an outcropping or put an arrow on a wall when the old man wasn't looking. Who knew when such a route would be useful again?

"Listen, boy," the old man said as they went. "When you do go down into the Cave of Wonders, you must *not touch anything* except for an ugly old brass lamp you will find down there. There will be rooms of gold and chests of rubies and ancient treasures worth a thousand kingdoms. Touch nothing but the lamp, or you won't come out of it alive."

"Wait, I'm just supposed to walk by piles of gold?" Aladdin scoffed. "You promised me riches, Grandfather."

"*Imbecile,*" the old man muttered, for just a moment sounding like someone younger. "The lamp gives one power over the Cave of Wonders and its treasures. If you touch anything before it's in hand, you will die. Bring the lamp to me and I assure you, you will get what you deserve."

"If you say so," Aladdin said, shrugging.

When they finally arrived at the surface, it was night. The passage ended in a rather inglorious drain hole near where the workhorses and camels were stabled at the back of the palace, beyond the outer wall. It reeked of horse muck, and Aladdin had to let the old man clamber onto his shoulders to get out. On the bright side, no one was around to see them.

Aladdin leaped out and took a deep breath of the fresh air. Although the sky was clear, the stars twinkled madly with desert sand and dust that was blown across them. He frowned. Not a good night to go adventuring in the desert. But fortune favoured the brave, and he certainly wanted a fortune.

He looked at his companion with a critical eye. The old man seemed like he was going to collapse in a pile of bones right there.

Aladdin murmured softly to the animals in the stable. He picked out an unflashy, sturdy little horse and lifted the old man onto it.

"The stable boy whose charge is this horse will receive 50 lashes for losing him," the old man said, cackling in delight as he gripped the reins.

"We will be back before dawn if your stories are true, Grandfather," Aladdin said, dislike for his partner growing. "And I will tip the poor boy well."

In the desert the winds swirled the sand into choking dust devils, and Aladdin had to cover his face with his vest. His feet kept slipping into the shifting dunes. The horse was slightly more accustomed to the terrain but whinnied and protested constantly.

It was not an easy trip.

The old man looked up at the stars. He muttered into the hump on his back, as if confirming his calculations. Eventually they arrived at a solid cliff of bedrock. Below it was a wide bowl a valley of sand, beautiful in the starlight, but desolate and deadly. There were no plants here, no lizards, not even stray stones.

Aladdin helped the old man down from the horse. Muttering and murmuring, the man drew something out of his rags, cupping his hands as if it were alive. As if it was something that might escape. Finally he spread his fingers and revealed his prize.

A golden scarab beetle rested in his palm. At first Aladdin thought it was a piece of jewellery or a statue, maybe with a treasure map on its back.

Then it opened its golden outer wings to reveal a set of flight wings also made of gold. It sparkled and glowed and flew into the air with a heavy buzzing sound.

Aladdin jumped back.

The beautiful, frightening thing flew off into the valley with the directness of something not entirely insect-like. It circled around a large mound as if deciding what to do and then plunged deep into the sands.

Almost instantly the dunes slid forwards in a rather disturbing way. Something large, something very *unnatural* was rippling and rising to the surface. A giant stone head of a tiger emerged, moving and growling and tossing like it was alive.

Aladdin prepared to run, but no more of the tiger appeared: just the head. It did not seem able to move and lacked the body of a sphinx.

Its eyes glowed like twin suns.

"Who disturbs my slumber?"

It was hard to say if the words were actually spoken aloud; the ground rumbled, the sky thundered, the tiger roared.

Aladdin backed away, almost tripping over his own feet.

This was *not* what he had signed up for. A dangerous trip into a deep, dark cave, yes. A jaunt into the middle of the desert at night, sure. *This* was too much. There had been no mention of a giant talking stone tiger with the voice of an ancient god.

The old man made an impatient *go ahead* movement with his hands.

"*What?*" Aladdin demanded. "Are you crazy?"

"You want the princess, boy?" his companion asked with a sneer.

Yes. Yes, he did.

Aladdin took a deep breath and tried to steady his nerves.

"Uh… it is I! Aladdin!" he shouted, feeling more than a little foolish.

The tiger was silent for a moment.

Aladdin got ready to run for his life.

"*Proceed.*"

The rumbles were softer, as if it was less angry.

"*Touch nothing but the lamp.*"

Its mouth snapped open, revealing a wide golden gullet. Down its tongue travelled a golden staircase. Aladdin couldn't see to the bottom. He took a tentative step forwards.

"Remember, boy, just fetch me the lamp!" the old man shouted, unconsciously imitating the tiger. "Get me the lamp and I shall make sure you get your reward!"

Aladdin thought of Jasmine.

He set his jaw.

"C'mon, Abu," he said, and began to go down the steps.

The golden stairs very quickly revealed themselves to be disappointingly normal stone, only lit golden by whatever was below. But the sheer number of them was breathtaking: the path dipped and curved through the darkness as far as the eye could see. Several times when Aladdin thought they had reached the end, the stairs began again into a deeper descent.

Aladdin was more than a little relieved to see an absolutely enormous, *normal* cave. Not a stomach.

At the far side of the cave was a stone doorway that glowed so brightly from whatever was in the room behind it that Aladdin had to cover his eyes as he went in.

"Would you look at that," he said, when he passed through to the other side, a wide grin growing across his face.

Gold. Ridiculous, ludicrous, unimaginable piles of it. Entire hillsides of coins, cups, urns and statues. Giant golden cauldrons stuffed to overflowing with necklaces, rings, bracelets and other trinkets. Golden thrones. Golden tables. Golden bric-a-brac shaped like fruit for no conceivable purpose other than to look at.

And among all this, rugs of indescribable beauty and size

and chests full of jewels shaped like berries and flowers.

"Just a *handful* of this would make me richer than the sultan," Aladdin sighed.

Abu chittered. Light sparkled on the closest chest, bouncing off a ruby the size of an apple.

The little monkey made a beeline for it.

"Abu!"

Aladdin ran desperately after the little monkey and did something he never normally would have. He grabbed the monkey's tail and pulled him back.

Abu squawked at the indignity and tried to stop himself by digging his hind claws into the rich purple-and-blue rug they were standing on.

"Don't. Touch. *Anything*," Aladdin chastised, shaking his finger at his friend. "Remember what that big, scary tiger thing said? Whose stomach we are currently in? We gotta find that lamp. First. *Then* we'll get our reward."

He plucked the monkey off the ground and set him securely on his shoulder.

"It's got to be around here somewhere…"

He wandered the path around the treasures carefully, making certain never to come too close to any of them. He kept one hand on Abu, just in case.

The monkey chittered irritably.

"I don't know," Aladdin answered, as if it was a real question.

"A little oil lamp, I guess. The old man obviously thought we could carry it out easily. I see cups and pitchers and plates and vases and other house-y stuff, but no lamps yet..."

The monkey chittered again. He sounded nervous this time and kept glancing behind them.

"Sorry, I'm looking as fast as I can," Aladdin said, continuing their imaginary conversation. "It's not like I can *touch* anything to move it aside..."

Abu screamed and clawed Aladdin's neck.

"What *is* it?" Aladdin demanded, turning round to see what was bothering his friend. There was nothing behind them, just the path they were on. And also a carpet that looked suspiciously like the one near the entrance, by the chest Abu had almost touched. It even had the same golden tassels, one on each corner.

"Huh," Aladdin said. He turned and began walking again.

Abu was silent for a good 10 seconds before beginning to screech in fear.

Aladdin whipped round.

Again, nothing.

Except for the carpet.

Which was right behind them.

Again.

Aladdin frowned, looking at the thing.

As he watched, the carpet rose hesitantly off the ground. Like a fish, or something used to swimming in the air.

Aladdin's eyes widened in wonder.

"A *magic carpet!*" he said with a whistle. "Mum used to tell me bedtime stories about djinn and their magical treasures."

He put a hand out to it, delicately, slowly.

The carpet responded, sliding forwards as if propelled by an invisible breeze. Its rear flapped gently like a flag. Aladdin found himself scratching and ruffling its nap as he would a cat's fur.

"Good... *carpet.* There's a boy. Good boy. Hey... may we get on you?" he asked politely, getting an idea. It would be *much* faster to scour the cave from above, gliding among the dangerous piles of gold without needing to go near them.

The carpet sensed what he wanted and lowered a little, like a trained elephant going down on one knee to enable a rider to easily jump up.

Aladdin grinned.

He stepped on carefully. It was a strange feeling; the rug both gave and held under his feet, like he was walking on a pile of hay waiting to dry. He crossed his legs and settled in, putting Abu in his lap. The monkey was not entirely happy about this turn of events, but since Aladdin didn't seem scared, he remained relatively calm.

Whether or not Aladdin won the princess, this was the best adventure of his entire life.

"We're trying to find a lamp," Aladdin said. He felt a bit like an idiot talking to a rug. But then again, the rug was flying. Who knew what it could understand or do? "A... *special* lamp?"

The rug rippled for a moment, as if thinking. Then, without a sound, it began to drift higher and higher into the air, picking up speed. Soon they were dipping and gliding around the mountains of treasure as easily as an eagle through the clouds. Abu gripped Aladdin's arms until his tiny claws drew blood, but the boy just laughed.

Following a series of tunnels and passageways he would never be able to remember, full of treasure he would never forget, they eventually came to a cave even larger than the first one. Aladdin couldn't see the far walls; it all drifted into darkness. The bottom was filled with a lake of perfectly still, clear water. Rising out of the middle was an island made up of boulders that looked like mushrooms, one on top of another, with steps carved out of their middle. At the very top, a single shaft of light from somewhere high, beyond sight, illuminated a small bronze object.

The lamp.

The carpet didn't fly to it, however; it gently set itself

down on a rocky outcropping on the near wall. A narrow causeway led from there to the mound. An ancient golden shrine guarded the way; some unknowable god who looked like an ape with too many teeth. It held aloft a ruby the size of an orange as if it was a lamp lighting his way.

"All right, here we go," Aladdin said, adjusting his vest and trying to put the image of the angry god out of his mind. Something about the place, whether it was the size, the silence or something else, kept him from just running across the causeway. Something demanded silence and respect. He found himself walking quickly but carefully, as if he was in a procession he couldn't quite see.

He slowly and solemnly climbed up the stone steps on the island. When he finally made it to the top, Aladdin picked up the lamp carefully with both hands… but it was as solid and sturdy as any modern household lamp. Morgiana decorated her hideout with dozens of these.

"This is *it*?" Aladdin swore, an incredulous smile on his face. He turned to Abu and the carpet. "Look at it, guys. *This* is what we came all the way down here to—"

He was just in time to see Abu grab the giant scarlet gem and try to wrest it out of the golden ape god's hands.

"Abu! *No!*" he cried.

"INFIDELS!"

The very ground itself spoke; the air, the earth.

"You have touched the forbidden treasure!"

Aladdin watched in horror as the ruby melted into dust in Abu's tiny hands. The monkey screamed as if it burned him, and scampered away from the golden statue, which tipped forwards, also melting.

"Now you will never again see the light of day!"

The light shaft that had illuminated the lamp in gold now turned a bloody red.

The cavern began to shake.

Aladdin hurtled down the steps back to the causeway. Stones fell away under his feet. What had been a stairway quickly dissolved into a ramp; he slid down it, barely keeping his balance as the whole cave shuddered and began to collapse. He pitched forwards.

A deadly heat hit him from below. He chanced a look down and saw to his horror that water no longer filled the bottom of the cavern, now it was all lava.

That one look was enough to throw him entirely off balance. As if the cave could sense his instability, a particularly big quake sent Aladdin flying towards the red-golden furnace below.

"Carpet!" he cried.

Aladdin windmilled his arms and legs, trying to slow his fall. He felt the heat singe the hairs on his legs, the roar of the molten stone rushing up to meet him...

...and then the soft, firm cloth of the magic carpet beneath him.

He didn't have time to relax: in a panic Abu had tried to run towards Aladdin and was now stranded on the last of three remaining stones in the causeway. The tip of his tail was smoking.

Sensing Abu's need, the carpet dived towards the monkey. Aladdin grabbed Abu by his poor burning tail and swung him aloft.

The carpet flew up, away from the heat and through the air, picking up speed. A hot wind surged against their backs. Aladdin turned round. The lava had pulled back into one huge roiling wave that rose above their heads, ready to crash down.

"Faster!" Aladdin urged.

The magic carpet doubled its speed and ducked them through the cavern's doorway. A split second later the wave crashed behind them. Lava exploded through the door and kept coming, boiling up from some immense pit as if it had no end.

They dived through each of the incredible burning caverns of treasure like a falcon hurtling towards its prey. Aladdin and Abu both ducked as the carpet shot through the final door that led into the first treasure room.

Aladdin started to sigh with relief.

And then the giant piles of gold began to explode.

Each priceless hill swirled into a molten pile of fire and ash that shot towards the ceiling and at the carpet. Aladdin helped steer, torn between fear for his life and heartbreak at the destruction that was being wrought there. As the explosions hit the ceiling, it began to cave in, boulders and square stones that had shaped the giant cat head now falling like bombs. The earth screamed in anger, frustration and pain. Lava began to shoot like blood from every tear in its surface.

Aladdin covered his face and let the carpet find its way to the top. It followed the rapidly disappearing stone staircase up the cat's throat, keeping close as if it was safer.

They had almost reached the top when a falling stalactite caught the back of the carpet. It plunged down with the stone. Aladdin threw himself and Abu off and managed to catch the end of the stairs at the edge of the cat's mouth. The cave was shaking too much for him to be able to pull himself up and over the side.

Like a miracle, the old man appeared.

"Help me out!" Aladdin cried.

"Throw me the lamp!" the old man demanded.

Aladdin could barely process what he had said, it was so insane.

"I can't hold on! Come on! Give me your hand!"

"First give me the lamp!" the old man insisted, a wild look in his eyes.

Survival won out over logic. Aladdin managed to reach into his sash, where he had stashed the lamp, and pulled it out with his free hand, holding on desperately with the other.

The old man grabbed it and cackled triumphantly. *"Yesss!"* he screamed. "At last!"

Aladdin managed to get one leg up into a crevice. Abu scampered off his head, making it easier.

The old man came forwards to the edge, a menacing gleam in his eye.

He began to hammer at Aladdin's fingers with his cane.

"What are you doing?" Aladdin cried.

"Giving you your reward. Your *eternal* reward."

The old man now standing strangely straight pulled out an evil-looking black dagger and raised it above his head.

Abu bit the man on the toe.

He screamed but managed to kick Aladdin's fingers.

Aladdin tumbled back into the cavern, falling into the darkness and lava.

A soft *thump* let him know the carpet had managed to find and catch him. A quick monkey scream meant he'd collected Abu, too. Slowly and shakily, as if the magic carpet was tired and injured itself, it lowered all three of them to a cliff, high above the lava. Aladdin watched in dismay as the cavern above them, the stone cat's mouth, yawned and screamed one last time before snapping shut and settling down beneath the sands.

Aladdin was stuck, sealed hundreds of metres below ground, with no way out, no treasure…

… and *no lamp*.

Jasmine and a Genie

THE SUN ROSE ABOVE the palace of Agrabah, seeming to dim before the gold-and-white greatness of the house of the sultan.

The princess Jasmine was seething.

She had, in fact, been seething since the evening before. Since the boy she had been just about to kiss was whisked away by the guards. Since she had stalked back to the palace on foot herself, not caring who saw her.

When she had arrived at the palace, Jasmine immediately demanded to be taken to the royal prison, where mostly harmless troublemakers and tax evaders were kept.

The boy was not there.

She demanded to be taken to the dungeon, where thieves, goat stealers and murderers were locked up.

The boy was not there.

Losing patience, she demanded to be taken to the secret royal oubliette, where the worst traitors, enemies of the state and caravan raiders were thrown to be forgotten. Forever. Reluctantly, a pair of the stoutest guards armed with two scimitars apiece took her down to investigate.

The boy was not there.

So she had started questioning the guards themselves. The younger ones, the lower-ranked ones, clearly had no idea about the boy or anything that had happened. Those higher in command were evasive. The ones who had actually brought the boy in could not be found. And Rasoul was silent on the matter.

"My lips are sealed," he said, somewhat apologetically. "By orders of Jafar himself."

"He is not an *enemy of the state* or a *spy*," Jasmine cried in exasperation. She almost lost her temper and stomped her foot like the angry little girl she felt like. "He's just a boy. A harmless boy who was showing me around Agrabah."

Rasoul continued to say nothing. But his eyes betrayed something at the last thing she said.

Jasmine realised with horror where this whole thing and the boy was going.

"I was *not* going to run off with him!" she yelled. *Probably.* "He wasn't going to… We weren't going to…"

Rasoul looked uncomfortable.

She composed herself quickly.

"I will go and find Jafar and clear this up immediately," she said, stalking off.

"As you will, Your Highness," Rasoul called after her. But he sounded relieved.

Several hours later Jasmine had failed to find her father's creepy adviser. If she hadn't known better, she would have thought he was purposefully hiding from her and her wrath. It was time to go and see her father, officially, and make some princessy demands.

"He will no doubt be in his playroom," she growled. Then she stopped. *"Study,"* she said, correcting herself. Who knew who was listening?

She stalked down the halls, not caring who heard the stomp of her feet in their silk slippers. *Seething* and trying to track down the boy hadn't left her a chance to bathe or change since the night before. Her thick black hair was coming out of its bands. Tendrils waved behind her like snakes. She scratched the side of her nose with a very unprincessy rub of the back of her hand. She had sweated in the hot streets of the market and the Quarter of the Street Rats, and it had dried; the feeling of its *still being there* and not immediately washed off was new to her. Not bad, necessarily, but new.

She threw open the carved doors to the giant, airy 'study' where her father spent all his time since her mother had passed away. She sighed as she passed the table with the giant clockwork model of Agrabah whose tiny water clock really *did* work, making miniature suns and moons rise and fall with the day. She rolled her eyes at the colourful silk kites hanging from the ceiling that were brought from the far east and looked like dragons.

She found her father with his latest favourite toy, an intricate balancing game that had come from somewhere in the far west. Tiny carved animals like puzzle pieces had to be placed carefully on top of each other in descending order of size, finishing with the mouse.

Currently he held a yellow duck in his hand and was frowning at it.

"Father," she said politely, trying not to startle him. She ground her teeth and reined in her impatience.

"Oh! Jasmine!" the sultan said, beaming. He was a fat, old little man with a beard as white as the snow on top of far-off mountains. He had been old when he married Jasmine's mother, but the white was less then merely streaks of clouds on the same dark mountains. His turban was also white and topped with a smooth round ruby and a blue feather. Cloth of gold trimmed his robes, and turquoise decorated his sash.

He paused, taking her in: her own turquoise trousers were dusty and had a tear near her ankle. Her sash was askew.

Her top might have been turned just a little.

"Dearest, is everything all right?"

Jasmine took a deep breath and smoothed back the hair around her face, at least.

"No, Father, everything is *not* all right. I slipped out of the palace last night—"

"Jasmine!" her father admonished.

She took another deep breath and continued. "And Jafar had his guards arrest a boy who saved me from having my hand cut off at the market."

The sultan blinked.

"Jafar," she began again slowly, "had his guards... arrest ... a boy—"

"Your hand cut off?" the sultan said, in something between the outraged yell of a sultan and the shriek of a father.

"A misunderstanding," Jasmine said, waving her still-attached hand like it was nothing. *A* big *misunderstanding,* she allowed, thinking about it for a moment. *Like not understanding how things work in the world outside these walls. Money. Poverty. The cost of an apple.* "The point is, he saved me..."

"Jafar did?"

"No, the boy," she said, finally unable to conceal her

impatience anymore. "A boy, I don't know his name, stopped a merchant from cutting my hand off, and then was showing me around Agrabah, and Jafar had him arrested—"

"*You went out of the palace unescorted?*"

"Which is probably *why* Jafar had the boy arrested," Jasmine said through gritted teeth. "But he wasn't hurting me, he was helping me, and he deserves a reward, *not* to be locked up, and I can't find him, and I'm worried."

The sultan looked at his daughter wordlessly for a moment.

"Well," he finally said, "I haven't heard anything about an arrest. But I shall speak to Jafar about this immediately."

"*Thank* you," Jasmine said, bowing her head.

"And while we're on the subject of getting your hand almost chopped off," the sultan continued, a little bit of a growl in his throat, "let's talk about you *leaving* the palace… unescorted… *running away…*"

"Well, I guess it's irrelevant, because Jafar can apparently track my every move," Jasmine growled back.

"Ah, yes, I shall *thank* Jafar for that, you can be sure."

"Thank me for *what*, Your Majesty?"

Jasmine glowered as Jafar swept into the room, cool as a melon. She had been looking for him *all morning* and yet here he was, suddenly, almost as if he had been summoned. Dressed from head to foot, as usual, with a black and red pointy-shouldered cape over his robes, and high white collar, as if it wasn't high summer in the desert city of Agrabah. Tapping his long staff with the cobra head and its evil eyes. Frightening to some, it looked like theatrical silliness to Jasmine.

At least that stupid parrot wasn't around.

On anyone else, the affectation of such a ridiculous bird might have been endearing. On Jafar, it was just another sign of his near insanity. The brightly coloured thing often sat on his shoulder all day, sometimes eating the crackers her own father delightedly offered it. And then it relieved itself down the back of Jafar's otherwise immaculate cloak. Long white disgusting streaks.

No one in the palace or city dared say a word about it.

"What did you do with the boy?" Jasmine demanded, crossing her arms.

"What?" Jafar looked genuinely confused.

"The one you had arrested!"

"Oh. *Him.* He's dead by now, I should think. But I came here for something far more important."

"Dead?"

"Yes, dead. Taken out to the desert and executed for laying hands on the royal princess. Or whatever," Jafar said impatiently, waving his hands.

"Who gave you permission to conduct an execution?" the sultan demanded.

Jasmine was barely listening. She had known the boy for less than a day but could summon his face at will, every detail of it. His large brown eyes that crinkled into a smile so easily. The tiny scar just above the left side of his lip. The way his hair moved when he laughed.

And it was all gone now. Dust.

Because of her.

"*Silence*, you useless little old man. I didn't come here to discuss the fate of one Street Rat," Jafar said.

Jasmine's father stared, speechless. *No one* treated the sultan that way. Not even Jafar. Not even Jasmine.

"*I* came to tell *you* that your reign, I'm afraid, is now at an end."

"Watch your tongue, Jafar," the sultan said warningly. "Obviously there is something wrong with your head today. But even you aren't above accusations of treason. What on earth do you mean?"

"I mean," Jafar said, drawling his words, "*your reign. Has come. To an end*. And mine is beginning."

"Explain yourself!" the sultan exploded. His face turned red and he balled his hands into fists at his side.

Jasmine forced herself to pay attention. She was still in shock about the boy, but strange things seemed afoot everywhere in this situation.

"With *pleasure*," Jafar said. He reached dramatically

into his cape and pulled out…

…what looked very much like a beaten old brass lamp.

"Is this some kind of joke?" the sultan asked curiously. "Is it my birthday today?"

Jasmine was also confused at first.

Then, with the hot prickles of creeping horror, she began to figure it out. Her nurses had told her tales of the magic of the djinn and the things that lurked in the deep deserts. She had also read many books of legends herself. The language etched into the base of the lamp was old. *Very* old…

As if she were in a story herself, Jasmine watched Jafar do exactly what she knew he would: he took the cuff of his sleeve and began to rub the lamp.

At first nothing happened.

Jasmine started to release the breath she had been holding.

Then a tiny wisp of blue smoke began to curl up out of the spout.

The sultan leaned forwards, intrigued.

"Oh, no…" Jasmine whispered.

Suddenly, more smoke poured out of the lamp, like bees escaping a burning hive. Jafar held the lamp delicately away from his body. The sultan jumped back. The lamp began to spark and shake. Tiny lightning bolts shot out of it. It began to scream.

Or *something* began to scream.

Something streaky and blue that shot out of the lamp and raced around the room like a wild dog that could fly.

Jasmine turned and covered her face.

"YYYYEEEEEEEEOOOOOOWWW!"

The scream resolved into something human-sounding.

The band of blue slowed down and expanded and became... a person.

Half of a person.

Half of a very big blue person, with a golden earring and the golden wristbands of a slave. He was bald except for a tiny black topknot held with a golden thong and a beard with a scrolly, pointed tip. His eyes were almond shaped and glittery.

His bottom half was smoke.

"Ten thousand years!" he cried in a booming voice. "Ten thousand years have I been imprisoned in the lamp."

"Genie," Jafar said with an oily smile. "Genie, I—"

"Oy, it feels good to get out," the genie continued in a more normal voice, stretching and grinning. He spun, feeling the air around him. "You know what it's like spending 10,000 years without a massage? Or a bath? Or a—"

"Genie," Jafar interrupted. "I am your master. Heed my words."

"Well, here's a man who obviously knows what he

wants," the genie said, smoothing what little hair he had and straightening his sash. "Lay it on me, Master!"

Jasmine started sneaking to the door. She kept her attention, seemingly rapt, on the genie. It wasn't hard. Besides his being so incredibly *improbable*, there was something also instantly likeable about him. Although she knew that djinn were supposed to be more or less exactly like regular people – magical, ancient regular people – she always imagined them stern, dignified and vaguely frightening. Not charming and goofy.

She slipped her hand over the doorknob.

It didn't turn.

Jasmine frowned. She lightly shook the door. *Locked.* From the *outside*. It must have been Jafar's doing.

"I am granted *three* wishes by you, is that not correct?" the sorcerer was asking, drawing out the words with relish.

The genie drew himself up and suddenly had on the robes of a scholar. He started to count things out on his fingers, as though he were giving a lecture.

"Absotively. Of course, there are a few provisos, a couple of quid pro quos—"

"Yes, yes, whatever," Jafar interrupted. "Genie, my first wish *is to rule on high and become sultan.*"

Jasmine's jaw dropped. The sultan looked aghast.

The genie noticed their reactions and gave a low whistle.

"Sorry, buddy," he murmured to the sultan. "Nothing personal. Looks like your time is up."

With a flash of blue smoke the room grew dim. Outside the window, Jasmine could see the sky become dark and stormy like it did before a monsoon. A strange energy filled the room. She felt the ends of her hair lift.

The sultan's turban rose into the air.

"Confound it! What is this trickery?" the sultan demanded, jumping up and trying to grab his turban. "Jafar, I order you to stop all of this nonsense at once!"

Jasmine gritted her teeth. Her father didn't seem to understand what was happening. He was so used to being the supreme ruler of Agrabah he couldn't imagine anything disturbing that. He actually believed he could still order his adviser around.

She shook the doorknob again futilely. She had to get out of there somehow. Jafar still had two wishes left and already ruled the land what came next could only be worse.

"Yes, *Sultan*, but there is a *new* order now," Jafar sneered. "*My* order."

Smoke circled around him and around the sultan. As Jasmine watched, her father was summarily stripped of his royal robes and cloth of gold. Soon he stood in nothing but his underwear.

Jafar grinned while he was kitted out in the finest robes

of state by the swirling smoke.

"Bow to me!" he screamed at the sultan and Jasmine, fixing Jasmine with his insane eyes.

There was no escape. That much was obvious.

Jasmine suddenly found herself wondering what the boy from the market would do. He had been a natural at thinking on his feet and surviving with nothing but his wits. If they played along, would that buy them time? Would Jafar swallow their act? Maybe they could distract him and grab the lamp...

"I will *never* bow to you, you *impersonator!*" the sultan spat.

Well, there went that possibility. Jasmine wilted with despair.

Jafar's face turned purple with rage. At any other time, Jasmine would have thoroughly enjoyed the sight.

"If you will not *bow* before a sultan, then you will *cower* before a *sorcerer*! *Genie!*"

The genie, who had been watching them quietly, his blue smoke thumping nervously a bit like a tail, suddenly leaped to attention.

"I wish to be the most powerful sorcerer in the world!"

Jasmine should have given the man more credit; insane, vain and repulsive he might have been, stupid he was *not*. Suddenly, things were a *lot* more difficult.

The genie widened his eyes, all the good-natured humour extinguished from them, as if he understood what a terrible, terrible mistake this was. He looked away, embarrassed by what he was about to do, and pointed a finger at Jafar.

A billow of blue smoke and tiny lightning bolts erupted from its tip. Hellish red fire climbed over his limbs and entered Jafar's eyes. Now the man was no longer in the white robes of state, but in robes so black it was more like looking into the void than seeing an actual colour. His turban was strange and angular. His cobra staff slithered as if alive and then froze into a sharp ebony-tipped thing.

"And now, *abject humiliation*," the sorcerer said, pointing his staff at Jasmine and her father.

She found herself thrown down to the floor, onto her knees, prostrate before him. Her father protested the humiliation and his nakedness in incoherent, blubbering gasps.

"And finally," Jafar said casually, stroking his staff, "my last wish."

Jasmine found herself magically lifted up. It was not a nice feeling at all. She was set on her feet, and her hands were arranged in a pious manner.

"For the princess Jasmine to fall desperately in love with me."

Everyone in the room was shocked into silence.

Even the genie.

Jasmine heard strange noises coming from the back of her throat, like she was about to throw up.

"No!" her father shouted angrily.

Jafar sneered and waited.

Jasmine waited.

She mentally assessed herself. Did she feel different? How did she feel about Jafar?

The urge to vomit returned.

Jafar's look of smugness began to slowly fade into confusion.

The genie coughed quietly.

"As I was *saying* before Mr High and Mighty Sorcerer of the Entire World interrupted me, you know, limitless powers don't excuse you from manners, Your Worshipfulness, there are a few provisos, a couple of quid pro quos. To your three wishes."

He hung in the air, his blue smoke calmly waving back and forth.

Jafar didn't say anything, but Jasmine saw the edge of his mouth begin to twitch in anger.

"Here are the basic laws of magic, students. Listen up. Rule number one: I can't kill anyone. Rule number two: I can't make anyone fall in love with anybody else." He looked pointedly at Jafar, then gave Jasmine a kind wink. "And rule number three, which I suspect is *not* going to apply to you; you don't seem like the, 'I made a terrible mistake, let's bring him back from the dead' type, I can't bring people back from the dead."

The sultan looked relieved. He stood next to his daughter and squeezed her arm.

It *was* a big relief. There was no worse fate she could currently think of than being a love-slave zombie to that hideous shell of a man.

But they weren't safe yet. Jafar was not someone who reacted well to disappointments.

Jafar worked his jaw, trying to control himself.

"What is the use of a genie who has limitations?" he growled.

"Hey now…" the genie said, getting offended.

"*I'll* show you what *real power* looks like! *Hold them, Genie!*"

Jafar threw his cape aside and strode forward. Jasmine found she suddenly had golden shackles round her wrists, drawing her hands together. So did her father. The genie swooped in behind them, and she found herself compelled to march, trailing behind Jafar.

The genie leaned forwards to whisper to them.

"Sorry. You guys seem like a nice couple."

"The *sultan* is my *father*," Jasmine snapped.

"*Oh.* Whoops. My bad. It's not so unusual, you know

old kings, young girls. Not totally my fault."

"At least I won't be married to anyone against my will now. Not even Jafar," Jasmine said grimly.

"Yeah, how about we not give Mr Revengey-pants here ideas?" the genie suggested archly. "There's a substantial legal and magical difference between *forcing to love* and *forcing to marry*."

He had a point. Jasmine kept her mouth shut.

Jafar continued to the royal balcony. As the strange procession passed through the halls, things changed in subtle and not-so-subtle ways, according to the sorcerer's tastes. Flowers disappeared or wilted; decorative paintings turned black and jagged. Even the stones they walked on became dark and shiny, like polished onyx.

Jafar threw open the curtain to the Public Balcony and glided onto it. He beckoned and the genie shooed Jasmine and her father out there as well. They made a strange quartet, the mostly naked sultan, the blue genie, Jasmine in her shackles, and the crackling-with-power Jafar.

People were running to the square below them from all quarters of the city like ants to a dropped piece of melon. How had Jafar summoned them? The sky swirled madly with the promise of a coming storm, and lightning arced overhead. Not the sort of weather anyone would willingly venture into...

Jafar smiled, his one gold tooth glimmering in the strange light. He raised his staff, waiting patiently for what looked like *everyone* in Agrabah to assemble and quiet down.

"*People of Agrabah,*" he said. Although he wasn't shouting, his words echoed off every building. "*At long last, the suffering you have endured at the hands of the old sultan is over.*"

Jasmine couldn't help sneaking a look at her father to see how he reacted to this accusation. He seemed mildly surprised. And just two days earlier, she might have reacted the same way. But since then she had *seen* starving children dressed in rags. She had seen organisations of thieves that only existed because there was no other way to make a living. She had spent the day with a boy who had only ever eaten what he had stolen.

"*With the support of the palace guards, an incredibly powerful genie and Princess Jasmine... I, Jafar, am the* new *sultan of* Agrabah!"

If he was expecting a cheer, with his arms uplifted, he was disappointed. His eyes flicked left and right. But rather than panicking, he continued speaking.

"*I will be a sultan of the people. Attentive to their... to* your *every need.*"

There were a few murmurs from the crowd below.

"We've heard that before," someone shouted back,

hands around his mouth to make his voice carry.

"Yes!" shouted someone else. "Remember the wedding? The new sultana promised us decades of prosperity!"

Jasmine felt her breath catch. Her mother had said that?

"You doubt my word?" Jafar asked thoughtfully.

Jasmine didn't like the tone of his voice. The sudden receiving of absolute magical power didn't seem to do anything to stabilise the sorcerer or quell his violent tendencies. He raised his arms again, brandishing his cobra-headed staff.

Jasmine and her father drew back.

"Let me, in my first act as sultan, prove my good faith!"

He cast an eye back at the genie. The genie, still looking a bit shocked by the turn of events, distractedly wiggled his fingers.

The clouds cracked apart with lightning. It began to rain.

A *golden* rain.

Small golden coins fell out of the sky and tinkled on rooftops and cobblestones.

There was a gasp from the crowd. Then people were diving for the money, holding their hands in the air to catch the coins, grinning. Jasmine turned her face away, repulsed by the show of greed.

When the initial rush was over, they finally began to cheer.

"Long live Jafar!"

Jafar visibly relaxed, finally getting something that he really wanted out of the day.

After a moment, he turned to the three standing behind him. He put a hand on the old sultan's chest.

"There, you see?" he said with a sneer. *"That* is *real* power."

And then he pushed Jasmine's father over the balcony.

Genuflect, Show Some Respect

DEEP UNDER THE DESERT, Aladdin was digging.

Digging. Removing rocks. Pushing slippery piles of scree and sand aside. Digging again.

He had been doing it for two days.

A lesser man might have given up.

He was so thirsty that his tongue was swollen and he couldn't swallow. He was so hungry he could barely even sit up; most of his scrabbling was done while lying down. He was so tired that the difference between *asleep* and *awake* was becoming hard to distinguish.

The blackness around him was absolute except for the occasional red flicker of lava from far below. Time had ceased to have any meaning. Aladdin slept very little, afraid that if he did, he would never wake up.

But he didn't give up hope. The same endless expectation of good things that had kept his mother struggling until she died was in his blood, as well.

He wasn't *so* deep under the sands, right? And whether it was dormant or alive and moving, the giant stone tiger still kept its basic structure, right? So he was probably still in the 'throat', which was close to the 'mouth', which led to the surface. And the thing was so broken up and destroyed that there were probably holes all over its granite skin…

Right?

Aladdin also had two more things besides endless optimism that most other people didn't have.

One was a tiny monkey. He wasn't *really* that much help. But Abu kept Aladdin sane and gave him a reason to push on.

The other thing he had was a magic carpet, which *was* useful. It neatly carried piles of stones out of the way and occasionally even lent a tassel to working out a stuck rock. Aladdin curled up on the carpet when he rested, and he could have sworn the thing rocked him a little.

He also had his thoughts to keep his mind busy while he worked. Sometimes they turned to the crazy, evil old man and his attempt at murder. But Aladdin wasn't one driven by revenge; he had seen that emotion use up and destroy others in the Quarter of the Street Rats. He just couldn't figure out why, once the old man had the stupid trinket he wanted, he had felt it necessary to *kill* Aladdin. He had what he wanted and Aladdin couldn't care less what happened to him and his dumb lamp. It wasn't like he was going to try to take it from him. There was something else in play there, a mystery he would solve as soon as he was out of the cave.

But mostly Aladdin thought about Princess Jasmine. If he had never met her, he wouldn't have been thrown into prison by the royal guards, he wouldn't have fallen in with the crazy, evil old man, and he wouldn't be there now, trying to dig himself out of a black, suffocating pit in the middle of the desert.

And *still* he wouldn't have changed a thing.

He thought about her eyes when she was looking into his. He thought about her eyes when she had seen the beggar children. He had witnessed the single moment she began to comprehend the world he lived in. He replayed the graceful skill with which she handled her tiny silver dagger. He thought about her descending from the sky at the end of her pole vault like a warrior angel.

Thinking about all that made him forget that his fingers were rubbed raw and the inside of his mouth felt like the sand he dug through.

———

At the end of the second day or maybe it was the middle of the third; it was hard to tell, Aladdin began to hallucinate.

He imagined there was a tiny monkey with him that wore a tiny vest just like him. He imagined there was a magic carpet helping him and waving its tassels around like a worried mother hen.

Aladdin decided to keep his eyes forwards and continue to dig. Things that weren't real would just distract him.

Some undetermined amount of time after that he began to hallucinate that there was light coming in from somewhere. Yellow light. *Clean* light.

A few minutes of pushing rocks aside and scraping away sand revealed that this, at least, was not a hallucination. A tiny pinhole, no larger than an ant tunnel, was filtering in sunlight that the cave greedily sucked in.

"I see the sun!" Aladdin croaked excitedly to his friends, forgetting for a moment that they weren't real. "I see it!"

He scrabbled faster, pulling away loose stones and trying not to get so overexcited that he caused an avalanche. If he imagined that the carpet and monkey helped him, so much the better.

After tearing off several more fingernails in desperation, Aladdin finally managed to force open a hole large enough to fit his head and shoulders into. When the stones refused to budge any farther, he croaked in frustration. He would *not* be stuck in the cave until he died. That wasn't going to happen.

With a final push that used all of his remaining strength, he shot through and into the daylight.

He lay there for a moment, blinking into the blindingly blue-white sky.

Then Aladdin laughed like a madman under the deadly desert sun. Its heat on his face felt *alive*. Far more natural than the searing flames of the lava. At least if he were to die, it would be outside, looking up at the heavens.

But he wasn't going to die...

Tumbling into the sunshine next to him were Abu and the magic carpet.

How could he ever have doubted their existence?

"Guys!" he cried happily, gathering them both into his arms. "You're real! We're all real! And alive! C'mon let's go home!"

The carpet spread itself out and Aladdin rolled on, barely able to keep his head from spinning. "*Agrabah*. Take me to Agrabah."

The carpet rose into the air and headed east.

Although exhaustion threatened to claim him, Aladdin kept his eyes open and forced himself to acknowledge the appearance of Agrabah on the horizon. The walls were too decrepit, the scene too dusty to be imagined. This wasn't a dream.

They covered the distance through the desert air far faster than he and the evil old man had on foot and hoof. Soothing wind lapped at Aladdin's face, and golden sand skimmed just below them like water. He wished he was feeling better and up to enjoying it. He bet that with a little nudging he could get the carpet to take some of the curves faster and the dives harder. It was like riding an eagle.

The carpet stopped in front of the camel watering station perhaps a little harder than it needed to, causing Aladdin with a bit of a flourish to tumble into one of the troughs with a splash.

"What are you trying to tell me, Carpet?" Aladdin said with a grin, glorious water trickling down his neck. Abu was already guzzling it down, but Aladdin waited until he got out and made his way to the well itself. He pulled up the bucket and ignored the ladle, pouring the sweet liquid directly down his throat.

It was only after he wiped his mouth with the back of his hand that he suddenly noticed they were still alone. He looked around suspiciously. There were no caravans arriving and watering their camels after the long, dusty road through the desert. There were no caravans leaving after filling up their water skins and letting their camels prepare for the journey. There were no vendors selling pastries to hungry and weary travellers. There were no hawkers trying to get the newly arrived to stay at *their* inn, or to pitch their tents at *their* property. There were no children offering to carry things or guide people through the city for a tip.

"Huh," Aladdin said slowly. "All right... let's go and grab a bite to eat. But, subtle-like." He twirled his finger and the magic carpet neatly rolled itself up. It flew over and positioned itself on Aladdin's left shoulder. Abu hopped up onto his right. They set off as casually as they could down the empty road.

As the three kept going deeper into the city, the streets remained silent. The desert wind blew mournfully through abandoned stalls, houses and squares. Far off there was the sound of *something* that he couldn't quite make out. Like the distant whisper of a hot breeze before a storm. Other than that, nothing.

Agrabah wasn't usually a quiet city. There was always someone shouting: a merchant selling his wares, a rag collector begging for people's refuse, mothers yelling at children, men screaming at each other. Very rarely was it in anger; that was just the way the people in his city communicated.

Aladdin scratched the back of his head. In his experience, creepy things that didn't make much sense usually added up to something bad. Like that day years ago when all of the doves and sparrows in the city flew up into the air at once. It had been an amazing sight and then there had been an earthquake straight after.

He resisted the urge to whistle, to fill the air with some sort of sound.

He jumped when a lone cat meowed from the top of a wall.

It wasn't until he was practically in the city centre that he began to see signs of human life. People stragglers, it seemed like were running. Towards the main square. Towards the palace.

"Hey, friend," Aladdin said, grabbing a man by the shoulder. A little harder than a friend might. "Where's the fire?"

The man looked at him with confused black eyes. "Have you not heard? There's going to be a great parade for the new sultan! Let me go, I don't want to miss it."

"There's a new sultan?" Aladdin asked, surprised. "What happened?"

"The old one is gone! Long live Jafar!" the man called out, and pumped his hand in the air in a strange, almost military salute. He broke out of Aladdin's grip and went scampering down the road to the palace.

"Gone?" Aladdin repeated in wonder. Just a week ago he wouldn't really have cared one way or the other what happened to the sultan or maybe he would have cheered a little for the regime change. Things couldn't have become much *worse* under someone new.

But then he had met Princess Jasmine.

The sultan might have been a bad joke at best, but he was still her father. She never had anyone else.

And, not irrelevantly, there was the little question of what happened to Jasmine now that her father was no longer the sultan.

Aladdin began to run in the same direction as the man. There would be answers to at least some of his questions at the parade, or at least more people to ask.

Worry for Jasmine and curiosity did not deter him, of course, from zipping through a couple of hastily abandoned stalls and helping himself to a quick kebab, a square of flatbread and half a dozen apricots. It had been at least three days since he had eaten and it wasn't just riding the carpet that was making him feel a little light-headed.

The noise that he thought was the wind eventually resolved itself into the murmurs of a crowd. And then… music? Someone… a whole chorus… was singing.

He creeped quietly up to the side of a building and slunk round the corner. But he needn't have worried about being seen; no one was looking at him.

Down the very road that seemed to begin at Aladdin's

hideout and end at the palace, the biggest, strangest parade in the history of Agrabah was taking place.

The music was deafeningly loud and *everywhere* at once. There were drums and horns and people in colourful clothes belting out the usual sort of praises for the sultan, with extraordinary claims and lists of unlikely feats thrown in.

But… it looked like at least some of the people in the crowd were singing along. As if they already knew the words somehow. That was more than a little strange.

When the singers in the parade passed they were followed by a dozen fire-eaters and acrobats. These leaped and capered about with manic grins on their faces and flames in their eyes. The crowd oohed and aahed as the performers swallowed blazing swords and blew puffs of smoke.

But… Aladdin had often seen fire-eaters in the market, and knew many of their tricks. These looked like they were actually… breathing fire…

Behind them a hundred men in shining ceremonial black armour marched like beetles in perfect synchronised time. Instead of swords they shook silver bells, ringing like all the angelic warriors of heaven were coming through.

Or maybe not quite *heaven*. Their eyes seemed fiery as well.

Behind *them* was a battalion of people juggling silver scimitars that looked sharp enough to slice the sky. Despite their wielders' unbelievable skill Aladdin found himself flinching.

Behind these were several dozen scantily clad dancing girls. They were beautiful, voluptuous. They all looked oddly alike. Not like sisters, not like cousins, not like members of an all-too-closely-related harem. It was more their bearing. The grins on their faces were the same and didn't quite reach their eyes.

Aladdin felt as uneasy about the girls as he had about the scimitars and the fire-eaters.

Close on their heels rolled what looked to Aladdin's practised eye like a perfect replica of the palace in gold. Possibly *solid* gold, from the strain of the horses pulling it. Tiny clockwork figures including a miniature Jasmine waved from its miniature balconies.

Behind this marched an entire zoo of albino animals. Which was more than a little weird, because many of the animals weren't the kind you could train for marching. Like the crocodiles, for instance. And the peacocks, which kept perfect formation. There were a few handlers, a few whips and a few leashes, but everything seemed oddly in order.

Following these were elephants. Not normal elephants.

These were huge, *much* bigger than even the ones from the western jungles across the sea. All had tusks that swooped and curved out longer than the length of a man. Some of them had four tusks. And their eyes were much, much smaller than a normal elephant's. And they had fur.

On top of the largest of these was a jewelled, canopied saddle. And atop *that* sat Jafar. The sultan's closest adviser. Some said the scariest man in Agrabah.

The one Rasoul had said was responsible for Aladdin's arrest and subsequent dismissal to the dungeons.

Jafar was grinning, a look that was as unnatural on him as it was on the dancing girls below. With his left hand he waved to the cheering crowds. Whenever he gave an extra flourish with it, small golden coins and bread rained out of the sky.

The people went wild, adults and children falling over themselves to grab the bounty.

Aladdin frowned. Jafar, though widely rumoured to have dealings in the dark arts, had never exhibited any powers like this before.

The explanation might have been with the creature that floated sadly behind him, just above his monstrous elephant. It looked mostly like a man, a blue man whose bottom half was smoke.

A *djinn*.

Jafar had found himself a djinn. Aladdin had thought

they were the stuff of legend. His mother used to tell him bedtime stories about them and all sorts of other unlikely creatures who had all been dead for a thousand years.

This one looked like he *wished* he was dead. His body drooped and his face was a study in misery. Every time Jafar wiggled his hand, the genie would point his finger sadly, another shower of coins and bread would appear, and the crowds would cheer.

Aladdin craned his head, trying to see why Jafar only raised his left hand.

He mounted the carpet so he could be raised up for a better view. *There.*

In Jafar's right hand he clutched an old brass lamp like it was his most treasured possession. Like a baby, or a fistful of gems.

Old brass lamp?

Suddenly, the pieces began to fall together, far too quickly for Aladdin's still heat-addled brain.

Jafar was the evil old man. In fact, now that Aladdin was actually looking at him in person, the resemblance was unmistakable. All it would take was a fake beard and some robes and some surprisingly good acting. Jafar had thrown Aladdin into the dungeons under false pretences specifically to get him to retrieve the lamp… the lamp in which the genie was imprisoned, just like in the stories. And genies granted wishes.

One of those wishes must have involved making Jafar the sultan and allowing him to take over Agrabah, wield power over the citizens, and organise this very, very weird parade.

Aladdin let the carpet slip him back into the shadows.

Things were confusing. Where *was* the old sultan? Where was Jasmine? Were they prisoners? Had she run away? Was she... no, he wasn't going to think about the third possibility. He just wasn't.

He needed to rest, regroup and think for a while. But he was reluctant to return to his hideout. Jafar *probably* thought he was dead in the desert, but Aladdin didn't like the way the sorcerer somehow had known where he and Jasmine were before. Almost like he was watching them from afar. Magically. Aladdin needed to blend in with the crowd, go back to being an unseen Street Rat.

Street Rat.

Hmmm...

The magic carpet drifted down the empty street slowly, as if sensing Aladdin's contemplative mood. Abu chittered questioningly.

"I think it's time I finally paid a visit to some old friends," Aladdin decided. "Carpet, we're going to the lair of the Street Rats!

"If they don't kill me first," he added in a mutter.

The Plans of Jafar, the Fate of the Djinn

ACROSS A CITY baking in the white-hot sun, people were staggering home from the largest party Agrabah had ever seen.

In the palace, Jasmine lay on her bed alone and tried not to weep.

She wasn't *entirely* alone, of course; Rajah was with her. She stroked her tiger's thick fur and pushed her face into it. The softness comforted her in a way that nothing else could.

She had just… *just*… started to come to terms with her father being someone who wasn't only her father. He was also a human with human failings. She was only starting to figure out how she could love him and judge him and accept him all at the same time.

And now he was dead.

She kept hearing his laughter and seeing his face. If she closed her eyes and buried her head in Rajah's side and pretended really hard, it was like it all never happened and was just a terrible dream. Her dad was out there, playing with his toys, coming in to see her soon.

Once in a while she would look up, hoping.

But of course he wasn't there. He was gone forever.

Someone knocked at the door.

Rajah let out a growl.

Jasmine didn't have time to sit up, shout "Go away!" or prepare herself at all before Jafar came gliding in. The miserable genie trailed behind like a dog on a lead. He gave her a weak smile.

Rajah bared his teeth at Jafar.

The genie snapped his fingers and immediately a stuffed mouse that smelled suspiciously like catnip bounced into existence. Rajah was instantly distracted and began to bat at it with his big paws. Jasmine gave the genie a grateful look. Both of them knew that Jafar would zap her beloved pet to dust if he so much as nibbled the sorcerer.

"Hello, beloved," Jafar said in his oily 'cheerful' voice. "You look a little pale today. Did you get enough beauty sleep?"

"You killed my father," Jasmine said dully.

"Oh, is that still bothering you? Forget about it." He grew thoughtful, looking almost concerned. "I could *make* you forget about it, if you like..."

"No!" Jasmine cried.

"Well, then." Jafar grinned. He came over to her bed and *actually sat down on it next to her.* How dare he invade her most private of places! She would have to wash all the sheets. And then burn them. "I just came by to tell you *again* how *pleased* I am to be marrying you... and cementing my claim to the throne."

"You already have the throne," Jasmine said listlessly. "What do you need me for? Let me go. Or kill me. Or something. You don't need me to marry you. You've taken what you wanted by force."

"And normally, I agree, that would be enough," Jafar said with a tired sigh, patting her knee. Her skin crawled under his touch. "But even the strongest sorcerer in the world has some limits when it comes to tradition... and history... and religion... and *public opinion.* This really is the easiest way. You were going to marry some arbitrarily chosen prince who would inherit the throne anyway. It might as well be me."

"I wasn't—"

"Oh, yes, you were," Jafar growled. "Your father coddled

you, but in the end he would have caved to *tradition*. To *law*. He was a coward. And you would have been handed over like so much chattel to the prince you hated the least. Trust me, girl, I know what it's like to be considered worthless, somebody else's property. But unfortunately you are the royal princess and I am the sultan and I need your hand to cement the throne. And once again you have no say in the matter."

"If I were the 'strongest sorcerer in the world' I would," Jasmine growled.

Jafar laughed. It wasn't, surprisingly, a particularly evil laugh. "I am not sure you have what it takes to seek that path. I remain unfrightened. Do not worry, beautiful Princess Jasmine. In time you will grow to love me."

"I. Will. *Never*. Love you," Jasmine spat through gritted teeth. "Or have your recent experiments in dark magic failed to convince you of my position?"

Her eyes still hurt from the 'hypnotic gestures' Jafar had attempted like a silly teenager, albeit a teenager consulting a book bound in human flesh.

Her derision didn't upset Jafar in the slightest.

"Well," he said, "the genie may not be able to make you love me, the weak fool that he is, and I may have failed so far, but there… are… other ways." His eyes grew distant. "Soon I will *break* the pitiful laws of magic that bind him…

and me. Then I shall raise the dead from their graves to do
my bidding. Then I shall kill those who oppose me with a
snap of my fingers. Then I will make not just you, but *all of
the people of Agrabah* love me!"

He wasn't paying attention to anything or anyone in
the room, now shrieking and staring off into space like a
madman. The hand not holding his cobra staff balled up
into a clawed fist.

Jasmine watched this transformation in horror, the
genie in resignation.

Even Rajah had looked up from his toy to watch the
human who was acting so strangely. A low growl formed in
the back of his throat.

Jafar glanced at the tiger out of the corner of one eye.
Seeming to recover from whatever fit had possessed him,
he rolled his shoulders and relaxed his hands. His expression
straightened back into Jafar's normal snide superiority.

Then he snapped his fingers.

Rajah went flying across the room like a giant had picked
him up and thrown him. The tiger smashed against the far
wall, head first, and fell down like a lifeless sack of bones.

"Rajah!" Jasmine cried. She rushed over to him.

Rajah lifted his head woozily. He made little mewing
noises, hurt and confused. Jasmine threw her arms around
his neck.

"If I cannot have *love* yet, I'll at least have fear and respect," Jafar snarled. "The strength of a tiger is *nothing* compared to the magic I now wield. You would do well to remember that."

Jasmine whispered in Rajah's ear and stroked his neck. There was a black and bloody gash over his left eye and a giant lump forming behind an ear. When he went to stand up it took several tries and he swayed uncertainly.

The genie shook his head in sympathy.

"You're a monster, Jafar," Jasmine hissed.

"You have no idea, *Princess*," Jafar hissed back.

Then he smiled that thin, closed-lip smile that reached to his ears but not to his eyes. He strode over to the genie, gesturing widely with his arms. "But I initially came here for a *much* happier purpose. Genie, I want you to create the most magnificent wedding dress the world has ever seen for my blushing bride! When we are joined as one I want the entire world to look on in awe and wonder."

"I thought it was going to be a private ceremony," the genie pointed out dryly.

Jafar ignored him. "I shall leave you two to it… bad luck to see the bride in her dress before the wedding and all." He waggled his fingers and swept out of the room, striking his ebony cobra staff against the floor as he went. Self-importantly. The doors slammed shut magically behind him.

Rajah let out a mewling whine.

Jasmine glared at the genie.

Suddenly, he was wearing the garb of a tailor, holding needles in his lips and stretching a ribbon critically against her height.

"I… don't suppose you know your measurements already?" he asked weakly.

That finally put her over the edge.

"How can you do this?" Jasmine demanded, coming very close to shrieking herself. The hysteria that had been building inside her for the past week threatened to burst forth and take over. She stood from where she had been cuddling Rajah and began to pace back and forth, trying not to explode. She crossed her shaking arms, trying to still them.

The genie shrugged apologetically.

"He has the lamp. He has the power. I have to do his bidding. That's why I say: 'What is your bidding, *Master?*' Or did you miss that?"

"You have made the *worst person* the most powerful sorcerer in the world! He is mad! Agrabah is doomed! And I have to marry him! And you don't *care?*"

"Of course I care. You think I don't care? For a snippy little princess you don't actually seem so bad and, yeah, I'd say your city is two shakes away from being a dystopian nightmare. *But,* and pay close attention now, *I have to do what he says.*"

Jasmine opened her mouth to say something, but the genie wasn't listening. He was staring into space dreamily, lost in memories.

"I had a master once. *Nice* guy. He wanted… are you ready for this? A bigger flock of sheep and a *house*. He had a hut. He wanted a *house*. I gave him a house. And the sheep. And a wife who, I might add, was totally into marrying a guy with a bigger flock of sheep. No breaking the laws of magic there. All I had to do was find her. Three nice little wishes and he was happy to let me go. They should all be so modest."

"*Stop!*" Jasmine screeched. "*Stop* with your jokes and stupid little stories! This is my *life* here, Rajah's life, the life of everyone in Agrabah, and you're treating it like it's just another joke! You're *ridiculous!*"

"*I'm* ridiculous?" the genie growled.

Blue smoke roiled. He grew in size until he was towering over her. Jasmine tried not to cower. Dark clouds filled the room and tiny lightning bolts flashed around the edges.

"I *do not* think you have been listening to the subtext, *Your Highness*. I. Am. Trapped. I am a living, thinking, sentient being who has been trapped in that lamp for *10,000 years*. Only let out to be ordered around by you *ridiculous* humans with your greedy, deranged desires. Do you think *you* could stay sane under those conditions for that long?"

Jasmine had never thought about it that way. Genies

were just… magical creatures, often caught in lamps, you could demand wishes from. She never thought about them as *people*. They were never *people* in stories. They just did as they were told.

The genie was far from being done.

"Also? *All of my people are gone.* The djinn are dead as a race. Disappeared from this world. Completely. Yeah, so *that* happened sometime in the last 10,000 years. I'm not sure exactly how or when since I was *in a lamp* when it happened. I'm the only one left. So I'm alone in the world, and even if by some *magic* I managed to get free, I have no home left to go to and no one to see.

"Oh, did *that* little detail escape Your Royal Highness's notice, too? The 'get free' part?" The genie brandished his forearms in her face. She tried not to shrink back from the golden wristbands that came perilously close to breaking her nose. "En*slaved.* These are *manacles*, sweetcheeks.

"But… what would you understand about that?"

Suddenly, he looked exhausted. He physically shrank in size, seeming to somehow draw into himself and away from Jasmine at the same time. "You're a princess among men. You have no idea what it's like to feel *trapped*."

Jasmine took a deep breath. She walked forwards and put a hand on the genie's arm, right above his manacle.

"Genie." She looked up into his eyes, set in a face that

was larger than a bull's head and a violent shade of blue. It was difficult trying to see him as a human, no, a *person*. But she had to try. "I am *extremely* sorry for not understanding your situation. I had no idea about how genies, or djinn, truly live. Or lived. As you said, I'm a snippy little princess. I'm an idiot. What do I know?"

He started to look contrite but she shook her head to stop him.

"You've lived over a hundred lifetimes more than I. It was rude and presumptuous of me to judge you. *Grandfather*," she added, a twinkle in her eye.

"Hey, now..."

"But as long as we're on the subject of being *trapped*... before all this with you and Jafar started, my father was going to hand me over, as Jafar so nicely put it, to whichever prince I hated the least. And then my job would be to make babies until there was a male heir. Assuming, you know, I didn't die in childbirth first. I'd be lucky if I made it to 40, much less 10,000. And currently I'm locked in my room waiting to be married to a man I hate and will continue hating for the rest of my life unless he finds a spell that will make me love him like a brainless puppet. If *that's* not the definition of trapped, what is?"

The genie quietly regarded her for a long moment.

"Apology accepted," he finally said. Making *not quite*

a joke out of it. But she could see in his alien black eyes that he understood.

Jasmine suddenly felt all of her energy, all of the fear, sadness, hysteria, anger drain from her. She collapsed as gracefully as she could on her bed and rubbed her eyes. She had a comrade in the same position as she who was just as powerless as she. They could sympathise with each other and not much else. What kind of comfort was that?

The kind she would have to make do with, for now, Jasmine realised.

"A whole race of djinn? Just like in the legends?" she asked, weary but curious. Rajah clambered up onto the bed next to her. She stroked his head and lay against his firm, warm back, as if preparing for a bedtime story.

"Yep. People just like you," the genie said wistfully. "I mean, not *just* like you. We all were what *you* call magical, but what *we* called normal. And we didn't all look like you humans do. My wife was purple, and…"

"Your *wife?*" Jasmine gasped, sitting up.

"Yeah. She's gone, too," the genie said sadly. He snapped his fingers and a silver mirror appeared and floated in the air between them. Instead of reflecting the room it showed a grinning purple girl. She had what looked like tiny horns behind her ears and claws on her feet.

As Jasmine looked closer she tried to remind herself that

this wasn't just a creature of legend; this was a woman who was once alive and married to the genie and had whatever a normal life was for a djinn. If she focused, Jasmine *could* begin to see the person behind the purple: tiny laugh lines around her eyes, a smattering of deeper purple freckles across her nose, frowny marks between her brows. The sort of round belly and arms that people often got when they had been married for a while and were content with their lives.

"She looks happy," Jasmine said, carefully not choosing the platitude *beautiful*. Plus, the horns…

"Yes, well, that's because she wasn't screaming at me right then. Or throwing things," the genie said fondly. "I kid. We fought, but we loved each other. Very much." He blew the picture a kiss and then it faded away into blue smoke.

"What… happened?"

"Oh, you know." The genie waved his hand dismissively. "Same old story. Dark prophecies about the end of the world. The end of *our* world, I mean. Time running out for the djinn. The Age of Man beginning. A young, greedy djinn who already had a bit more power than those around him and used that as an excuse to seek even greater power. Saving our world. 'I'm doin' it for the wife and kids', you know?"

"You had children, too?"

"No, it's just a saying. I'm telling a story here, sweetcheeks. You mind? Anyway, long story short, the quickest path to infinite power is... infinite wishes. Right? A wish is the most powerful thing in the universe. If you know how to work around the limitations. So I went down the path of becoming what you folk call a genie, the most powerful being in this world.

"Only there was one tiny problem. I hadn't quite understood the catch: you can't make the wishes yourself. The universe has a way of keeping things in balance. Which, yes, I should have understood better as a student of the great magics. I thought I was above all that. So wham, bam, thank you, Kazaam, here I am. Still paying for my hubris 10,000 years later. And the djinn still died out. The, as they say, *end*."

Jasmine was silent. There was too much to think about. An entire race gone, one man attempting to stop it and losing. The genie's story was sad and horrible.

And yet, if one ignored the fact that he was *sort* of thinking about saving his people when he went seeking unlimited power, one could *almost* see similarities between his and Jafar's paths.

The genie still wound up losing everyone and, by trapping himself in the lamp, set things in motion for a greedy Jafar to attain almost limitless power himself. It was like a never-ending cycle of greed, power and insanity.

And unhappy endings.

The universe certainly had a terrible way of keeping balance if this was how it chose to do so, Jasmine reflected.

She shivered, wondering if Agrabah would end up like the empire of the djinn: forgotten and legendary.

"So… again with the long story short… I would help you in a heartbeat, if I could," the genie said gently. "But this is all I can do right now."

He waved his finger sadly up and down. White smoke trailed out of the tip and became a silken thread. The thread rose up and down and then began to circle around itself. Faster and faster it ran, its point becoming sharp and golden like a needle. The whisper of cloth against cloth grew louder as a form began to take shape.

Jasmine watched, mesmerised, as a dress appeared in mid-air.

It was *not* the most magnificent gown the world had ever seen. It was a natural off-white, the rough threads woven so loosely it was like layers of netting. Instead of normal sleeves the material was gathered once at the shoulders, once at the elbows, and once at the wrists, draping down to the floor and exposing most of the arms. There no rosettes, no embroidery, no tiny mirrors sewn into the fabric, no pearls or jewels on any trim. The hem ended far above the ankles.

"It's beautiful," Jasmine said, standing up and drawing it close to her, to see how it would hang. She spun and the layers bloomed out. It was *perfect* for dancing in.

"It's the dress my wife wore on our wedding day," the genie said sadly.

He turned and drifted out of the room like so much smoke, barely needing to open the door to go through.

Jasmine watched him leave, still holding the dress. Somehow her grip had tightened. She had to make herself relax so her nails wouldn't ruin the beautiful cloth.

No more crying on the bed for her.

She was the royal princess. She had to start acting like one. She had to stop talking about being trapped, about being handed over from one man to another. She had to start *acting*.

She had to start being the hero.

The Street Rats

THE CARPET FLEW DOWN an empty street. Aladdin stood tall and barely needed to move his arms to balance, even when they took corners fast. Once again he wished he had time to *really* see what it could do but more pressing things awaited in the Quarter of the Street Rats.

If the section of it that Jasmine had seen was frightening, well, Aladdin pressed on through neighbourhoods that were downright terrifying.

Tall old buildings toppled towards each other and blocked out the sky overhead. At mid-day the streets were in shadow, which was a relief from the sun but left everything in a strange, hot twilight. There were a *lot* of places to hide. Black windows on vacant houses looked like empty eye sockets. Grim, broken statuary and crumbling piles of bricks made it seem like an ancient war zone. The only open space was one of the few graveyards inside the city walls. Its creepy, spiky stones stood like broken teeth, pointing in all directions.

The whole place was flooded with loneliness and desperation... and yet at the same time there was a constant feeling of being watched by someone, or something, unseen.

The only people visible had shifty eyes and a palpable sense of mischief about them. Aladdin jumped off the carpet in front of an abandoned building that looked like all the others. Growing used to their routine, the carpet helpfully rolled itself up and slung itself over his shoulder.

It had been, quite literally, *years* since Aladdin had set foot in this place. As he carefully stepped over the dusty threshold, he saw that it was all almost exactly as he remembered it. Although the windowless rooms should have been nearly pitch dark, strangely convenient cracks in the walls and loose stones illuminated necessary things. A doorway here and a stairway there. And a deadly booby trap *there...*

...which Aladdin remembered at the last moment, pulling his foot back just before stepping onto the rope that would snap around him and fling him aloft, trussed up like a rabbit.

With a shuddering release of breath Aladdin proceeded

more carefully through the building to a back room. Counting by threes, he found the right board to lift up and revealed an old storage cellar. Once down there he tiptoed around what looked like a nest of scorpions and slipped behind some old broken clay amphorae. Finally he jumped into a black, slanting tunnel, landing on a slippery metal slide that he surfed down with ease.

Receiving him at the bottom was a cave, which, while he remembered it fondly, now seemed a little too similar to the Cave of Wonders. He tried not to panic, swallowing several times and trying desperately to notice the differences. This was smaller, and not full of wonders at all, but dozens of flickering oil lamps, and pairs of glittering eyes.

"Nice place you still have here," Aladdin drawled, trying not to let his voice crack. "Love what you haven't done with it."

"*Aladdin.*"

Morgiana's tiny, tightly muscled and very familiar form resolved itself from the shadows. She was dressed differently from the last time Aladdin had seen her; a pair of black harem trousers was belted tightly across her belly so they moved with the slightest bump of her hips. She used to wear a close-fitting top that exposed her midriff and arms, but now had a loose black shirt made of the same material as the scarf that tied up her mass of impenetrable black curls.

Her normally aristocratically hooked nose was screwed up as if she had smelled something bad, and her ample lips were pursed. The dimple on her cheek that used to appear when she smiled was nowhere to be found.

"I don't remember asking you over to dinner," she said.

"I was in the neighbourhood, so I thought I'd drop by," he quipped. "What's cooking?"

"Aladdin!" Duban came forwards with a much more genuine smile. It faded after a moment, as if he only just then remembered something about his old friend. The thief looked exactly the same as he always did, if a little taller: square, thickset, with surprisingly intelligent eyes in an otherwise wide and open face. His long black hair was pulled back into a ponytail and held with golden rings. Golden rings were in his ears now, too. "Come, sit down, break some bread with us."

Aladdin looked at the additional sets of eyes watching him from the darkness. Morgiana and Duban he had known forever. He couldn't say that about everyone else. Their little gang of thieves had grown over the years; if for some reason anything got ugly, it would be hard to escape.

But he was already this far in…

"Absolutely," he said with forced jollity. And yet even the fake smile slipped from his face as he approached the pile of pillows and rugs. Safe for the moment, exhaustion almost overwhelmed him. He still hadn't eaten much, and the events of the past several days were taking their toll.

Morgiana's expression softened.

"Are you all right?"

"I'll be fine," he said, waving a hand at her. He collapsed as gracefully as he could at a low table and tried to reach for some grapes as slowly and nonchalantly as possible.

"We'll get you some water," Morgiana decided. She made a clicking noise and raised her chin at one of the *much younger* thieves in the dark. "Another cup for our guest. Hazan, go!"

A little boy leaped up, quick as a shadow, to fulfil her request.

"What's been going on with you?" Duban asked, settling down next to him. "You look like you've been in combat."

"Aw, it's nothing. Just in trouble, as usual," Aladdin said. When the boy reappeared with his drink, he sipped it slowly as if it was no big deal. Then he threw five grapes into the air and caught them in his mouth, swallowing without chewing. "I think a bigger question is, what has happened to *Agrabah* in the last few days while I've been… otherwise occupied?"

Duban laughed. "Wouldn't we all like to know! It seems as if creepy Grand Vizier Jafar is now creepy Sultan Jafar."

"I noticed that," Aladdin said, nodding.

"It's actually been… surprisingly okay," Morgiana admitted.

"The regime change, I mean. Not too much violence. No military uprising. And life under the new sultan has, so far, been pretty good. No one in the city has gone hungry since he took over. Everyone in the Quarter of the Street Rats has had full bellies, for the first time in their lives, some of them. No one has had to steal food because of all the handouts."

"Which makes *our* livelihood a little unstable," Duban said with a wry smile. "Especially with Jafar's announcement about new Peacekeeping Patrols that will walk the city now. Crime is already down."

"But other than *us*, everyone's been pretty happy," Morgiana added cheerfully. "Nobody cares that Jafar killed ol' whitebeard in cold blood."

Aladdin choked on a grape.

"Killed?"

"Yes," Duban said with a philosophical shrug. "Despite the generosity, Jafar isn't exactly an angel. He called everyone in the city to gather in front of the Public Balcony and announced he was the new sultan. And then he threw the old sultan over the railing. Just like that."

"After he made it rain gold," Morgiana pointed out. With a familiar flick of her fingers a small coin appeared in her hand. It glittered ominously in the lamplight. Aladdin noticed piles of the same coins behind her. Like tiny versions of the mountains of gold treasures in the Cave of Wonders.

He frowned and took the coin from her. She didn't object unlike the old Morgiana, who would have yelped and grabbed it back. She merely watched him as he carefully held it between his thumb and forefinger, tilting it in the light to get a better look. It *felt* like real, pure gold: heavier than its tiny size would seem to have justified. Blank on one side. On the other was a strange, jagged symbol he couldn't figure out. Ancient and threatening looking. Almost like a stylized lizard, or a...

"Parrot," Morgiana filled in. "We think. A very angry one by the look of it. See? His beak opened there, and there, his claws, there... You sort of have to use your imagination."

"Oh, I see it now... Jafar has a pet one, right?"

Morgiana nodded. He gave the coin back to her. It didn't look much like a parrot, really. It looked evil.

"And they just... stay? They don't disappear after a while, like the treasure of an ifrit in old stories?"

Morgiana shrugged. "Nope. They stick around. It's all real."

Aladdin didn't like it. He couldn't get his mind off the mountains of ancient gold buried in the desert.

"What about Princess Jasmine?" he asked finally.

"Jafar is marrying her. To cement his claim, I assume."

"And she agreed to this? She *wants* to marry him?"

"Oh, yes, I'm sure she is all into a guy more than twice

her age who killed her dad and is generally known to be evil," Morgiana drawled. "When did you become such an idiot, Aladdin?"

"But she doesn't love him!"

"No kidding, Kazem," Duban said with a chuckle. "They say his own mother abandoned him at birth, he's so evil."

"But what choice does she have, exactly?" Morgiana demanded. "She should count herself lucky that he didn't kill her outright along with her dad. It was probably some sort of bargain they made. 'You marry me and seal my claim to the throne, and I *won't kill you*.' Why are you so surprised? It's the first thing you men do when you seize power. Punish all the women."

"I've got to stop the wedding," Aladdin vowed.

"Settle down, friend," Duban said soothingly, but whether it was to Morgiana or Aladdin, it was hard to say. "Aladdin, it's not going to be a public ceremony you can just go to and say, 'I object to this wedding!' It's going to be held in the sultan's private chambers of the palace tomorrow night, only the highest high-born are invited. That's why there was that parade today, to publicly celebrate it."

"And by the way, just why… do *you*… have to stop the wedding?" Morgiana inquired sweetly. "Have you suddenly taken it upon yourself to defend women's rights across the sultanate, or is there something you're not telling us?"

Aladdin thought about lying. He was good at it, to other people. These used to be his two closest friends.

"It's a long story," was all he allowed.

"Aladdin disappears for a few days, Agrabah is overthrown, and suddenly he has an interest in rescuing a royal princess," Morgiana mused. "I'll *bet* it's a long story."

"Well, you have until tomorrow night to play the hero," Duban said, spreading his fingers to show the food, the pillows, and the other, younger thieves who were making themselves comfortable in preparation for hearing a good tale. "You even brought your own carpet to sit on," he added, looking at the magic carpet doubtfully. "What's up with that?"

"Part of the story," Aladdin admitted.

"Yes, tell us the story. Let's catch up. I haven't seen Abu in *ages*," Morgiana crooned, taking a grape and handing it to the little monkey. He accepted it from her with a politeness he didn't usually demonstrate.

"I don't—"

But Aladdin was prevented from having to say anything else by the sudden arrival of a swarm of tiny thieves: sliding down the ramp, leaping into the room, rolling and scuttling to present themselves to Morgiana and Duban.

"Mistress," the first one said, opening up his hands.

In it was a golden bangle and an emerald necklace.

"Well done, Deni! Excellent. Who's next?"

All of the thieves lined up to present something to her, even things as little as an empty leather purse or a single copper coin.

"I thought you said Street Rats didn't have to steal food for the last three days!" Aladdin snapped accusingly at Morgiana.

She shrugged.

"Yes, I said they didn't have to steal *food*. The parade was a perfect place to… *remove* the valuable possessions from all the idiots hypnotised by the magical buffoonery."

"This was always my problem with you!" Aladdin swore at his old friends. "Yes, I steal, too, but only what I need. What I can't get for myself. You do it *as your day job*. You have a whole little… organisation of apprentices here who are going to grow up thinking this is an acceptable thing!"

"If there continues to be food and gold from the palace, it *will* no longer be an acceptable thing," Morgiana said agreeably. "But history has shown time and time again that it is generally unwise to rely on others, especially those in charge, to provide for the poor. I give this new sultan a week or two at most before he realises he doesn't want to keep giving people handouts. At least not without getting something in return."

"Even when things are going *great* you expect the worst

out of people and think they *deserve* to be stolen from!"
Aladdin spat.

"My father didn't deserve to lose the use of his leg,"
Duban said mildly. "My sister didn't deserve to be beaten
by her husband."

"No one deserves anything they get," Morgiana
said, shrugging. "It is what it is. You just have to make sure
that at least sometimes you're on the *good* side of getting.
For you."

"And evil keeps going around," Aladdin swore angrily,
storming out. "There's another way. You don't have to *choose*
this life. You could be something more."

A Rescue of Sorts

NIGHT IN AGRABAH.

Was it quieter than usual? Were people recovering from the huge party, suddenly uneasy with something they couldn't quite put their fingers on? Did they pull out the tiny, funny little gold coins and stare at them in the lamplight, thinking deeply about the turn of events in their city? Did they leave the gold coins out on their tables and not hide them in shoes, under mattresses, inside pillows? Why bother? All of their neighbours had coins, too.

It wasn't just the religious and the superstitious who worried about the gold. The most educated scholars and wisest of old folk all knew that *something* was never created out of *nothing*. Not without consequences.

And that parade had been more than a little weird.

These philosophical issues were the least of Aladdin's concerns at the moment, however. And actually, he had to admit that the city's uneasiness was a great help to him. The streets were much simpler to sneak through with everyone lingering inside, close to doorways, staying away from the open sky.

Abu sat on his shoulder and the magic carpet glided silently behind him, it was too dark to be able to fly well without the risk of hitting something.

People had been trying to sneak into the palace for centuries. Some of their skulls could still be seen on spikes around the castle walls, bleached white into shiny marble balls by years of desert sun.

Aladdin was well aware of this. But he also had something those poor souls hadn't had, secret knowledge of the palace grounds. And though returning to the hidden tunnels made his heart quicken with fear, Aladdin gritted his teeth and pressed on to the stables on the far side of the palace, on the edge of the desert.

The horses and camels whickered and whinnied at his approach; he calmed them with some soothing noises of his own. Then he spotted a familiar-looking horse.

"You made it back!" Aladdin whispered with joy, patting him on the neck. The horse snorted, perhaps both pleased at seeing the boy again and also wanting nothing to do with the human who had led him out into a stormy desert in the middle of the night. But for all that, he seemed fine.

"I hope your stable boy is all right, too," Aladdin sighed.

He found the drain that hid the secret entrance and carefully moved aside the cover just enough to let himself in, sliding it just as quietly back over his head once he was down. *This* time he was prepared for the pitch darkness with a tiny oil lamp he had pinched from Morgiana on his way out. It seemed fitting somehow.

The stone passages were deathly silent but for the distant roar of lava. Aladdin still found himself treading softly. It was, however, a much easier trip made with his two friends. The magic carpet floated alongside, almost like a faithful dog, while Abu stayed on his shoulder.

Aladdin saw with relief that all the marks he had made with his knife were still there on the walls. He easily followed them back to the dungeons. A gentle tap of the correct rock sent it sliding aside and he was back where it had all begun.

Abu chittered with nervousness. There were the manacles that had held Aladdin; there was where Jafar had appeared from the shadows in disguise.

"Kind of brilliant," Aladdin admitted reluctantly. But he did wonder why Jafar had found it necessary to go to all the trouble to get *him* for the lamp business. Any Street Rat would have done it for a single golden coin. Or less…

Thoughts for another time. He had a princess to rescue! The door leading out was locked, of course, but Aladdin had his little kit with him. He worked with his picks in the flickering lantern light for many long minutes, sweating and swearing. When the lock finally gave it was with a nearly silent, anticlimactic *click*.

The passageway outside was short, murky and dim. He stared at what looked like an infinite number of stone steps spiralling upwards to the hazy ceiling. It was as though he were at the bottom of a tower buried underground. Even the design was similar to the Moon Tower, the tallest building in the palace. *Jafar's* tower…

Across from the entrance to the dungeon was another door that was covered in strange carvings. The edges were highlighted with an evil orange glow from whatever was in the room behind.

"Another time," Aladdin promised himself. He would explore what was very obviously Jafar's secret study when things weren't quite so dire.

He snapped his fingers and the carpet obligingly lowered to let him step onto it. They drifted upwards through the dark, above the steps, like a dandelion head borne aloft by a soft breeze.

At the top was a strange sliding door that was unlocked with the press of a lever. Aladdin opened it the smallest crack and peeked through. The room beyond was dimly lit and mostly empty except for a few pieces of finely wrought furniture. There were no guards.

Aladdin drew back in surprise. What sort of dungeon didn't have guards?

He slid the door open just wide enough to let his body, and Abu and the carpet, through. When they were out he turned round and saw that what looked like a door from the dungeon side looked like a completely normal wall panel on the other. In fact, when the door closed itself with a quiet click, it was impossible to tell where it had been.

A *secret* dungeon! Secret even from the sultan himself, Aladdin wagered. Jafar's personal, evil, sorcerous laboratory and prison. It seemed like all of the whispers about him were true...

And if they *were* true, Aladdin realised grimly, then Morgiana was probably right, and Agrabah was in worse trouble than before. There was no way someone this secretive, treacherous, murderous and evil would turn overnight into a generous and doting benefactor. Aladdin *knew* people. He had to, as a thief. And people didn't usually change that much.

The marble floor was chilly under his bare feet; suddenly Aladdin understood why rich people owned so many carpets.

The soft click of heels on stone alerted him to the presence of others nearby. Aladdin dived behind a velvet sofa. The carpet laid itself on the floor. Abu climbed up a screen on the side of the room and stayed silent and still near the ceiling.

A pair of guards marched through, stiff as rods and carrying deadly looking spears across their chests. They were clad head to toe in black and red, Jafar's colours. These were not the unruly market guards that Aladdin was used to dealing with; these were inner palace guards, with quick, intelligent eyes, nervous hands and not an extra ounce of body fat on them. Very, very dangerous men.

As soon as they were gone Abu started to descend. The carpet curled up one corner in anticipation of rising.

"Shhh! *Not yet,*" Aladdin whispered.

He counted his heartbeats and his breaths.

Almost 10 minutes later, the guards came through again. Exact same route, exact same wary glances, exact same march.

Aladdin smiled at his own forethought.

"Okay," he whispered as soon as they were out of sight.

The three of them tiptoed or glided on to the next room. What he found made Aladdin pause… and then raise an eyebrow in wonder.

The space they were in *could* have been a banquet hall

that easily held a hundred revellers. Instead, it was furnished with tables covered in... things. Miniature palaces. Models of mazes on tilting platforms you worked tiny silver balls through. Puzzles that made brightly painted jungle scenes when they were done. Balancing games in which the blocks were intricately carved animals and fantastic beasts. And above all this hung the gorgeous silk kites the sultan flew when he deigned to leave the palace on one of his famous picnics.

So these rumours were true, too. The old sultan was nothing but a crazy, decadent old man who played with toys while Agrabah starved.

Or... he was Jasmine's sad, lonely old father who wanted more kids, or grandkids, or his wife back. It was complicated.

A quiet *tick* from the corner of the room sent Aladdin flying behind a table and Abu and the carpet into other hiding places.

No one appeared.

The ticking continued.

Aladdin lifted his head and saw that on one of the tables was a model of Agrabah, a different one, an imaginary clean one, that was accurate down to the calendar clock-tower that rose above the central square. *That* was what was making the noise. A tiny working version of the real thing: a miniscule golden half-moon popped out and turned a degree on the dial.

Aladdin shook his head either at himself or at the dead sultan and his hobbies.

Ten minutes. He heard the scraping of shoes again.

He gestured frantically to the room beyond the one he was in. The carpet and Abu followed close behind as he ducked down and crab-walked quickly to what looked like a room with no discernible purpose. There was a brazier with coals smouldering in the corner and an incense burner sending smoke up to the ceiling; next to the burner was a low day-bed, but no one was on it.

More footsteps. From the *other* direction!

Aladdin dived under the divan, sucking in his breath to fit.

He couldn't see the faces of these new guards from his position but was pretty sure there were more of them this time, three, maybe, or four, walking in perfect synchronicity. The guards he had avoided twice before met up with them in the middle of the room; Aladdin watched their feet and heard the smart smacking of spears against each other in a military salute.

Then each set of guards kept going in the direction they had been heading.

Aladdin started counting again, frustrated. This was bad: he hadn't allowed extra time to wait for guards to complete their circuits. Impatient to move, he got up, deciding to take

a risk; he knew he had at least 10 minutes from the one set
of guards and thought they would all probably be on the
same clock.

Wrong!

Aladdin slammed himself against the closest wall as
the second set of guards passed by the door, moving in an
entirely different direction.

Abu scampered across the cold hall to be close to him,
his tiny toenails clicking against the floor.

The guards stopped.

"Abdullah, wait. Did you hear something?"

Aladdin closed his eyes and tried to still his heart.
The silence was so complete and profound he was certain
they could hear it beating.

"I heard something in the room with the incense."

"It was probably just a mouse, or a monkey."

"I will not lose my head over something which turns out
not to be a mouse."

Aladdin winced as the concerned guard walked to the
door, spear raised.

All he had to do was step four inches farther into the
room.

The guard made a thorough scan of the place, turning
his head slowly back and forth.

Aladdin opened one eye and almost caught his breath

when he saw how close to him the shiny, sharp spear tip was.

The silence stretched on.

"It's nothing," the guard decided.

As he stepped back to rejoin his companion, Aladdin practically crumpled with relief.

He wasted no time, scurrying out of the room and ducking under a window through which the moon shone like a spotlight. Then he stopped, caught by the view outside.

Spread over a huge area was the most beautiful garden he had ever seen.

There was a miniature forest of cedar, cypress and other sweet-smelling pines that couldn't normally live in hot, dry Agrabah. There were rows of delicately petalled flowers. There was a garden just of mountain plants. There was a pool filled with flowering white lilies and their pads, and pink lotuses taller than most men. There was a fountain as big as a house and shaped like an egg. There was a delicate white aviary that looked like a giant's birdcage. Strangely, there were no birds in it.

And everywhere, entwined around every tiny building and every balustrade and every topiary ball, was jasmine. White jasmine, pink jasmine, yellow jasmine, night-flowering jasmine… The smell was heady enough to make Aladdin feel a little drunk.

Jasmine.

This was her garden.

She had to be close. Aladdin hurried on.

There was definitely a feminine change to the decor as he tiptoed through the dusty twilight of the slumbering palace: more soft rugs, more shapely urns, more wall hangings, more flowers and plants. He passed through a sitting room filled with silk cushions and low tables scattered with bowls of nuts, scrolls and even a few games. Apparently the sultan thought the palace was safe enough from the eyes of outsiders and didn't consider a screen or the usual huge female guards necessary.

Of course, it was said that Jasmine's best friend was a tiger, so maybe guards really *weren't* that necessary.

Past this room was a short hall that ended in a pair of beautifully carved golden doors that flared out like butterfly wings. On either side of them stood a pair of the usual male guards in black and red, Jafar-style.

This was a problem.

Aladdin clenched his fists in frustration. Of course he could take them out, somehow, and in doing so make noise that would summon every last man in the palace. He found himself thinking of Morgiana, 'the Shadow', and how this was exactly the sort of situation she would have excelled in.

Something must have clicked somewhere; some invisible clock or quiet chime. The two guards raised their spears and saluted each other, then turned and marched out of the room.

Aladdin had no idea when they would return, but the instincts of a thief told him to *act immediately*. He might never get a better chance.

He rushed forwards and pulled out his lock-picking kit again. This lock was beautiful and intricately decorated, but quite basic underneath all that. It would take him only a minute or…

The door suddenly opened inwards.

Surprised, Aladdin looked up into Jasmine's equally surprised face. She was pulling a pair of sharp hairpins out of the lock on *her* side.

"Uh, hi," Aladdin said.

He didn't understand, but didn't object to, the sudden embrace she wrapped him in, hugging him more tightly than the Widow Gulbahar did on special occasions.

"You're alive!" she whispered with joy.

"Of course I'm alive," Aladdin started to object. Then he thought about the past few days of his life. Maybe it wasn't such an obvious conclusion. "I came back to rescue you. Which… though… now doesn't seem that necessary."

At that moment, her famous pet tiger appeared and glared at the intruders with flashing yellow eyes. He seemed violent and mean, with an evil-looking wound on his head. He uttered a deep, disapproving growl. Abu hopped up and down and began to chitter on Aladdin's shoulder in hysterics. Aladdin quickly put a hand over his friend's mouth to keep him quiet.

"Really. You seem to be fine," Aladdin continued as calmly as he could.

"It's the thought that counts." Jasmine grinned, putting the hairpins back under her tiara and a hand on Rajah's neck. "I'm... Jafar told me you were executed, because of me."

"*What?*" Aladdin's mind raced. "Huh. Things are starting to make sense. Sort of. Let's talk later. We have to get out of here."

"We have about nine minutes before the relief guards come back," Jasmine said, nodding.

"Right." Aladdin grabbed her hand and turned to go. Abu chittered in agreement. The carpet rose up.

"*What is that?*"

Jasmine tried to confine her shriek to a whisper. Aladdin was about to make some joke about her being a girly girl, afraid of monsters, but stopped. A girl who was locked up in her own bedroom by a madman forcing her to marry him probably didn't need to imagine monsters. She could probably be forgiven for being a little jumpy.

"Oh, this?" Aladdin asked casually. "Say hello to

Magic Carpet. Magic Carpet, the royal princess Jasmine."

"A real… flying… carpet…" Jasmine said in awe, eyes wide. "Amazing. We have a *lot* to talk about."

"Yeah, *Royal Princess Jasmine*, we sure do," Aladdin agreed with heavy irony. She had the decency to blush a little. He set off down the hall. "We can talk back at Morgiana's."

"Who… never mind. But first we have to rescue the genie."

"Uh, *no*, Jasmine. We can't right now. We don't have time."

"He's trapped. Just like me," Jasmine said desperately. "Jafar is *making* him do all these horrible things, making him into the sultan, a powerful sorcerer. He doesn't want to. We just need to grab his lamp…"

"From a *powerful sorcerer* who is *also the sultan*, has a *secret dungeon*, and has already transformed the palace into his own personal… uh… *palace*. No way, Jasmine. Not now. We can come back better prepared and with a plan but just getting you out of here is going to be tough enough. You think he's going to let his most precious possession lie around for the taking?"

Jasmine's face fell. "But…"

Aladdin put his hand on her arm and looked into her eyes. "I promise: if it's that important to you, we will come back for him. But right now, there is only so much a thief, a princess, a tiger, a monkey and a magic carpet can do."

She nodded sorrowfully and took his hand.

"Now it's more like seven minutes," Aladdin said. "I have a secret way out. We just need to get back to the room with the red panels."

Jasmine nodded and hurried alongside him, keeping her quickly moving feet silent.

"But Jafar isn't finished with everything yet," she whispered breathlessly as they went. "He has a plan."

"But he has all of Agrabah!" Aladdin said in an exasperated whisper. "What more could he want?"

Jasmine's face darkened. "What do people like him always want? *More.* More power. More adulation. More..."

She stopped as Aladdin drew up short. The carpet and the tiger skidded to a halt. Abu grabbed on to Aladdin's neck at the sudden cessation of movement.

Standing in the room with the brazier, looking as surprised as they did, was Rasoul.

"Run..." Aladdin suggested weakly.

"Guards! To me! In the Room of the Scintillating Brazier!" Rasoul roared.

"Room of the Scintillating Brazier?" Aladdin muttered in disgust as they took off down the hall.

The heavy stomp of feet seemed to come from

every direction. If they had been outside in the streets of Agrabah, Aladdin would have known where they were safe, what roads were too crooked to be seen on, where there were easy escapes. Now he was just leading them blindly.

"Can we get outside?" he asked Jasmine in a gasp.

"Straight ahead," she said between breaths. "There is a columned loggia that leads to the Courtyard of the Rose-Scented Footstools."

Aladdin looked at her.

"Just kidding," she said with a quick smile. "They don't really smell."

The tiger bounded ahead as if he knew the plan. The carpet stayed behind them as if he were guarding the rear.

Aladdin wasn't sure what a *loggia* was, but ahead there was a hall dotted with columns that opened up into a large courtyard, with no ceiling overhead. There were lemon trees, sweet-scented myrtle and pots of roses. More columns, ornamental and abstract, decorated the interior of the courtyard along with statues depicting ancient river gods. There were indeed footstools carved into the shape of roses.

There were also about a dozen guards waiting for Aladdin and Jasmine.

"Halt!"

Aladdin fell back as the pair in front leaped at them. One guard got his arms around Aladdin's waist and brought him down. Jasmine leaped out of the way of the other one.

The tiger roared and raised his paw.

"No, Rajah!" Jasmine cried. "It's not his fault. It's Jafar's orders!"

"*Now* she gets all 'protect-the-people-y'? Couldn't she wait 10 more minutes?" Aladdin wondered aloud as he tried to shimmy out of the guard's grasp. When that failed, he curled himself into a ball. He aimed his toes at the man's privates. With a muscle-taxing burst, he pushed out his arms and legs as hard as they would go.

The guard screamed and fell to the side. Aladdin climbed over his back.

"Split up!" he ordered, diving to the side.

A blade sliced through the air above Aladdin's head. He fell into a roll. He kicked his feet out at his attacker and managed to topple the guard into another pair of guards. Scimitars flew like deadly missiles.

A scream from Jasmine brought him to his feet. A guard had managed to grab her sash and was pulling her. She held on to a statue for dear life with one arm... but reached for her silver dagger with the other.

Rajah turned and roared.

"*Fool!*" Rasoul yelled at the guard as he finally caught up with the fight. "The sultan will have your head if you touch the princess in such a manner!"

Rajah leaped.

Aladdin didn't see what happened next because a pair of guards ran straight at him, swords aimed directly for his chest.

Aladdin crouched and spun like a dervish. He managed to sweep the legs out from under one of the guards, causing him to trip into the other. They both came crashing down, landing on the stone floor with a sickening crunch.

"*Carpet!*" Aladdin ordered the moment he could take a breath. "*Get Jasmine!*"

The carpet paused where it was dancing in the air. It was just out of reach of some easily distractable guards who were poking at it with the tips of their scimitars. Finished with whatever he had done to the other guards, Rajah was silently stalking them from behind, getting ready to pounce.

At Aladdin's words, the carpet immediately slalomed down between the marble columns towards Jasmine. The guards turned to chase it and came face-to-face with the tiger.

Before he could turn to do anything else, Aladdin was grabbed violently from behind by a pair of familiar, professional and very adept hands, Rasoul's.

"*Street Rat.* You are in way over your head!"

"At least I still have one," Aladdin countered. But as much as he kicked and struggled, Rasoul held him tightly. Another guard levelled his blade so the tip was just touching Aladdin's belly.

Things did not look good.

But he saw that Jasmine was free from her own pursuers. The princess threw herself at the carpet and grabbed its tassels. The carpet dipped under her weight, then raced for the skylight with Jasmine hanging from it like a rabbit from an eagle's talons.

Aladdin let out a sigh of relief. He would be fine, of course or not. It didn't matter. At least she was safe.

With a scream, Abu dropped down onto the head of the guard with the sword.

That was all the distraction Aladdin needed to kick off the floor and fling himself backwards with Rasoul's hands still gripping his arms, and land on Rasoul's back.

Aladdin tried not to cry out at the pain of bending his arms in such an unnatural way.

Sputtering, Rasoul's grip lessened. Aladdin twisted wildly like a weasel until he found a weak spot and was free.

"*Hey!*" a voice called from above.

Aladdin looked up.

Completely at odds with his awesome rescue plan, Jasmine was leaning over the edge of the roof, *not running away*. Or flying away. Like she was supposed to. She pointed: the magic carpet swooped back down towards Aladdin.

"Are all princesses so disobedient?" he shouted with a grin and went to leap aboard.

With an angry howl, Rasoul threw himself at Aladdin, sword drawn. The tip of it caught Aladdin in the side.

Aladdin staggered from the pain. Blood ran down his body.

Jasmine gasped.

He sucked in his breath and forced himself to stay upright. The carpet was close enough to step on.

But Rasoul's next blow wasn't aimed at Aladdin.

Despite trying to scoot out of the way, the magic carpet didn't quite make it.

Rasoul's sword sliced off a corner, ripping away one of its tassels. The carpet gave a terrible shudder, then drifted away lopsidedly, trying to recover. Rajah growled.

Aladdin cursed.

"I don't want to kill you, Street Rat," Rasoul said, his sword raised.

"Sure looks like it, Rasoul," Aladdin shot back.

"If the princess disappears it will mean my head, as well as those of my men."

Out of the corner of his eye, Aladdin saw the carpet slowly drifting back and forth past a *very* interesting row of statues and columns. An idea began to take shape.

"If the princess *doesn't* disappear, she will be forced to marry a man *you know* is a monster. Even worse than you!" Aladdin cried, ducking around him.

Rasoul spun faster than a man his size should have been able to and sliced his sword at Aladdin's back.

Aladdin ducked and avoided it. With a leap like a frog, he put his hands on the head of the first statue and propelled himself up to the second.

Without pausing, he executed a flip onto the third.

Too late, Rasoul realised his plan and ran to stop him.

On the last, highest decorative column, Aladdin leaped with all of his remaining strength. The column rocked under the force of his push.

His hands came down on the roof, grasping at clay tiles that crumbled beneath his fingers. Jasmine grabbed him by the arms and helped haul him up.

Below him in the courtyard, the column rocked too far and began to fall. Aladdin watched in horror as Rasoul spun and looked up, confused about what was happening.

"Carpet! Get Rasoul!" Aladdin screamed. "Knock him out of the way!"

The carpet, slow and confused, moved to the captain of the guards. It didn't so much knock into Rasoul as get tangled around his ankles.

Abu managed to scurry up the column's side and leap out to the roof just before it crashed to the courtyard floor.

Rasoul was not so lucky.

The large man turned and looked up and screamed.

And then there was a terrible, terrible crunch.

Aladdin turned his head, but not before he saw Rasoul's one free arm lift weakly and then fall to the ground.

The Birth of an Army

A TRIO OF SILHOUETTES tiptoed across the top of the palace walls: the night was so dark they could only be seen by where the stars did *not* shine. Noises were beginning in different towers and offices of the capital. Orders were being given, a chase was mounting, explanations were being offered, heads were literally beginning to roll.

Aladdin, Jasmine and Abu made it to a section that came close to some high-growing palm trees, where Jasmine had made her escape not that long ago. It would have been impossible to make the leap with the tiger and a lot easier with the magic carpet. It wasn't right leaving them behind; the party felt light and lonely.

Aladdin lay flat on the top of the wall and lowered Jasmine down as far as he could reach. She had to fall the last three metres onto the prickly treetops. Her landing, while not perfect, was good enough, and the part of her hair that got caught on the sharp fronds would grow back.

Aladdin leaped down straight after, his wound burning as the skin stretched. Blood trickled down his side.

When they hit the ground, they ran as fast and as lightly as their feet would take them to the Quarter of the Street Rats.

They hadn't gone far when a strange sound grew out of the dark like the scuttling of an enormous centipede. One with large, pointy shoes.

Jasmine paused, a finger to her lips, when Aladdin looked at her questioningly.

"We have to hide!" she whispered.

Aladdin looked around and found what seemed to be an abandoned house. *Seemed* because all of Agrabah, apart from the palace, seemed abandoned that night. Every house was black, either with shutters and screens tightly closed or only a few lamps lit. Even in the wealthy quarters, the teahouses and bars and wine gardens were empty. The silence that Aladdin had first encountered when returning from the cave in the desert was somehow deepened by the eerie, regular *tap-tapping*.

Stepping through the door that hung broken on its hinges, they saw little furniture inside, and what remained was broken and smashed. Dust and the endless desert sand covered everything. The place was obviously empty. Jasmine sank wearily on a rotten old pillow that was probably full of insects but it didn't look like she cared.

Aladdin stayed close to the door so he could watch through a crack.

Passing by only a few metres from the door was a phalanx of six... *guards*. Aladdin couldn't figure out what else to call them. Their uniforms were shiny and black. Their movements were perfect and synchronous. They held unusual shiny metal weapons that were long but only had blades at the tip. They wore boots like horse riders did, with metal worked into the leather at the heels.

But it was their faces... and their eyes... that made Aladdin wonder. They all looked the same. Like the pretty girl dancers in the parade. Again, more than just like cousins or brothers... There was a perfect similarity to their expressions, from their strangely blank black eyes to their straight-as-a-line mouths. Like statues, or puppets, or...

Aladdin shuddered without knowing why.

"What *are* they?" he murmured after they passed by.

"Jafar's new Peacekeeping Patrols," Jasmine said with a weary sigh. "They are... well, I don't know what exactly they are. They just kind of keep showing up. More magic, somehow."

As she spoke, she took her hair out of its clasps and bands and began to run her fingers through it. Dusty and ragged though it was, Aladdin still would have very much liked to do it for her. To brush it back from behind her ears…

"The patrols are only part of Jafar's big plans for Agrabah. They march through the city on rounds all night. To keep crime down. So he says. Some people like it, I guess. They feel safer. So he says."

"They seem a little… weird."

Jasmine's face was pale and listless. They had escaped and should have been revelling in triumph, but she didn't seem that excited. Actually, now that he thought about it, Aladdin didn't feel that excited, either. He was *relieved*, of course. But he felt terrible about the magic carpet. And he had seen other things in the past week that were much harder, much *heavier* than anything he had ever had to deal with before.

"I'm sorry about your father," he said softly, sitting down next to her.

Jasmine's face hardened. There was a light in her eyes now, but it was angry and ominous. She stretched her fingers out and back, like a tiger unsheathing its claws.

"Jafar killed him. Right in front of me. I had no idea he… hated my father so much. He could have done anything else to him. With all of his power, he could have banished him, or turned him into a mouse. Or *anything*. Instead he just pushed him over the railing. Just like that."

"I think Jafar has been nursing some very high ambitions… and some very angry thoughts for a long time," Aladdin said gently. "This was all extremely *planned*. Arresting me for being with you was just part of it. He needed me to get the lamp with the genie in it."

Jasmine blinked. "*You* got the lamp for Jafar?"

"It's a long story. Funny, I've been saying that a lot recently. Someday maybe I'll tell you the whole thing. Suffice it to say that I *never* want to go inside another cave again."

Jasmine frowned. "So… it wasn't my fault? He would have found someone else to do his dirty work anyway?"

"I have no idea. It's something I've wondered about. But it *is* your fault for not thinking of the consequences when you went out and about in Agrabah in disguise," Aladdin said gently. "I just thought you were a pretty rich girl slumming it. *Your Royal Highness*."

"You think I'm pretty?" she asked, eyes wide.

Aladdin paused with his mouth hanging open, unsure what to say.

"*Ha!* I'm kidding, of course you do," Jasmine said, cracking a very unprincessy smile. She pushed him on his shoulder and for a moment Aladdin was reminded, not unfavourably, of Morgiana. "You're as easy to read as a book in Aramaic.

"You need to tell me the truth about one thing, though," she added, suddenly serious.

"Anything," he promised.

"What is your *name*?"

Aladdin laughed.

"I guess we never formally introduced ourselves, did we?" He leaped up and gave a deep bow. "I am Aladdin, son of Hatefeh, who was the daughter of Twankeh, who was the son of Ibrahim, who was the daughter of a whole lot of people you've never heard of. *No one's* ever heard of."

"And I am... well, you already know who I am," Jasmine said, growing gloomy again. "I'm really, really sorry for everything you've been through."

"It's been worth it. Mostly," Aladdin said, sitting back down on the ground next to her. He winced at the pain in his side. Jasmine saw it and sucked in her breath. But when she reached out to touch it, he lightly pushed her hands away. "Besides, I lived through it to fight another day. We'll get Jafar. And get you back on your throne. Somehow. In memory of your father."

"To avenge my father," Jasmine hissed through her teeth. She clenched her fists again and stared into the distance with burning anger.

Aladdin rubbed his hands over his face. Too much had happened too quickly. Everything was changing too fast. The old sultan was gone, not a great man as sultans went, but at least he was consistent. Jafar, the creepy vizier, was now a creepy and insane dictator. Agrabah was, different. Everything felt uneasy.

And Rasoul was gone.

Aladdin didn't have especially deep feelings for the man. Especially since he had given Aladdin the wound in his side. But, like the old sultan, he had been a constant in Aladdin's life. A *personal* one. Rasoul had been chasing him since he was a boy. Now Aladdin was a young man, and Rasoul was captain of the guard. It was almost like they had grown up together, on different paths.

A strange ache formed in Aladdin's stomach. He had never wished the man dead. He had never been responsible for *anyone's* death before. That was different, too. This guilt was new. And everything new seemed terrible.

Except for Jasmine.

Just looking at her made him feel better about everything. Her hair was now in a braid wrapped around her head like a nomad girl's, tendrils coming down around her ears in a ridiculously charming way. Her face, streaked with dust, still glowed.

In another time and place, he would have reached over to kiss her.

But she was different, too. She was *seething.* He realised he was watching the happy and generous, albeit naive, girl turn into something dark and terrible.

He had to stop it.

"We have to stop him," she said, her voice cracking, strangely echoing his own thoughts.

"All right, we will," he said softly, his arm around her. "But I don't think we can stop him on our own. Let's get somewhere safe. Morgiana's. We can figure stuff out from there."

He stood up and gave her his hand. She took it, struggling with an exhaustion that threatened to pull her back down.

He checked outside but the danger seemed to have passed; he could hear Agrabah reawakening behind the patrol, like scrub grass full of timid insects that start chirping again once mounted raiders have gone on their way.

They had slipped only about four houses up the street when Jasmine suddenly asked:

"Wait, who's Morgiana?"

Aladdin sighed.

"A friend," he decided.

"A 'friend'," Jasmine said sceptically.

"We've known each other since childhood. We grew up together. And then we sort of... went down different roads."

"What, she became a scholar?" Jasmine teased. But she sounded relieved. "A mother? A priestess?"

"No, worse. A *thief.* Much worse than me. She and Duban organised their own little crime ring. They started off training the small, uncared-for Street Rats to be better beggars. Remember the ones I showed you? Yeah, those. And then they trained them to be thieves. And sometimes *other* not nice things. I didn't agree with their... philosophy of life. Between that and what was going on with my family, we went our separate ways."

"A fortnight ago I didn't understand markets, thievery or poverty. Today I'm learning there are different *levels* of thievery," Jasmine said, shaking her head.

"Yeah, try getting stuck inside the belly of a stone tiger," Aladdin suggested. "That will *really* open up a whole new world for you."

Jasmine was delighted by their entry into Morgiana's hideout but not by the daggers that were suddenly pointed at her and Aladdin as soon as they arrived in the main room.

"Twice in one week, Aladdin," Morgiana drawled. She and Duban had obviously been engaged in some sort of tense discussion: they stood close and looked unhappy. "I'm honoured."

"You should be," Aladdin hissed, trying not to flinch when a little girl's dagger poked his wound.

"Oh, let them go," Duban said wearily. "Aladdin and his girlfriend are no threat to us."

Morgiana nodded at the children and they melted into the darkness like dreams. She flashed a quick smile at her old friend. "And a mighty impressive girlfriend at that, Aladdin. Tell me, how are you and the *royal princess Jasmine* acquainted?"

Jasmine looked startled. Aladdin was surprised, but only a little. Under the dirt and blood her clothes were still silk and satin; above her braids she still wore her crown, and those giant golden earrings were pretty much a dead giveaway. Morgiana was just faster on the uptake than he had been, undistracted by Jasmine's beauty from seeing who she really was.

Although, in his defence, Jasmine was no longer wearing a headscarf.

Jasmine went cross-eyed trying to look up at what Morgiana was indicating with a tilt of her chin. When she realised that it was her crown, she quickly took it off. She threw it at the thieves' feet, where it hit the dirt floor with an ominous *thud*.

Duban and Morgiana, and even Aladdin, jumped in surprise.

"Take it. I don't care. I've lost my father, I've lost my tiger... I've lost my kingdom. What's a crown going to do for me?"

"Whoa," Duban said.

"You didn't have to get rid of the crown," Aladdin said quickly. "We could have—"

"If I wanted your crown, I would have taken it myself, Princess," Morgiana said. She used the heel of her foot to neatly snap it into the air, catching it one-handed. Then she walked over to Jasmine and held it out. "What's mine is yours, in my house," she said in the traditional welcome. "If you thirst, I have water."

Jasmine took the crown back. Slowly she began to smile.

"I do, in fact, thirst. I would love a cup of water."

"Please," Morgiana said, indicating the low table. Jasmine collapsed as gracefully as she could into lotus position. Aladdin sank down as well, in his own graceful yet jerky way. Duban and Morgiana followed suit. The boy Hazan came forwards with two cups of water: a plain silver one for Aladdin, a golden one for Jasmine.

"Many thanks," Jasmine said, toasting them. She took a long drink, finishing it. Then she turned the cup over and looked at the bottom. "Ah... I knew it. This goblet comes from the palace. It's from the lesser banqueting set. There's my father's seal."

Morgiana spread her hands out and shrugged. "You can't move those very easily, because of the seal. No one will buy them. They can be traced back to the palace, and the punishment for theft from the palace is death. So we use them here."

"Uh," Aladdin began. Duban also looked nervous.

Jasmine waved her hand tiredly at them. "It was just an observation. I find my standards for *right* and *wrong* shifting greatly these days."

Duban and Morgiana exchanged a glance at the jaded tone in her voice.

"You guys seem nervous," Aladdin said, shifting on his pillow and helping himself to some persimmons and a quail leg from a platter. It was surprisingly juicy and well cooked. "Extra guards, lookouts on the street corners, yes, I saw them. Even the well-disguised young woman in blue. I thought Agrabah was *wonderful* under its new ruler."

"Not all change is good," Duban muttered, drinking something that was very obviously *not* water out of his own cup, and then shaking the droplets out of his beard.

"We thought the Peacekeeping Patrols would be the usual market guard trash," Morgiana said. "But they are something else. Something unnatural. Nobody knows who they are, or where they come from. And last time I checked, there weren't caravans coming into the city carting dozens of identical soldiers from foreign lands."

"And they have been keeping the peace very well,"

Duban growled. "Just an hour ago a thief was found tacked to the city wall like an insect, a dagger in each of his wrists and feet and neck and heart. Not one of ours," he added hastily.

"There's also the little problem of inflation," Morgiana drawled, pouring herself some wine out of a leather flask. "It's no joke."

"Inflation? Like money?" Jasmine asked. "What has that to do with anything?"

"Do you see this orange?" Morgiana asked, spearing one from the table with her dagger. "A week ago you could get a dozen for a single silver shekel. Now? This one orange will cost you *20* golden darics. Or golden *jafars*, or whatever you want to call the sorcerous coins."

"When you can bring forth gold from the sky," Duban explained, seeing Jasmine was still confused, "when anyone can reach up and take as much as they want, gold stops having value. Like sand."

Morgiana pointed her chin at the tiny piles of gold in the corner of the cavern. "That is all basically worthless now."

Aladdin was reminded once again of the mountains of treasure now buried under the desert. A strange thought occurred to him. Had this all happened... before? Was the treasure buried not because of some mad old sultan who wanted his wealth to die with him, but because someone nearly destroyed the world by bringing too much gold into it? With the help of a genie, whose lamp was the only 'worthless' thing in there... Maybe it was all hidden to protect people from the power of wishes.

He rubbed his head. Deep thoughts were not usually his thing. He suspected *that* was changing, too.

"This can't have been part of Jafar's plan," Jasmine murmured. "I don't think he foresaw this."

"You said there was a bigger plan, though, right?" Aladdin prompted. "Something worse?"

"Worse than worthless gold?" Morgiana asked archly. "I have a hard time imagining anything beyond that."

Jasmine nodded. It was as though, with a moment's rest and a single cup of water, she had regained her former energy.

"We need to stop Jafar. Listen: he has a lamp with a genie enslaved to it. So far he has made *two* wishes: one to become sultan, another to become the world's most powerful sorcerer. The genie wasn't able to grant his third wish, because it broke the laws of magic."

"What was it?" Duban asked breathlessly.

Jasmine blushed, faltering in her role as storyteller.

"Jafar wanted a *willing* bride," she finally said, forcing the words out. "He wanted the genie to make me fall in love with him."

"Oh," Morgiana said, disappointed. "Is that all? Why?"

Jasmine didn't take it as an insult, Aladdin was relieved to see.

"Because that's what he wants, besides power," she explained. "More than anything Jafar seems to want to be loved and admired, that's why he has those parades, and gives all the coins out, and makes those speeches from the balcony. He wants everyone, including me, to love him."

"That's not what I would wish for. No offence," Duban said, equally dumbfounded. "What about all that good stuff you hear about in myths and legends? Like a horse faster than the wind, or a ship that can fly through the stars? That's what *I'd* want."

Morgiana's eyes narrowed at Aladdin.

"I'm sorry, do I understand correctly that you have brought the object of obsession of the *world's most powerful sorcerer* into our secret hideout?"

"Um. Yes…?" Aladdin offered with an embarrassed smile.

"She could be a useful negotiating point," Duban offered.

"If he knew I was here, he would have attacked already," Jasmine said quickly. "I don't think he possesses the power to see through walls. But let me continue.

"He was enraged when the genie couldn't, when he

couldn't make me fall in love. Magic can't do that, or directly kill people, or bring them back from the dead. So right now Jafar is dedicating all of his resources to figuring out how he can *break* the laws of magic. He has already sent dozens of servants all over the world to find ancient, evil sources of knowledge that may help him. Jafar wants everyone to love him, but he also wants to raise an army of the dead. To conquer the rest of the world."

Everyone was silent as the significance of what Jasmine had just said sank in.

"You're joking," Duban said, wide-eyed.

"I'm not," Jasmine said grimly. "I've seen his initial attempts. It's… really not a joke."

Morgiana spat a curse in her mother's language.

"Black magic of *Shetan*! This is serious business, Jasmine," she said, almost accusingly.

"I'm not sure what is worse," Duban mused. "Raising the dead to walk again and serve him, or a spell that would compel all of us to love Jafar unconditionally. Forever."

"*Both* sound equally awful to me," Aladdin said. "We have to stop him. Or get out of town. Or die trying."

"Will you help me?" Jasmine pleaded. "Will you help me stop Jafar from getting the things he needs to make this nightmare happen? Will you… will you help me overthrow him and reinstate me on the throne?"

Morgiana and Duban looked at each other.

"We're *thieves*, Jasmine. What can we do?" Duban asked.

"You're not just thieves, you're a whole *network* of thieves," Jasmine pointed out. "You're practically an army. And we don't need military strength, we just need to stop Jafar from gaining the ability to break the laws of magic. Like by stealing the stuff he's looking for before it gets to him. I'll bet you guys know a thing or two about holding up a caravan."

"I have no idea what you're talking about," Morgiana said mildly, taking a sip from her goblet.

Jasmine ignored her. "In the meantime, I can circulate among the people and build up support for my retaking the throne. Build a real power base."

The two thieves didn't say anything. Jasmine looked back and forth between them.

"What's in it for us?" Morgiana asked, sounding reasonable.

"Limitless thanks of a grateful sultana?" Jasmine asked archly. "*Not* having your mind taken from you and your body used as an undead soldier in a mad sorcerer's army? How about that?"

The thief shrugged. "Maybe it's time for us thieves to simply disappear. Relocate. I hear Baghdad is nice this time of year…"

"Come *on*! This is Agrabah! And the rest of the *world* we're talking about saving!" Jasmine said desperately.

"I don't particularly care about the rest of the world. The army of dead can have 'em," Duban said with a shrug.

"Yes, but I don't *particularly* care for the Peacekeeping Patrols," Morgiana sighed, as if she were talking about a kind of plum. "They make it damn hard for a body of thieves to get any work done."

"I'll give you that," Duban agreed, toasting her with his cup. "And honestly, I have no particular love of ghouls. A whole army of them might be unpleasant."

Jasmine despaired at their casual, offhand remarks.

But Aladdin grinned. He recognised the careless-sounding banter from his longtime friends: they had already made their decision and were talking around the subject. Like it was no big deal to take on a sultan, a sorcerer, a genie and a guarded palace.

"So… you *will* help us?" Jasmine asked hopefully, seeing Aladdin's amusement.

Duban reached over and slammed his fist into the table in front of her. Jasmine jumped back. When he pulled away, his dagger was left standing deep in the wood: dark and short and deadly, like Duban himself.

"*Nobody* takes Agrabah from us. No devilish sorcerer

and his dark arts. Not an *army* of them."

Morgiana did the same thing, slamming her dagger into the wood in front of Jasmine.

"For Agrabah," she pledged.

"For Agrabah!" everyone in the cavern echoed. A half dozen daggers and knives were embedded in the table in front of and around Jasmine by surprisingly adept little arms.

"Well, Princess," Morgiana said. "You have an army of Street Rats. Now, what is the plan?"

Unravelling

"I DON'T *EXPECT* YOU to understand what I'm doing. Just watch and learn."

Lit harshly red from below by lava that flowed through his secret workshop, shears in hand, Jafar looked like a terrifyingly evil tailor. He pursed his lips and raised an eyebrow, pulling back from his work to get a better perspective. Then he made his decision, chose a point, and starting clipping.

The cloth he was working on shuddered.

The brightly coloured carpet was stretched taut across a rack usually reserved for human victims, its three remaining tassels pinned with cruel, barbed nails into the head and footboards. As Jafar squeezed the shears and tore its fabric, the poor thing bucked and rolled. Bits of thread and fluff from the nap fell to the floor in a strange liquid stream like blood.

"The problem is," Jafar said, getting to the end of the carpet and struggling with the thick pile. "The problem is, Iago, you still don't understand how you need to keep your mind open and be ready to seize whatever life hands you. How you can turn disappointments and failures and setbacks into triumphs. It's all about perspective. It may *look* very bad that we lost Jasmine, but turn it round. We have *gained* a very interesting and valuable resource. Do you think I would be sultan now if I hadn't been able to come up with some... *creative* responses to the problems life threw at me?"

A final *snip* and the cloth was cut in two; both sides wiggled strangely, like an insect whose head had come off but whose legs still moved for a while after.

Jafar had more than a little experience with that sort of thing. Seeing it made him nostalgic. He sighed and then went back to cutting.

"You have no idea. None at all, Iago. You've lived your life pampered and plush in these gilded halls. Everyone gives you treats and crackers, even that stupid old sultan used to spoil you. When *I* was a boy, my mother gave me nothing but my name. I was sold as a slave to the first person who would take me. I didn't get crackers, I can tell you *that*, Iago. I had to work hard, and plan constantly, and be *creative* to get out of my lot."

He grew quiet, concentrating on pushing the shears through the next piece of resisting cloth. With more slack it could now also struggle more, and Jafar had to grip it tightly. Beads of sweat popped out on his pallid forehead. The room was silent except for the sickening sound of blades against thick, crunching fabric. The pile of strange glistening threads pooled out over the floor.

When he finally made it all the way through again, Jafar cackled in triumph. He held up a wide strip of carpet that was frayed on its two long edges. It weakly twisted and squirmed in the air.

"Perfect! Don't you think so, Iago?"

But of course the room was empty except for the carpet and the sorcerer, and no one answered him.

A Heist

A STRANGE, HEAVILY GUARDED cart rolled slowly through the dust to Agrabah. Silhouetted against the sky behind it were the Mountains of Atrazak, tall, sharp, grey and mostly lifeless. Whatever the caravan had brought back from the lands beyond those mountains was important enough to require two armoured drivers, two black-and-red palace soldiers marching on either side and the genie, hovering silently above them, blue hands spread in readiness for *something…*

When this strange procession, quiet except for the squeaking of the wheels and the occasional chuffing of the camels, came through the rarely used northeastern city gates, the silence was immediately broken.

A dozen little kids ran to greet them, armed with pails,

cups and pitchers. They clanged and brandished these over their heads to get attention.

"May I quench your thirst, honoured guards?"

"Water your camels, esteemed effendi?"

"Good sir, have a drink?"

"Want some water?"

One of the drivers leaped down. He was covered in sweat and dust; his lips were cracked. The padded armour he wore stuck to him unpleasantly, and the hair that crawled out from underneath his pointed helmet was plastered in place like a statue. His face was an ugly portrait of sunburn, dirt and exhaustion.

And yet he did his duty and swept at the children with a small whip.

"Away, Street Rats!" he snapped. "If one of you so much as *touches* my camels or cart, I will beat you to within an inch of your worthless little lives!"

The children immediately backed away, some bowing, some throwing themselves in the dust, some prostrating themselves at his feet.

"Tell me, how is it you urchins knew of our arrival?" he demanded. No ordinary caravan guard, he was smarter than average, with a gleam in his eye. "Our coming and going were secrets known only to Jafar and his most trusted associates!"

"Your path left a plume of dust in the sky, good sir," answered one brave voice.

A girl stepped forward, a young woman, really. An urn of water was balanced on her curvy hip. Her shiny black hair flowed out from under her headscarf and around her ears like a waterfall. Her robe was dark, dark blue like an ancient river.

The caravan driver turned to look behind him: indeed, she was correct. The clouds of dust and sand their camels' feet had kicked up lingered for miles behind them and rose gently to the sky, unfettered in the still air.

"Huh," the man said gruffly. "You, bring me and my men a beaker of water. The rest of you may fill the troughs... but no one is to come *near* the cart or camels themselves, under pain of a whipping. Am I clear?"

Murmurs of assent mixed with the sounds of bare feet slapping the dirt as the children scattered to do his wishes.

The girl carefully and slowly poured a ladle of water for the man and held it out to him. "When I am done with your men, is there no one in the cart to attend to?"

The driver drank the water with the slow, measured pace of one who was used to self-control. He would not make himself sick by gulping cold water.

"No one," he said shortly, handing the ladle back. "I suppose you'll want a coin for this."

"None of us want coins from Agrabah," the girl said, moving on to the other driver. "Coins can buy you nothing in this town anymore, unless they are foreign. Foreign coins we will take. Or food."

"Huh," the driver said again, acting neither surprised nor upset by this fact, but not refuting it, either.

Another girl appeared with an urn of water and hurried to the men on the other side of the wagon. Her hair was short and curly and her smile had a dangerous-seeming dimple at its corner. The girl in blue immediately began to shout at her.

"I was here first!"

The new girl shouted something extremely impolite back. Soon their screaming fight rose over all the other noise.

A monkey added to the chaos by leaping off a nearby building, onto the helmet of the driver.

"Get off me, insolent vermin!" he sputtered, shaking his head and using the butt of his whip to whack at the monkey.

"*Did you see any foreign devils?*" one child demanded of a guard. "*Any monsters?*"

Up in the hot, dry loft of an abandoned warehouse that overlooked the scene, Aladdin grinned.

"That's my cue!"

He scrambled out of the window and scurried down the

wall, keeping one eye on the scene below him. In the loud, chaotic activity, no one had noticed his spider-like descent. At least, no one who wasn't meant to. The children and the water girls, and Abu, raised the level of confusion with more running, shouting and sloshing of water.

Then Aladdin's foot caught on an old trellis. A piece weakened by dry rot clattered down to the road.

"*The floating djinn,*" the girl with the dimple said loudly, breaking off her fight with the girl in blue, when the guards started to turn round to look. "Does he require water, too?"

It worked: the guards turned back to her. One gave a lascivious grin.

"I'll bet you'd like to wait on a djinn, wouldn't you, young lady? But no, he doesn't require food or water or… anything else real men require."

Aladdin breathed a sigh of relief.

He let himself fall the last three metres, landing softly on his toes. While the girl in blue was tipping a ladle of water towards a guard's mouth, he slipped into the back of the cart.

It had the usual stores that nomads and desert travellers carried with them: dried meat and fruit, leather flasks of water and wine, rope and extra cloths and harnesses… But in the dark, dusty back, there was a chest with multiple locks on it that seemed too delicate and strangely out of place in such a rustic outfit.

A Whole New World

A behind-the-scenes look at the characters and world of *Aladdin*.

Text adapted from The Disney Book *written by Jim Fanning and published by DK.*

A Genie in the lamp. A magic carpet. An evil vizier. These are just some of the things that spring to mind when thinking of the 1992 animated film *Aladdin*. Based on the Arabian Nights tales, and set in the fabled city of Agrabah, the Disney artists created a signature style for the film.

To accurately and authentically recreate the Middle Eastern world in the 15th century, Artistic Supervisor and native Iranian Rasoul Azadani travelled to his hometown of Isfahan to take photos and inspiration.

Concept Art: Peter Gullerud

Meanwhile, Production Designer, Richard Vander Wende, incorporated design elements from ancient Persia, such as their love of bright colours.

"Inspired art direction, layout and background paintings give *Aladdin* a look unlike any other animated feature." – Roy E. Disney

During the character development process, Richard Vander Wende had the artists use the thick and thin 'S' curve seen in Arabian calligraphy to inject a fluid caricature style, which worked particularly well with the Genie.

Bold and brave, Princess Jasmine was the first Disney princess not to be based on a European fairy tale. Her confidence and outspokenness created a whole new world of challenges for Supervising Animator Mark Henn, who looked at several live models for inspiration.

Story Sketch: Disney Studio Artist

Ultimately, Jasmine became a young woman who was courageous enough to jump over any wall and discover life on her own terms.

"You're not going to find another girl like
her in a million years." The Genie

Concept Art: Jean Gillmore

Every great film needs a great villain; after all, villains define our heroes.
Voiced by Jonathan Freeman, Roy E. Disney called Jafar "Mr Evil
Himself". Jafar has ambitions to take over the universe at whatever cost,
but his desires and arrogance blindsight him from the technicalities of

Story Sketch: Disney Studio Artist

Story Sketch: Disney Studio Artist

The Disney artists ensured that Jafar's appearance reflected his many, somewhat-lacking personality traits. His oversized turban signifies his oversized ego, while his cobra-shaped staff embodies power and a poisonous personality. The sharpness of his shoulders hint at Jafar's dangerous nature, and sit in contrast to the Genie's more curvaceous appearance.

Aladdin pulled out his lock-picking kit and worked quickly. These were serious locks, not like the ones in the dungeon. He listened as the sounds of chaos rose and fell outside the wagon and the genie began to get involved, shooing off the water-bearing beggars. A single drop of sweat rolled down his elegant nose and landed unpleasantly in the dust.

Finally, the locks sprung. Aladdin threw open the chest.

Inside there was nothing but a few old books. He couldn't help feeling a little disappointed; he had been hoping for enchanted jewels or a staff that granted access to an all-knowing oracle or something like that.

Aladdin gave a low click of his tongue that could have been the sound of camels' feet against the dirt or a sword settling into its sheath.

Immediately a Street Rat's head appeared at the wagon's door. Aladdin tossed a book to her. In what seemed like a completely random fashion, other Street Rats formed a human chain zigzagging through the hustle and bustle. The first girl threw the book to a second child, who caught it in an empty bucket. He passed the bucket to a little boy, who scrambled with it under the legs of the camels. A girl grabbed it from there and ran away into the streets as fast as she could.

Five times they did this. Once for each book.

From the level of the noise outside, Aladdin could tell

the driver and guards were getting restless. Now that they had slaked their desert thirst, they were ready to go back to the palace to report and then retire to the baths, probably. The crowd of water bearers was being driven off with words and whips.

As soon as the chest was empty, Aladdin closed it with a snap and refastened all the locks, making sure the pins fell in the same way he had found them. He grabbed the edge of the cart floor and flipped himself under it.

The guards tossed foreign coins and oranges as far away from themselves as they could. The children went flying after the goodies. The driver whistled and slapped a camel on its flank. The cart slowly lumbered off. The two water girls stood close behind to watch them go...

...and also to quickly drape Aladdin in a woman's robe that he rose up into as soon as he came out from under the wagon, like a magician appearing from a basket.

When the wagon, guards and camels were some way down the street, the genie looked back at Aladdin. He gave a nod. Aladdin nodded back. Then the genie turned and continued following the cart, looking serious, almost sad.

There was something about the genie's face. It was instantly likeable, more suited to smiles and grins than the frowns and grimaces he seemed always to have. He was far more *human* than Aladdin imagined a djinn would be.

In a different time, he could almost see the two of them becoming friends. Or at least talking, or…

Aladdin shook his head. Another time, another place. Meanwhile, the Street Rats had to disperse and go their separate ways back to Morgiana and Duban's secret lair.

Without even saying a word to each other, the three 'girls' melted into the shadows. Within moments, except for the marks in the dust, it was like no one had ever been in the square at all.

Robber Queen

ALADDIN ALLOWED HIMSELF a few moments of being alone and relaxing a little; he practised walking down the street the way he imagined girls did, robes curling about his feet. Abu chittered happily, sensing the change in his friend's mood.

"You make a pretty believable girl," someone drawled from the corner.

Morgiana stood there, arms crossed, watching his antics with a raised eyebrow. She had taken off her disguise and now wore her usual trousers-and-top outfit.

"So do you," Aladdin quipped without missing a beat.

"Idiot," Morgiana growled, walking over to help him out of his costume.

"I mean, not as believable as that *other* girl. She was amazing. Where did you find *her*?"

"Her name is Pareesa, and she is one of the most skilled thieves in our little band. Also? Shut up," Morgiana said pleasantly. "A man who has the attentions of an attractive royal princess should probably keep his eyes to himself."

"I'm just kidding, Morgiana. I really only have eyes for Jasmine," he said seriously. Then: "No offence."

"None was ever taken. You're too skinny for my liking, anyway. Put some meat on your bones and then we'll talk."

They walked down the street as casually as two thieves could, shoulders occasionally bumping like they didn't care, eyes searching out quick exits *just in case.*

"We've missed you, you know," Morgiana said eventually.

"I… missed you, too," Aladdin admitted. "I just wish…"

"We weren't *professional* thieves. Mr High-and-Mighty," Morgiana said, rolling her eyes. "We just do what you do and refined the process a bit. Neither one of us has the moral high ground, Aladdin. The law treats all kinds of theft equally."

"I never cared about the law," Aladdin said. "Only what my heart tells me."

Morgiana shook her head. "It is very easy to steal only what you need to eat and live when you are a strong young man. The starving three-year-olds and dying grandmothers *cannot* steal to eat. So we steal extra, and, yes, coins and jewellery."

"Do *not* tell me all those trinkets in your cave are just for your destitute charity cases," Aladdin said, but with a twinkle in his eye.

"I'm not denying that I have bigger plans and a penchant for moving shiny objects," Morgiana said with a shrug. "I'm just saying that we aren't as *purely evil* as you think us, Aladdin. There are shades of grey and goodness to us as well."

"I never thought you were evil, Morgiana. Just that you made bad choices."

She laughed. "Now you sound like my mother. When she was, ah, clear-headed."

Aladdin smiled. Was it possible to be friends with someone you didn't agree with?

They turned a corner, and with thieves' instincts, both immediately shrank back into the shadows.

There was a tent set up ahead in the wide street. It was squat and square, black and red: Jafar's colours again. The angular, evil-looking symbol from the coin was painted on its side and flew on a pennant at the top. A long line of people, hot and desperate-looking, snaked away from the tent and down the street.

"What's this?" Aladdin asked uneasily.

"Something new," Morgiana said, also worried.

"Let's investigate."

Realising that they looked like nothing more than a young couple strolling down the street, they came out of the shadows and linked arms. With the casualness of two experts casing a joint, they let their lazy eyes slip over everything and every*one*.

"What's going on here?" Aladdin asked a father standing in the queue, hands on the shoulders of his two children.

"You haven't heard?" the man asked, his eyes darting around nervously as he tightened his grip on his daughters. "They are giving out bread. Better get in line fast."

"I thought Jafar just gave it away. Like, everywhere. Like tossed it to the crowds at parades and off the balcony at the palace and stuff."

"Not anymore. Jafar said too many... of the *wrong* sort were *preying on his generosity*." The man said the last part slowly and clearly and a little louder than the rest, so that anyone listening would be sure to hear.

"Hmmm," Morgiana said. "I guess we will get in line. Thank you, friend."

The man inclined his head, then turned as if they didn't exist anymore.

As the two turned to walk away, Aladdin gestured with his chin at the tent. Morgiana followed his look.

A man with a narrow face and narrow eyes sat at a makeshift table within. Two giant guards stood on either side of him. Behind him there was a pile of bread sloppily thrown on a sheet on the ground. A young woman in an oft-mended purple robe tried not to stare at it as the man spoke to her.

"Do you swear your entire allegiance to Jafar and his new government, Agrabah Ascendant?"

"Yeah. Yes. Of course," the woman said. She was still staring at the bread.

"Do you swear to uphold his laws and revere him with the respect and love due to the rightful ruler of the lands inside the Atrazak Mountains?"

"I do. I mean, what? It's not like I'm marrying him, right?" the young woman suddenly said, for the first time looking at the man before her and not the bread.

"No. You are not marrying him." The smile in the corners of the man's eyes was not a twinkle of amusement. It was a malicious, knowing gleam. "Do you swear?"

"Yes," the woman said.

"Excellent. Next."

The woman blinked, then laughed like a girl when one of the guards slapped *two* loaves into her hands. She practically skipped away in delight.

"I think she would have sworn away her own mother," Morgiana murmured.

"I don't think she cared *what* she said or figured it

meant anything," Aladdin said. "And it probably doesn't."

They wandered slowly down the street, turning off as soon as they could to get away from the breadline.

"I don't like it," Morgiana said when they were far enough away to feel comfortable. "That whole setup was creepy."

"It felt very weird," Aladdin agreed. "I can't put my finger on it. But really, what do words mean? Like you said, that woman would have sworn away her own mother and not meant it."

"Yes, but what happens when *Jafar* realises that?"

The rest of their walk home was uneventful until they entered the hideout. The moment they were inside, a monster in orange and black with teeth the size of daggers barrelled out of the dark into them.

"Rajah!" Aladdin said in surprise. He gave the large cat a scruffle through his neck fur. The tiger growled happily. "How did he get here?"

Morgiana shook her head and rolled her eyes. "Duban said he showed up at our doorstep this morning, right after we left. There was a ribbon, a *ribbon*, around his neck and a note saying that we should be on the lookout for a particular book in Jafar's wagons. *Al*-something-or-other. It was signed, 'the genie'."

"Ha!" Aladdin nuzzled Rajah with his own nose. "I like this new way of getting us intelligence. It's *much* safer than having him and Jasmine meet."

"Well, I think we'd need a lot more tigers," Morgiana said sceptically. "But that would make Ahmed and Shirin happy. They've already adopted Rajah for themselves. And Maruf does *not* trust the big cat with his grandchildren."

"Maruf is here? Where?" Aladdin asked delightedly.

"At this hour? Probably in the kitchen making breakfast."

"Of course! I'll join him there."

"Of *course*," Morgiana muttered. She wandered away, waving her hands in the air and continuing to talk to herself in exasperation. "Genies? Tigers? Magic books? When did my life come to this?"

Aladdin took off down several labyrinthine passageways and confusingly connected cellars, ending up in the surprisingly spacious and airy kitchen of some large old-fashioned house that had no windows, only skylights. Over a giant stove with an equally giant pan was Maruf, Duban's elderly father. He was grinning and talking and jumping around a crowd of hungry kids, managing not to spill a drop of oil on his crazy beard or miss a hungry outstretched hand. It was especially amazing considering his stiff left leg that didn't move, he used it as a pivot, twirling round on his heel.

Everyone got a piece of hot bread and, from a giant jar in the corner, a dollop of sweet cheese.

"*Aladdin!*" Maruf called the moment he saw him. "I'm just reheating your favourite *nan-e sangak*. Made 'em last night. Here!"

He spun the pan and a round piece of bread flew through the air. Aladdin snatched it and tossed it to the other hand immediately; it was too hot to eat.

Maruf threw his head back and barked out laughter. "You never change, Aladdin. Always trying to bite into things that are too dangerous."

"*Me?*" Aladdin asked, licking his thumb. "What about you? When you were my age?"

"*Ha!* I was just telling them, these kids, they have no idea," Maruf said, shaking his head. "When I was their age... why, even if I was just a few years younger, I'd show them a thing or two about evading the market guards!"

Two of the children ran forwards and leaped onto Maruf's legs, clinging despite the danger of the hot oil and fire.

"Ahmed! Shirin! You're going to kill me!" But the old man was grinning.

Aladdin looked at the kids. They seemed familiar... but from where? Then he placed them. They were the ones he had given his bread to just a week or so earlier.

"Are they...?" he said slowly.

"Kazireh's kids. My grandchildren," Maruf said proudly.

Aladdin kneeled down and tickled each one on the nose.

"I think we've met," he said.

"We have a pet lion!" the little boy, Ahmed, told him.

"Tiger, Ahmed. He has stripes," Shirin corrected gently. "And we've been taking care of Abu for you."

"That's great. The poor thing could use a little extra love," Aladdin said, popping the now-cool piece of bread in his mouth. "Er, speaking of, does anyone know where Jasmine is?"

Maruf looked at him slyly.

"Yes... she's in the... 'study'. I'm sure you're eager to discuss *important business* with her."

Aladdin pretended he didn't hear the implication in the older man's tone and gave him a little bow in thanks, hands pressed together. He backed out of the room and returned the way he had come, into the twisty maze of storage spaces and secret tunnels the Street Rats had carved underneath the abandoned neighbourhood. The 'study' was a large room with a plain rectangular rug spread out in the middle. Drawn on the rug in chalk was a sketchy map of Agrabah. Small bricks and square blocks of stone highlighted important buildings and landmarks. Around it stood an attentive group of Street Rats.

Jasmine was on her hands and knees, pushing around little piles of pebbles that represented the thieves and beggar children who made up her troops. She carefully explained the plan to her audience and then had them repeat it word for word before they skittered off to do her bidding. Soon they were all gone and Aladdin sat down beside her.

"Hey, what's that?" he asked, suddenly noticing several chalk marks on the wall. He initially thought they were random, but then he realised that they were four elongated triangles... like claw marks from a giant beast.

"The Mark of Rajah," Jasmine said, not looking up. She continued to ponder her map, one finger to her mouth. "Some of the Street Rats thought that if Jafar has a symbol, we should have one, too. It's supposed to mean *resistance*. Also, because Rajah resisted Jafar himself and was wounded. It's to honour him."

"Oh. Clever," Aladdin said.

"Yes, yes, but listen," she said impatiently. Little tendrils of hair waved, unkempt around her head, like a wreath, and Aladdin had a hard time concentrating on her words. "In the genie's note he said that Jafar is looking for one book in particular that deals with magic of the dead and the *un*dead. If it's not in *this* shipment, it may be in one coming from Kajha, by the sea. They are expected to return tonight, but we don't know if they will stop off at Midrahf for supplies first. So the Street Rats are going to disrupt caravan arrivals at both the southern gate *and* the western gate as a distraction."

"What's the book?"

"*Al Azif,* by Abdul Alhazred."

Although they were in underground passages where no winds blew, Aladdin found himself shuddering in sudden cold. Jasmine didn't look particularly pleased to say the title aloud. There was just something about it...

"Maybe it's one of those books we just lifted, they definitely looked serious."

"Yes, let's go take a look at them," Jasmine said, getting up and stretching. "It will be a welcome break from playing robber queen. I don't mean that, ah, meanly. This whole thing would be utterly impossible without Duban and Morgiana and the Street Rats."

Aladdin was silent, thinking about his discussion outside with his old friend. About layers of complexity, and good and evil, and choices. If Morgiana *hadn't* gone down a path he didn't approve of, she wouldn't be able to help him now. Where did that fit in the great moral scheme of things?

"You guys took a long time to get back," Jasmine said, poking him in the stomach. It was as if she could read his thoughts. "You and Morgiana."

"We were catching up. Jealous?"

"Only because she's known you for so long," Jasmine said with a smile, giving his hand a squeeze.

"We saw something," Aladdin said reluctantly, not wanting to break her mood. "Jafar is now having people line up for bread and swear allegiance or loyalty or whatever to get it. He's not just handing it out anymore. Things are taking an… unsettling turn."

"What, and the whole 'wanting to create an army of the undead' thing isn't unsettling?"

"No, that's horrific. But it's *so* horrific it's like it's unreal. But this… these were normal, desperate people suddenly afraid the free food they had *just got used to* was being taken away. I can't speak to genies and ghouls and ancient books of magic. But I don't like what Jafar is turning the people of Agrabah into."

"He killed my father in front of me, in *front* of the people of Agrabah," Jasmine reminded him with gritted teeth. "There is *nothing* he is incapable of."

They came to the main room of the headquarters, the one with the tables and braziers. A guard stood next to the chest of pilfered items and the girl in blue from the heist. Now she wore trousers and a long dagger slung on either hip.

"Thank you, Pareesa," Jasmine said with a warm smile. "We'll take it from here. You deserve a break after everything you've done today already."

"Of course, Jasmine," the girl said with a bow before she left.

Aladdin opened the chest and carefully took out the musty leather-bound books. They were still a relatively novel concept for him; he was more used to scrolls or notes written on shards of dried clay.

"There's an imam from the Old Quarter named Khosrow, very learned, who said he would help us with any translations as soon as he could slip away," Jasmine said. They sat down at the low table, now clear of food except for a pitcher of mint tea and a plate of flat-bread. They put the stack of books between them and each chose one.

Aladdin opened his, *A Treatise on the Limits of Magic*, then quickly traded out the giant text-only volume for *Spellbreaker, a Compendium*, which had pictures and recipes for charms.

After a few minutes, Jasmine put hers down, disappointed.

"I don't think *any* of these are *Al Azif*. I can't be *sure* about these two, because of the languages. That looks like cuneiform, which is just mad… and that's hieratic Egyptian, which I definitely cannot read. But they seem to be about much lighter subjects, if the illustrations mean anything. We need that imam."

"But on the other hand, do you want to protect your

sheep against hoof fungus?" Aladdin asked brightly. He turned the book so she could see the ancient, brightly illuminated picture and recipe he had been looking at. "Because if you do, have I got the charm for you!"

Jasmine smiled. "I wonder if it works."

Aladdin put his book aside. "So what *is* this *Al Azif* all about anyway?"

"I guess it's a record of some ancient madman's travels to forbidden and dark worlds. He wrote down the knowledge he gained there about channelling powers from beyond the universe itself. Somehow the very act of recording it became the conduit of that power."

Aladdin blinked at her.

"Just possessing it lets you kill with your mind and raise armies of the undead," Jasmine re-explained, rolling her eyes.

"Ahh. I get it now. Bad stuff. So what do we do when we get it?" Aladdin asked, putting his book down. "Burn it or something?"

"Burn it?" Jasmine said in shock. "A tome of that importance? No, we can't do that. We have to keep it for ourselves."

"Um… what?" Aladdin said slowly.

"Just think. In it lies the power to break the laws of magic. What else can it do?"

"Nothing. Nothing good," Aladdin said firmly.

"It could give me the power I need to defeat Jafar and take back the throne."

"We're working on that. Here," Aladdin said gently, reaching out to touch her knee. "With people who believe in you and your cause. With children and thieves and beggars and tigers and genies. We can do it without any extra magic."

Jasmine looked doubtful. "More strength, more weapons couldn't hurt."

"Oh, yes, they could when the weapons are evil. And just because the book's in *our* hands doesn't mean it couldn't end up in someone *else's* hands. We need to burn it. That keeps it from *ever* being used for evil purposes."

"That's a daft reason to destroy it, because it *might* do damage someday. When we could *use* its magic to fix everything!" Jasmine yelled.

"You know who believed magic could fix everything?" Aladdin yelled back. "*My mother.* All of those stories about marids and djinn and houris and whatever granting wishes and fixing all of your problems with a snap of your fingers. Every single one ended happily ever after. Just like she believed my dad was going off to find some 'magical' thing or job or whatever that would save our family. *Magic doesn't do that.* Nothing does it. You're as crazy as my mother if you think otherwise."

"I could bring back my father with it."

Jasmine said it quietly, in a small voice. She wasn't looking at Aladdin or the books anymore; she was staring off into space with eyes that were suddenly wet.

Aladdin immediately felt his anger melt away like a sandcastle in the desert wind. She looked so tiny sitting there, not a robber queen or a sultana at all. He slid over next to her and wrapped her in his arms.

"Hey," he said quietly, kissing her on the cheek. "I know you miss him. I miss my mum, too, despite all those things I just said. But… you can't bring your father back. He wouldn't be the same. He wouldn't *want* it."

"You don't know that," Jasmine said, sniffling.

"Are you willing to find that out the hard way? He's gone now, Jasmine. Let him go."

Jasmine held Aladdin tightly for a moment, squeezing him harder than he'd thought possible for a girl her size. Then she sat back and tried to compose herself, wiping her nose.

"This is all *because* of my father, in some ways. Isn't it?" she finally said. "If he hadn't… brought Agrabah to the state it is now, with a huge population of incredibly poor people, and an even huger disparity between them and the wealthy nobles like us, there wouldn't have been an opening for someone like Jafar. No one would have supported him if the sultan had… done right by his people."

Aladdin really, *really* wanted to tell her it wasn't true. But he couldn't.

She saw the pitying look on his face and smiled wanly.

"I've... learned a lot of hard truths about him and my whole world lately. I think maybe, in the back of my mind, I always knew. In the history books *I* read, great rulers didn't spend all of their time playing with children's toys. And they didn't let their advisers handle everything. They kept an eye on their people and had a hand in day-to-day affairs. The great ones, that is. Even military leaders like Xerxes. They didn't just let ordinary people go hungry for no reason... ordinary people like you..."

Aladdin guessed what was coming next. He focused on his piece of flat-bread, carefully breaking it in half.

"What... happened with your family? With your mother?" she asked hesitantly. "What made *you* turn to a life of thievery?"

Aladdin sighed and put the bread back down on his plate. His usual glibness drained away under her scrutiny. Actually, a lot of his joking and irrepressible monkeying had disappeared in the past two weeks. He wasn't sure if he missed it or not.

"My father, Cassim, left us when I was very young. I barely remember him."

Aladdin hadn't mentioned his father's name aloud in

years. He half hoped he wouldn't be able to remember it, but it rose perfectly formed from the depths of his mind, immediate and whole, just waiting to be brought to the surface again with all of its accompanying pain.

"Imagine someone just like me," he continued. "Imagine an independent, roguishly handsome young man, quick with a laugh and a joke. Slow to find honest work. Imagine a... *me* with no thought for any other person, no thought beyond the moment's fun. *But with two people to be responsible for.*

"When it got too much, he just... left. And my mum... she was a *great* mum," he said forcefully, looking into Jasmine's eyes. "She could make soup out of dust and a drop of water. She could make clothing, *decent* clothing, from scraps she begged for from people only slightly less poor than us. She kept our nasty little house spotlessly clean and as cheery as she could."

"She sounds like an amazing person," Jasmine said gently.

"Yeah. But..." Aladdin sighed, his defensiveness gone. "Like I said, she was completely deluded. Insane and irresponsible in her own way. Another woman would have had people hunt her wayward husband down and bring him back. Another woman would have had him declared dead and found herself *another* husband. A better man.

But she truly believed, until the day she died, that Cassim would come back. That one day he would return and whisk us away to a fabulous new life. With a nicer house and servants. And he would stay at home and be the father and husband our family needed."

He looked up at Jasmine. She had a look of such compassion and sadness that Aladdin had the urge to reach over and comfort *her*.

"She died young, of course," Aladdin finished. There was no other way to put it. No 'nice' way. "She was overworked and came down with a wasting disease. It was... one of the other things that drove me apart from Morgiana and Duban and everyone. 'Street Rats take care of each other,' my mother always said. But no one took care of *us*. Maruf tried to help out a little... but by that point his leg no longer worked and he was scraping for food himself. And my *friends* were too busy putting together their little network of thieves and beggars to spend much time helping me or comforting my mother.

"Well, I guess that's not fair," he said, breaking his pieces of bread into smaller pieces. "Everyone's got something, like they say. Everyone had someone starving, sick or dying. Morgiana's parents would spend any money they got on wine. Duban's dad was lame and his older sister was married to a man who beat her."

"Good God," Jasmine murmured. "I had no idea…"

"It's all bad. It's the Quarter of the Street Rats, remember? Anyway, from the day my mother died, I decided I would never rely on anyone else for food or shelter or to fulfil my dreams *for* me. And that one day I would be rich and live in the palace. And all my troubles would be over."

"You dreamed of living in the palace?" Jasmine asked with a curious smile.

"Our house had a view of it, from the back," Aladdin said with a weak grin. "I used to gaze at it and dream. It looked like paradise. Golden and white in the sunlight, stark and imposing in a dust storm, lit up by a thousand lamps in the middle of the night. And then, when I moved out… after my mum died… I chose my hideout because it had a similar view."

"And all those years," Jasmine mused, "I languished in my beautiful gardens, and looked out of the windows at night at Agrabah laid out below me, and wished I could be *there*. I wonder if our thoughts ever crossed, like stray breezes."

"Or a pair of swallows." Aladdin made his fingers dance around each other in the air.

"But wealth isn't a magic lamp that suddenly erases all your problems," Jasmine said slowly, breaking off a piece of bread for herself. "Imagine being a large bird in a tiny, but golden, cage. If it weren't for the death of my father, I'd be happier now than I've ever been. I'm *free* here. Having the freedom to choose is better than having everything you want."

"You'd better convince the people of Agrabah of that," Aladdin said wryly. "Otherwise they'll never back you. So far they seem to prefer full bellies and *no* choice."

"When I am sultana, they shall have both," Jasmine vowed. "I will figure out how to feed the people *and* keep them free. They shall go to school, *all* of the children, no matter what religion, no matter what class. Boys *and* girls. They shall be given every opportunity to do whatever they wish when they grow up and not be forced to thieve and beg. This I swear."

Her eyes were distant, looking at some future sight, a world of her own building. Aladdin had no doubt that she would achieve that vision or die trying. She made him believe that it was actually possible… that a kind of paradise on earth could be possible.

And he was willing to do whatever it took to help her with that dream.

"I believe you," he whispered. "I believe *in* you."

He never would have dared kiss the royal princess Jasmine.

But it turned out he didn't need to.

The royal princess Jasmine leaned over and kissed *him*.

Her skin was warm and smelled of sand and mint. Aladdin melted into the kiss like his whole body had been waiting for it and he didn't even know it himself. She put her hands around his neck and drew him in closer. One of her hands worked up into his hair, the other onto his shoulder, with a need he hadn't realised she felt.

"So I guess we've finished fighting?" Aladdin whispered.

The royal princess Jasmine tweaked him on the nose.

Deadly Magic

"MORNING, FOLKS," Duban yawned, stepping into the room with slapping feet and big heavy steps. He had a large brass cup of steaming hot coffee and several tiny delicate-looking cups. Despite this, he fell like a donkey onto a floor pillow. Not a drop spilled. Blearily, he set out the cups and poured.

"Wait, it's night, isn't it?" Jasmine asked, looking up from her book. "It's so dark in here, you lose track of time."

"Dusk is morning to those who work in the shadows," Duban said, expertly pouring despite his narrowed eyes. "Sorry, oh great Robber Queen and Sultana-to-Be, I didn't ask how you liked yours. I made it with lots of sugar, the way Dad taught me."

"I would drink the dregs at the bottom of an army canteen right now," Jasmine said, delicately picking up her cup, "and I'm sure yours is much better."

"*Jasmine!*"

Two chaotic bundles of rags came rushing into the room and threw themselves onto the princess's lap. She laughed and put an arm around each.

"*Shirin, Ahmed*," Maruf chastised, coming in slowly behind them with the particular *tap-slide* gait his bad leg gave him. "Do not treat the royal princess like your personal auntie."

Aladdin cocked his head and looked at Ahmed, who had Abu sitting on his shoulder just as naturally as you please. Sort of like a miniature… Aladdin.

"It's all right, Maruf," Jasmine said, giving them a squeeze. "I never got to play with children at the palace. Even distant relatives were told to, uh, 'keep their distance'."

Shirin looked up at Jasmine with huge, adoring eyes. Then she found Jasmine's little silver dagger and played with it wistfully, singing a song that sounded suspiciously like the anthem they played in Jafar's crazy parade.

"They seem pretty happy," Duban said, indicating the children with his cup.

"Happier than they've been in a long time," Maruf said bleakly.

"Your sister hated thievery. She swore that neither she nor her children would ever have anything to do with it," Aladdin remarked. "And here they are, in the belly of the beast."

"Well, if she were still around, maybe she'd have a say in the matter," Duban growled.

"I meant no disrespect," Aladdin said, holding up his hand. Very few things could get the normally rock-solid Duban riled. The fate of his sister was one of those things, however. "I just meant... they seem to be thriving here."

"Well," Maruf said brightly, "what could be better than having a royal princess, a tiger, a monkey, other children to play with... oh, yes, and *food*. Almost forgot that. Having food in their bellies seems to be important to these little ones."

He held out his arms and Ahmed and the monkey leaped into them happily.

Shirin didn't seem like she was going to budge, however. One arm was locked firmly around Jasmine's waist and she was making the dagger march behind one of the golden clips taken out of Jasmine's braids.

"She doesn't have any dolls," Maruf explained in embarrassment. "I should... steal her a toy, or—"

"Where did all the people in the parade go?" Shirin suddenly asked. "All of those dancers and animals and soldiers… where did they go when the parade was done?"

"Um," Jasmine said. She looked to Aladdin for help. He shrugged helplessly.

"Ahmed and I wanted to see the animals when it was over, but we couldn't find their cages or pens like when the travelling shows come to the city. Are they like the Peacekeeping Patrols? Are they the same people? In different costumes?"

"I… think… the genie summons them. All of them," Jasmine said.

"But where do they go *after*?" Shirin pressed.

"Those are *really good* questions," Aladdin said quickly, squatting down and tweaking the little girl on the nose. "Maybe Jasmine can ask the genie the next time she sees him."

"I hope *I* get to see him one day," Ahmed murmured wistfully.

"Me too," his sister said. "I want to wish for my own tiger. One I can ride. Also my own silver dagger."

"Or a doll," Maruf said hopefully. "Er, *she* can have a dagger? A tiny one?"

"I hope you get to meet him, too," Jasmine said with feeling. "When this is all over."

Aladdin smiled and finished the entire contents of his cup of coffee in one gulp. Then he leaped up.

"Think I'm gonna go see if I can round us up some more recruits. Back at one of those breadlines. I'll bet there are some people there who aren't down with the whole thing and will want to see an exiled princess reclaim her rightful throne."

"Be careful," Shirin warned in a very serious tone.

"I'm always careful," Aladdin said sweetly, prompting a snorting laugh from Jasmine. It was delightful to hear. He resolved to try to make her laugh more often.

"My neck hairs all stood up on their own today," Duban said doubtfully. "And Shirin said she saw a white cat earlier, in the alley by the Egyptian's teahouse. Didn't you, Shirin?"

"You're as bad as an old mother," Aladdin groaned. "You and your superstitions. Later, Princess." He leaned over and gave Jasmine a quick kiss on the lips.

As Aladdin swung up and out of the secret door behind the chimney upstairs, he heard Duban say to Jasmine, "Right in front of the kids? Really? What kind of place do you think we're running here?"

"Well, aren't you glad you don't have Aladdin for competition with Morgiana?"

"*Morgiana?* He can have her. I'd rather marry a cantankerous she-goat with five horns. Be less hard to deal with."

Aladdin smiled to himself as he slipped into the blue

twilight of early dusk. From naive, lonely princess to winner of hearts and minds in less than a month, Jasmine managed to make people feel at ease with her while still maintaining her role as leader.

Abu caught up with him when he was less than a block away, and it almost seemed like old times: scurrying up trellises, bounding lightly across rooftops, sliding down conveniently placed poles.

But Agrabah was different. The giant red sun was half sunken into the horizon of the Western Desert and looked like it was swimming in a lake of blood. Those few people still out on the streets were rushing to get home, or inside, as quickly as possible. They were silent and glanced nervously over their shoulders in fear of something they hoped would never come.

From his high vantage point, Aladdin could see three separate Peacekeeping Patrols spreading out from the direction of the palace. They moved like strange insects, *click-click*ing in perfect unison, shields behind them like the shells of beetles. He thought about Shirin's questions. She, too, had picked up the weird similarity between the patrols and the people in the parade. Curious, he picked one patrol to follow.

By now, everyone in the city was so terrified of them that they had little to do *but* march down the apocalyptically empty streets. The *tap-tap*ping of their metal boots was an effective warning that preceded them. They walked, black eyes straight forward, manic grins on their faces as if they really, *really* loved their jobs. If there was a strange noise or something moving in the shadows, they reacted in *almost* human fashion: raising their weapons, dropping into fighting positions, sending one or two of their number down an alley to check it out.

With no words.

Not a single sound was uttered the entire time he followed them. They nodded to one another, but that was all. How were they communicating? It made Aladdin shiver just to think about it.

When the waning half-moon reached the peak of its ascent, the clock began to chime the hour.

The patrol paused.

Their identical faces began to appear a little unfocused. They didn't look away but seemed somehow no longer to be paying attention to whatever was in front of them.

With horror, Aladdin realised their faces were *really becoming unfocused.* Their eyes, noses and mouths were blurring, twisting and smudging like dirty clothes being wrung out in a stream.

Soon their features were vague thumbprints of tan and black.

Then their bodies grew puffy. They seemed to suddenly hang at the tips of their toes and sway for a moment in the breeze.

And then they popped.

Silently, like everything the patrols did, except for the *tap-tap*ping of their feet. Threads of hazy human colours spun out for a moment from the quiet explosion, one after another, six of them in all. These wavered and dried up in the air, disappearing with a final tiny curl of blue smoke.

Aladdin shivered. They weren't even a little bit human. Not even as real as the genie. They were golems. Unthinking magical creatures with limited existences that did what they were told until their clocks ran out. He forced himself to think about his task: to find new recruits for the resistance. Anything but the blurry faces that he knew would haunt his nightmares from then on.

But as he turned to go, the sounds of angry conversation drifted on the wind from several streets away. Something Aladdin would have ignored in normal times but was unusual at this hour under the new curfew.

He leaped quietly to the next roof and then dived down to a convenient balcony. From there, he swung on a clothesline and landed silently on an awning across the way. There he hid behind a pair of dangling harem trousers and watched.

It was the Square of the Sailor, so named for the ships carved into the corners of the civic buildings that surrounded the square. It was once a popular meeting place for the slightly less destitute of the ghetto; there was even a teahouse in one corner with rickety chairs and threadbare rugs and watered-down tea.

And now it had Jafar and six of his elite *human* palace guards, along with a small gathering crowd.

A silver tray of tea, wine and cakes, obviously *not* from the teahouse, was hovering in the air before the sorcerer. He wore a grin that would look false to the blindest, most foolish of observers.

Aladdin was neither. He leaned in close: he hadn't had a good look at Jafar since the parade. The 'sultan' rarely went into public anymore. The light of insanity glowed strongly in his eyes. What was worth risking his precious self and spending time out among the common people?

"All I am asking for," Jafar was saying with the soothing patience of a mother, "is the location of Princess Jasmine. Just tell me where she is and you will never go hungry again. You will sup on meat and delicacies and wine... not this watered-down muck your friend here serves you every night."

The crowd of skinny and shabbily dressed people shuffled uneasily. Some couldn't take their eyes off the silver tray of treats. Some seemed uneasy, glancing back and forth from the guards to Jafar's face. Some waited to see what others would do first. A few quietly drew back into the shadows, trying to disappear from what looked like a very bad situation.

Aladdin made careful note of *those* faces. They would be useful to find later.

"Who cares about the sultan's old filly?" one man called out. "You can have anyone you want. *My* daughter is twice as pretty as Jasmine and *she* won't hide from you, I swear."

Perhaps he was trying to gain favour with the mad sorcerer. It was a bad idea. Anger burned in Jafar's eyes, instant and complete.

"I don't particularly care for your opinion of my business," Jafar said with the careful enunciation of someone who really didn't care, someone who could take as long as he wanted with a group of ants before deciding to grind them into the dust under his heel. "Nor have I any interest in your daughter. Now, I ask again. Do. Any. Of you. Know. The location. Of the princess?"

The tray of treats waggled suggestively in the air. Aladdin could smell the intoxicating aroma of dates and honey cake even up where he was. He wondered if it was more magic.

No one stepped forwards.

"Let me put it another way," Jafar said calmly.

The silver tray clattered to the ground, treats rolling in the dust.

"You there." He pointed at someone with his ebony cobra-headed staff. The man, short and bony, looked left and right quickly to see if anyone else was meant. Without a word, two of the black-and-red clad palace guards approached him on either side and grabbed his arms, wrenching them behind his back. Unsure what was going to happen to him, the man began straining against them.

"Tell me," Jafar said. His eyes glowed red and so did the jewelled eyes of the cobra on his staff. The poor man seemed frozen like a mouse or small bird, hypnotised by the glow. His body still struggled as if he had forgotten to tell it to stop, but his face and head were completely still. "*Where* is Princess Jasmine?"

"In the palace?" the man asked in a daze.

Jafar's face broke from sorcerous concentration to crumble into annoyance.

"If she was in the palace, why would I be looking for her?"

"It's a very big palace," the man answered.

Aladdin tried not to laugh aloud. The poor guy was answering as honestly as he could under the spell. The problem was he wasn't a very *smart* man. And he didn't know anything.

With a sigh of frustration, Jafar jerked his staff. The red glow faded.

The man turned to look at his friends for help… but now it was like his *body* was frozen and only his neck and head could move.

The man's face went white as panic began to set in.

His head continued to turn.

Muscles stood out on his neck, sinews and tendons straining against his flesh.

Jafar kept looking at the man dispassionately. Only the tip of his finger moved, making the tiniest of circles.

The man's head kept slowly turning.

He screamed as his muscles began to tear and bones began to crunch.

People in the crowd watched in horror. Maybe they tried to look away, but couldn't.

The man's scream suddenly cut off in a gurgle. With a final *snap* the head was all the way round, the man's blank eyes looking at the crowd.

Aladdin turned away, feeling sick.

"Next," Jafar said with an indulgent smile.

"A plague on you, you murderous scum!" one man in the crowd shouted, terrified and enraged at the same time.

Jafar just rolled his eyes.

"Mmm-hmmm. *Next*," he repeated tiredly.

The sorcerer had gone from being an almost humourous villain to a madman of truly demonic proportions.

Aladdin had to take a moment to collect himself before heading back out into the night.

Tea with a Genie

JASMINE WAS, OF COURSE, *not* in the palace. Ironically, however, she was just barely on the other side of its walls, in a fashionable ritzy district that was now silent with fear.

She had often dreamed of going to a teahouse to play chess or argue esoteric scholarly points with students and feisty old men and women. It was a dream forbidden to a royal princess, of course. And now that she was finally in one... she was alone. Giant urns, empty of tea, made strange and monstrous shapes in the half-light.

A telltale wisp of blue smoke curled up from behind the bar. Soon the rest of the genie appeared with a tray full of glasses and dishes on his arm, a tea towel over his wrist.

"Coffee? Tea? Who got the Egyptian wine? Little early in the evening for that, don't you think? Have some of this instead."

He glided over next to Jasmine. The tray and towel of his little joke disappeared but two cups remained; he offered one to her. It was a pretty glass thing with gold curlicues on its sides, hot tea within. She looked at it curiously, feeling the warmth in her hand.

"It's not poisoned," the genie said archly. "Jafar's not that subtle. Trust me. If he knew we were meeting, you would already be strung up and saying *I do* against your will."

"No, I was just wondering..." she frowned. "If you can make food and drink out of thin air, why hasn't Jafar been doing just that? He was tossing bread to everyone at the parades, but that seems to have stopped. Now it's being rationed... he's only handing it out to people who stand in line and swear loyalty. And that whole thing with the inflation of gold has been making it hard for people to obtain food otherwise. Couldn't he, or you, solve that with a wave of your hand?"

"Aha, smart lady," the genie said, a smile of genuine warmth taking the place of his usual sardonic look. "The laws of magic aren't as simple as I may have made it seem. Even the most powerful sorcerers in the world cannot just summon infinite amounts of *anything* into existence forever, it has to come from somewhere. And gold is far more simple, in its own way, than bread and meat."

"All right, but *you* could do it, couldn't you? You did it before. That's what separates a genie, uh, a *djinn*, from a sorcerer, right? You're way more powerful?"

The genie pretended to look embarrassed by the praise, flushing. "Why, yes, I could. But Jafar's two wishes were fairly explicit. One could assume making him sultan involves the occasional parade and accompanying handouts. It might also come with his own personal disposable army. It does *not*, however, mean standing next to him and summoning meal after meal for everyone like some cafeteria lady."

"A what?"

"Nothing, never mind. The point is, if he were very clever and found a historic precedent, perhaps he could get me to do that. But he's not and I'm not making it easy for him. And on top of that… *Jafar doesn't* want *to give out infinite amounts of free food.*"

"Why not?"

"The free food is just bait." The genie mimed releasing the line of a fishing pole. A pole appeared in his hands, of course with a giant fish at the end of it that looked a little too much like an average citizen of Agrabah. "Everyone grabs the free food and gold and *bam*, he's hooked them." He jerked the line. The fish flopped onto the floor. "Now he just reels them in. Or tightens the noose."

The genie frowned, contemplating metaphors. Suddenly, the fish-person looked like a rabbit-person, with a noose around its neck.

"This isn't really working for me," the genie decided with a sigh. All of his props, including the rabbit, vanished. "Switching topics to a slightly more evil form of magic… a caravan is arriving from Carcossa three nights from now, when the moon is at a perfect quarter. It's got a load of books and other magical bric-a-brac in it. I think this may be the big one. The one with *Al Azif*."

"Why weren't you sent with the caravan this time, to defend it?"

"What Jafar is looking for may not be found in, how do I put this, *human* realms at all. Let's just leave it at this: djinn don't really travel to Carcossa very well. Matter of fact, no one does. Go easy on the guards when you take them down," the genie said with a shudder.

"All right. Thank you," Jasmine said, toasting him with her tea. She took a sip. It was hot and honeyed, comforting. "And thank you for returning Rajah, and telling us about *Al Azif*, and… everything else. We owe you so much."

The genie shrugged. "This is a pretty nasty situation. Just get the bad guy. Maybe set me free? Anyway, it's all good karma."

Jasmine tilted her head, looking at him. "How are *you*

holding up?" she asked gently.

"Oh, as well as can be expected," he said, waving his hand. "Considering I'm, like, the last of my race, enslaved to an insane, power hungry, evil – did I say evil? – dictator with delusions of godhood... who won't even make his final, insane third wish and let me off the hook from all this. Maybe my next master will be someone nicer. Like the sadistic tyrant of a kingdom of vampires. Or something."

"What *would* you do?" Jasmine asked curiously. "If you were free?"

"I'd travel," the genie answered promptly. "I'd get as far away as possible from here, and from my memories. It's too much. Maybe I could come back one day, but there's a lot out there to see first. *Snow*, for instance. I'd kind of like to see that."

"I don't know if I could ever leave Agrabah," Jasmine said with a wistful sigh. "It's so beautiful, and there's so much to do."

"Well, better here than on the Marie Celeste," the genie said, clicking his tongue. "No one ever figures out what happened to *them*."

Jasmine thought about the genie's strange mood switches, humourous jokes, and bitter hints at horrible things. Here was a creature who knew more than she would ever know, trapped in a place and a time where he didn't want to be.

"It must be really hard... being you," she said, fumbling for the right thing to say.

"Princess, you have *no* idea," he quipped, quoting Jafar but with a sad smile.

And with that he dwindled down to a curlicue of blue smoke and evaporated into the night air.

Friends in Unlikely Places

"I NEVER THOUGHT I'd be stealing with *you* again," Duban muttered as he stood on the back of a wagon and threw a sack to Aladdin. Their latest caravan heist held no magic books but something infinitely more useful to the poor people of Agrabah. Food.

Aladdin grinned, catching the sack and making sure the top was knotted tightly. *Street* Rats weren't the only kind of rat they had around here.

"I think Morgiana's idea is brilliant, to have Jasmine herself offering the handouts," Duban said. "It will make a real connection with the people."

"It's dangerous," Aladdin said, scowling. "Jasmine is too many things: a valuable prize to hand over to Jafar, a symbol of the old sultan, our de facto leader. I don't think she should be out in the open."

Duban shrugged. "You can't gain without risk. You of all people should know that."

The quiet noise of a throat being cleared interrupted their chatter.

Aladdin and Duban looked up in surprise to see a tall, middle-aged man standing there, quietly waiting. He was wrapped in a simple robe that was worn in places with what looked like all-too-perfect rips. His face didn't show any of the long-term effects of privation: while he was skinny, it wasn't because he was starving. His skin was clear and his greying beard well trimmed. His hands were clasped politely. He wore a plain gold ring on one hand... but Aladdin's expert eye saw that it didn't quite match the tan lines round his finger. And there were more pale areas on his other fingers...

"We were just..." Aladdin began.

"My father runs a bakery," Duban said. "We were just helping him. This is where... he keeps his..."

"*Baguettes,*" Aladdin supplied.

Duban looked at him as if he was an idiot. Which he sort of was.

"I am here to speak to the... 'Street Rats'," the man said politely. His accent was clipped and refined.

"I don't know of any..." Duban said.

"We aren't..." Aladdin said.

"You're talking about those *thieves* they named this

neighbourhood after?" Duban asked with interest.

"A travesty," Aladdin swore, "totally ruining property values."

They trailed off as the man just watched them in silence.

Finally, he spoke again.

"I am Amur, the head of the Jewellers' Guild, and I risk my own life by coming here."

He twisted the gold band around on his finger and, as Aladdin suspected, revealed a huge gem with the golden image of a perfect diamond incised on it.

Duban gave a low whistle.

"What is it you want?" Aladdin asked, confused.

"I would feel… more comfortable discussing it over tea," the man said, looking around obviously.

The two thieves immediately felt stupid. Of course a rich man who disguised himself to come to the most dangerous part of town would come with a purpose he didn't want exposed to the world.

"Yeah. Of course. Sure," Aladdin said quickly. "But how did you… know we were Street Rats, or we were here?"

The man gave a polite cough and nodded his chin at a wall.

There was the Mark of Rajah, four claws in bloody red paint.

Inside the labyrinth of passages that made up the world of the Street Rats, Duban and Aladdin managed to cobble together some tea and chairs and a table... without leading Amur too deep into their secret lair.

The head of the Jewellers' Guild sat poshly relaxed, looking around with interest as if this was just a new tea house and not the lair of the people who probably stole from him and his clients.

"We should do something about that," Aladdin suggested to Duban. "The claw marks, I mean."

"The kids love it," Duban said doubtfully. "It really makes them feel like they're a part of something."

"And here I was thinking you were concerned about security."

"I am, but it's a good symbol. For people to rally to. They just shouldn't... paint it so close to home."

Amur took a sip of tea pointedly, waiting for them to sit down.

"Sorry, we can discuss this later," Aladdin said.

"No, it *is* a good symbol," the jeweller said. "Maybe I'll have a couple made up in gold for those who support our cause."

"*Our* cause?" Jasmine asked, entering the chamber. She pushed her hood back from her face. Morgiana followed close behind. She scowled when she saw who sat drinking tea.

"Your Royal Highness," Amur said, leaping up and immediately executing a perfect bow. "There were rumours you were somehow connected with all this, in hiding..."

"The rumours are true," she said with a smile, indicating for him to sit down. She sat as well and took Aladdin's cup from him. He grinned and let her have it.

"I am gratified to see you are still alive and well. Underground, literally as well as figuratively," Amur said. "And this leads us nicely to what I came here to discuss... I want to talk about the little *situation* Agrabah has with Jafar."

"Why do *you* care?" Morgiana asked. "He's not bothering you. He's not making you swear an oath of loyalty for *bread*. At night, when curfew tolls, you guys just stay inside your mansions and wait until morning. How is he bothering you?"

Amur gave her a withering look.

"Life isn't that simple, thief. Let's start with *gold*, for instance. I am sure that *as* a thief you are aware of how much this magical influx of coins has devalued it?"

Aladdin chuckled, but not meanly. "He's got you there, Morgiana. Jafar is ruining *their* trade, too."

"A second thing," Amur continued. "And no less important. Jafar has closed all the libraries, all the religious education centres, and all the trade halls that deal with science or magic. The Alchemaics, I have it on good authority, are forbidden from meeting, on pain of death."

"But why would he…?" Duban began.

"Because he doesn't want competition," Morgiana said grimly. "He's looking to break the laws of magic and doesn't want anyone stopping him."

"And of course everyone who's educated knows how Jafar's 'benevolent' rule ends," Jasmine said, nodding.

"It's true. Imams, mullahs, priests, rabbis, teachers, scholars, students… they are… *dissatisfied* with the current state of affairs, to say the least," the jeweller said with a sigh.

"And you…?" Jasmine prompted.

Amur steepled his fingers together. "Let us say I am representing them. I come to speak for a certain segment of the population, which includes the religious leaders, and guilds, and others in various quarters of the city… people you might not normally have discourse with. Who have… heard of some of the caravan raids and other exploits carried out by your little band of outlaws here. Who are willing to support you in your endeavours as best we can."

"And they elected *you* to risk your sorry self down here?" Duban asked with a toothy grin.

"No," the man said calmly. "I volunteered."

Duban had the decency to look abashed.

But Amur wasn't done. "You know, thief, you are not the

only ones who value freedom. To do what you want where you want with whom you want. To read what you want, if you can read. To *live.* I have a pair of granddaughters I used to walk with *every evening* up the hill past the cloth market to watch the sun set. It seems like such a little thing not to do anymore… but it matters. For them, and for me. And even mansion walls do not keep out the fear of the night and the odious new things it brings."

"So we do the dirty work and you *secretly* support us?" Morgiana demanded. "Your talk about *freedom* is all well and good, but *living,* the freedom of that, is denied to many of the poorest in the city. Where were you before the breadlines when people were just hungry?"

"It's a fair point," Amur allowed. "But it's hard to gauge the severity of a situation when *your sorry self,* as your friend so nicely put it, is in danger every time you set foot in the poorer parts of town. When there is a *well-organised gang of thieves* bold enough to start infiltrating the gem and gold markets."

"And *that's* a fair point," Jasmine said with a gentle smile. "Can we, perhaps, agree that when this is all over, it is a problem we will all work on? Together? That Agrabah's problems are everyone's, and we need *everyone's* help?"

Amur and Morgiana glared at each other for a long moment.

"Yes," Amur finally allowed.

"All right," Morgiana said, not *quite* sullenly.

"All right," Jasmine said with a relieved sigh. "It's past time I got out there and started distributing bread to the families who have refused this whole swearing allegiance thing. Who are starving because of the decisions they made. Why don't you come along, Amur? And finally see firsthand the problems of a certain segment of the population of Agrabah *you're* not acquainted with?"

"Yes, I think that's a good idea," Amur said, surprisingly agreeable to the suggestion. "And... I'd *like* to help."

"Huh," Morgiana said.

"Princess *Jasmine*?" the old woman said in wonder, looking up into her face. Half a dozen grandchildren scurried around her feet in various states of undress, trying to stay busy and play while their parents were gone.

Jasmine stood before her like a supplicant, head covered, offering a small bag of bread and cheese. Morgiana stood behind her, hands on her daggers. Behind them Ahmed and Shirin carried more bags of bread; Amur had a giant one.

Jasmine smiled. "Yes. I've come to help."

"But... aren't you marrying Jafar, the new sultan?"

"No," she answered shortly. "He is a murderous usurper. I will have my vengeance upon him, and—"

Morgiana elbowed her discreetly in the ribs.

"And… he and I don't see exactly eye to eye on matters of governance," Jasmine added quickly, with a gentle smile. "And he's turning Agrabah into a prison, where everyone is scared of doing or saying the wrong thing."

The old woman continued to look at her with unreadable pale brown eyes.

Jasmine tried not to grow nervous.

"He's an evil, murdering son of a *pig*," the old woman finally said, spitting. "The old sultan may have been a fool who never did anything for us… but he never tortured anyone or demanded loyalty for bread. And what do the Peacekeeping Patrols keep us safe from, anyway? Each other? It's Agrabah! If you don't carry a dagger, it's your own damn foolishness."

"That's how I feel, too," Jasmine said. "Mostly. It would be nice if the streets were free *and* safe. But please, take this bread and cheese. I'm not demanding your loyalty in return. I just want my people fed."

The old woman looked at the bread warily. Then her face broke into a smile of a thousand crinkles. She cackled.

"The royal princess… the future sultana… bringing *me* bread and cheese. In my own home. And I didn't even have to get up and bow!"

"Peace be with you," Jasmine said, nodding.

"And to you," the old woman said with dignity. *"And death to Jafar!"* she added with a mischievous grin, her hand swiping the air in front of her like a tiger's claws.

When they walked back outside, Jasmine took a deep breath. She knew she should adjust her hood more tightly round her head... but she couldn't help taking it off for just a moment. She needed fresh air. It still felt strange to have anything covering her so completely, and the rough material pulled at her hair in its new braided updo.

"I know, I know," she sighed, seeing Morgiana's look. "Just give me a second. And... thanks for the little reminder back there. I just think of Jafar and... I get all crazy. It's like a rage that can't fit inside my own head. I want him to pay *so badly* for what he's done."

"I know," Morgiana said.

The two girls strolled side by side down the shaded part of the street, away from the baking-hot white wall on the other side. The rest of their team stayed a few steps behind, Ahmed and Shirin playing hopscotch with a small stone. Amur looked around interestedly at the part of the city he had never been in before. Shirin had to pause her game to show him the right way to walk in the Quarter of the Street Rats: face straight and forward, eyes darting everywhere, not showing that you were staring.

"You look like a tourist," she explained with the

patience of a much older teacher.

Morgiana watched them with a smile. Then she took a deep breath, trying to figure out how to say something politely to the princess. "See, the thing is... none of us... none of the Street Rats, even most of the normal citizens of Agrabah, really care who's in charge. No offence or disrespect to your father. But except for taxes and prisons, it doesn't really matter to the little guy. Jafar is playing a bad card with the patrols and increased violence. Nobody likes that. And you should bring that up. Often. But otherwise, I would stress the details of regime change less and yay-yay-happy-joy *nice* Sultana Jasmine who cares about her people more."

"You're right," Jasmine sighed, arranging her hair in preparation for putting the hood back up. Several people passed them and gave her a second glance. Most of the city was now aware that Jafar hadn't yet married the royal princess... and everyone wondered how she had got out of it and where she had fled to. In the poorer districts, rumours spread that she was among them somehow, but no one knew where. And that she was helping the poor, like some sort of heroine from legend.

Jasmine smiled at those who stared at her too hard.

"Although," she added with a sideways look at Morgiana, "I am a *bit* surprised that you, of all people, had to remind me to speak of peaceful things."

Morgiana grinned. Her face lost its characteristic tightness and scowl as though she was dropping a costume or a heavy pair of boots. "Aladdin may not approve of our 'little thieving organisation' and make fun of it... but what he fails to grasp is the *organisation* part. It's not all about gold and jewels and heists and stealing from 'the man'. It's also territories and percentages and fair shares... and not *quite* fair shares when someone's family is ailing and needs a little more. It's about loans no one is ever going to pay back. It's about conflict resolution because in our case, an unresolved conflict results in daggers coming out. It's about dealing with people, treating them fairly, and listening to them even if you don't agree. Sometimes it's about making everyone unhappy, the same amount."

Jasmine listened with interest.

"I've... only just begun to realise that myself. None of our plans, none of *my* plans to win the people, to stop Jafar from breaking the laws of magic, to overthrow him... would be possible without the network you have in place. Sorry about taking over."

"That's okay," Morgiana said, only a little ruefully. "I truly believe that it's the only way to keep Agrabah from falling down a very, very bad path."

"What will you do when this is all over?" Jasmine

asked, realising it was the second time recently she had asked someone that question.

Morgiana looked surprised. "I don't know. You'll be sultana and I guess I can't go back to thieving… now that you know everything about us…"

Amur was trying not to look like he was listening.

"I liked what you said before," Morgiana said slowly. "About everyone working together to make Agrabah"

She stopped short.

Amur misunderstood.

"I meant what I said about helping out!" he protested. "I was merely interested in what you were going to say; I wasn't…"

"No, look," Morgiana said, pointing without moving a muscle. Jasmine and Amur followed her eyes.

One of the passers-by didn't look twice at Jasmine; he looked *three* times. And then kept looking back. Jasmine wasn't sure what the big deal was, but Morgiana had tensed up and put her hands where her daggers were hidden.

The man saw the three of them looking at him and broke into a run.

It was like Morgiana had known he was going to do exactly that; she sprang after him almost before his legs moved. She let him get just far enough ahead so he could duck into a narrow, deserted alley off the street. Probably thinking he could escape her there. Probably thinking that there he could easily subdue a girl so much smaller than he, where no one could see.

But he wasn't a Street Rat.

Once they were alone in the alley, Morgiana doubled her pace and covered the last few metres in an astounding leap. She wrapped her arm round the man's throat and pulled him back into her. Her left hand held a dagger to his side.

Jasmine and Amur and the rest of the party rounded the corner just in time to see this. Amur drew back in shock.

"What's your problem, big guy?" Morgiana hissed in her captive's ear.

"Nothing, I am on my way to the market, *nothing at all*. Get off of me!" the man ordered.

"Try again." Morgiana dug the tip of her dagger deeper into his clothes so he could feel the prick of its point. She tightened her elbow at his neck.

"I am a citizen of the Jafar's Agrabah. Agrabah *Ascendant*. Let me go, you Street Rat! Or it will go poorly for you!"

"What were you doing staring at us like that?" Morgiana demanded. She twisted the knife so it began to tear his tunic.

"Come now," Amur began. "He just recognised the princess and was surprised. Let him go…"

"Yeah, the royal princess," the man said, choking a

little. "I was surprised."

Morgiana seemed unconvinced. The man's hands flew up to his throat as she gave it a quick squeeze.

"I'll give you one more chance."

"Morgiana, please," Jasmine begged. "Don't... wait, what's that on his hand?"

Everyone stopped and looked. Shirin ran forwards and grabbed his left arm, wrenching it so the back of his hand was exposed.

A strange symbol was burned into his skin so violently that it was still oozing and raw.

"The Mark of Jafar," Morgiana spat. "Like on his coins and flags."

Jasmine put her hand to her mouth, unsure if she was going to throw up or swear in frustration.

Amur swore.

"My apologies, Morgiana," he growled. "You know your business. You have the eye of a hawk."

"What *is* that?" Jasmine finally asked, moving forwards to get a closer look.

The man's slitted eyes raced back and forth like a crazed horse's. He tried to scramble with his legs but Ahmed sat on them and held them together tightly.

"It's a brand," Shirin said simply. "Like what they do to goats."

"Who did this to you?" Jasmine asked the man coldly.

"You get extra," the man whined. "The red light. He looks into you and sees that you really are completely devoted. And then you get the mark. And then you get meat and gold."

"But what about... the oaths?" Jasmine asked. "Don't you get bread just for saying the oaths?"

"Everyone lies," the man jeered. "But I'm pure. I'm safe. I'm one of Jafar's men now. A Branded One."

"Dear heaven," Amur murmured. "When did *this* start?"

"I am in the first hundred," the man bragged. "Soon all of Agrabah will be pure, but I am one of the first."

"He can't make them love him with magic or bread," Jasmine said. "So he's gaining their loyalty by torture and fear? *Where is he doing this?*"

"In the palace," the man answered sullenly. "It doesn't matter. I've seen you. I am the eyes and ears of Jafar."

"We'll have to kill him," Morgiana said.

"No," Jasmine said, more tiredly than righteously. She thought quickly. What would Aladdin do?

Lie.

"So Jafar knows I'm in the city he probably already knew that. He doesn't know where I'll be next. Because... I never stay still. I never sleep in the same place twice. I move like the wind and the shadows. I am sheltered by the good and faithful all over Agrabah, in *every* neighbourhood.

"Go crawling back to your master, scum. Tell him that *I* am the eyes and ears of my people, and they *do not want him.*"

Morgiana dug the dagger in one more time, drawing blood.

Then she let him go.

In a series of clumsy, desperate flops, the man got up and ran away from them, sandals hitting the ground loudly.

He didn't even shout a curse or promise back at them.

"Coward," Amur spat.

Jasmine wanted to crumple to the ground. The smell of recently burned flesh was still in her nose; the Mark of Jafar hung in the air before her eyes, bloody and pale.

Morgiana put her arm around the princess's shoulders.

"Jasmine," she said, "I believe it's time to rethink our tactics. He's building his own power base, a strong one with threats and rewards."

"You're right," Jasmine growled. "This isn't some heist-and-hijinks resistance operation anymore. We can't wait around patiently to win the hearts and minds of all of Agrabah. We need to do more.

"We need to attack Jafar directly and take back Agrabah."

A Declaration of War

BROTHER AND SISTER were in the sky together, if briefly: the sun was just sinking below the horizon in the west. The moon followed not far behind, slowly chasing the day away. It was a strange orange crescent that night, its tips pointed directly down like a bull getting ready to charge. Old people called it a dry moon and said bad times were coming.

As if the curfew, the patrols and the loyalty brands weren't bad enough, Aladdin thought cynically.

But the moon was also beautiful with the stars beginning to come out around her and palms below, waving in the hot wind. At least that's what he told himself and Abu.

This heist was going to be trickier precisely because it was at dusk. The Peacekeeping Patrols were just setting out, so the streets were empty. There was no chance of using the 'watering the camels' ploy or 'angry merchants arguing' gambit or 'flock of wayward goats' ruse to distract the drivers of the caravan.

'Injured child' would have to do: a girl lying in the street, moaning in pain and grabbing her leg. In some ways this was actually better in the early evening, because she would have more reason to be terrified, not wanting to get left by herself to be found by the patrols.

This was the big one, the caravan from Carcossa. In it they would almost certainly find *Al Azif*. Keeping that out of Jafar's hands was pivotal in the war they planned to wage against the sorcerer to take back the city. Once he got it and began to raise the undead, things would get a *lot* harder.

And besides the obvious advantage of depriving Jafar of a weapon he was counting on, a victory against the 'all-powerful sorcerer' would be huge for morale. It would be a sign to the rest of Agrabah that the good guys could win and that, in turn, would drive even more people over to their side. Jafar would begin to feel vulnerable. Then it would only be a matter of time before they could defeat him entirely.

Aladdin waited on a rooftop, watching the wagons that appeared on the horizon grow larger and larger. The warm, dry wind whipped around his face, bringing the resinous scent of desert scrub with it. He wished Jasmine could be there next to him, just the two of them, sharing a quiet moment on a rooftop together. Like they were originally supposed to, just a short time ago, when she was just a rich girl in disguise slumming it and he didn't even have a name.

He sighed, kicking his dry, bare feet against the dried mud roof. One day there would be time. When all of this was over. When Jafar was overthrown and the city was theirs and Jasmine was sultana... instituting her reforms... Yes, there would be *plenty* of time for hanging out on rooftops.

Right now she was back at the lair, working on plans to attack the palace. Amur had brought in the lead Alchemaic to discuss explosives. Morgiana had organised the sudden influx of new recruits, dividing them into squads. Duban was in charge of tactics, along with a new guy named Sohrab, who had defected from the royal guard. Maruf managed the flow of supplies to their incipient army and continued the generosity to families who supported the resistance.

Aladdin was in charge of making trouble, of course. That was why he was leading tonight's raid.

The wagons stopped just inside the city gates.

A girl lying on the ground cried up for them to help her.

"Please, esteemed effendi! Give me a ride, anywhere. Even a few blocks to the first empty house you see! So I might seek refuge from the night and the Peacekeeping Patrols!"

That was Aladdin's cue.

He leaped down lightly, Abu beside him. The drivers although strangely pale and hollow-eyed, were predictably more annoyed by the interruption of their routine than concerned for the little girl's safety. They got down to move her just a few metres out of their way and damn her fate to the patrols.

So Aladdin didn't feel *too* bad when Morgiana and Duban slipped out of the shadows behind the drivers and knocked the backs of their heads with silent leather-covered clubs. The plan was to tie them up somewhere after drawing all sorts of strange insignia on their clothes, as if they had been magically subdued by a rival sorcerer. As much as Aladdin didn't like those who worked for Jafar, he didn't want to see them lose their lives because they had failed their master.

Street Rats melted out of the scenery, hoisted the guards between them, and disappeared again. Aladdin gently took the reins of the lead camel, whispering and clicking his tongue. A little unnerved by the turn of events, the animals immediately followed their new human master. He would probably, like all humans, give them water and food. Abu leaped onto the back of one and chittered like he was driving the whole caravan himself.

Aladdin led them back out of the gate and round the outside wall. If Agrabah was quiet at night these days, the outskirts of the desert were as silent as death. The insects and little chirping lizards and animals that usually called through the dark hours were still. The only noise came from the wind whispering through the dry grasses.

Aladdin found himself shivering despite the heat and was relieved when they came to the crack in the wall where a whole crowd of Street Rats was waiting quietly to unload all the books and artefacts at once in one long human chain. He patted the lead camel on her neck.

"We'll get you all watered in a moment," he promised before going to the back of the cart and throwing open its cloth flaps. There were crates and urns and even western-style barrels sealed tightly for the trip. Someone handed Aladdin a metal-tipped construction hook and he went to work immediately, prying the lid off the first of the crates.

It was filled to the top with ancient mouldering…

…rocks?

He stared at the beige and grey desert stones, chunky and worn. They were all jumbled together like a giant child had picked up a handful of pebbles and stashed them away, pretending they were precious gems.

He opened another crate. More rocks.

He brought the tool down on a clay amphora, smashing the top off. Instead of holy water or magic potions or even wine or beer, *sand* poured out in a fine stream that mockingly replicated the thing it replaced.

Aladdin stared at it for only a moment before reacting. *"Get out!"*

He spun round and shoved the smaller Street Rats in front of him, trying to make them move faster.

"It's a trap! *Get out! Run! Hide!*"

Malicious laughter rose all around him. It grew like a dust storm: from the desert, from the city walls, from the streets, from the very air itself.

"Did you really think your little treacheries would go unnoticed by me?"

Aladdin tried not to pay attention to the voice of Jafar as he concentrated on getting the children away. He put two up on a camel and whacked its flank, causing it to scream in annoyance and gallop off into the city.

"Me. Sultan of this city and greatest sorcerer in the world. You thought you could hide from me?"

Duban and Morgiana had abandoned the original plan: upon hearing the voice, they had just left the unconscious guards and run to find Aladdin. They helped scatter and send off the rest of the Street Rats.

"We have to warn Jasmine," Aladdin said as the last little thief ran off. "Is she back at your hideout?"

In silent answer, Jasmine herself stepped out of the shadows, looking a little guilty.

Aladdin threw his arms around her and squeezed so tightly he was almost afraid of breaking her. He kissed her hard.

"And here I was thinking you'd be angry I came to see one of your heists," she said with a rueful smile.

"I'm just glad you're safe with me."

"But other people *are* at the hideout," Jasmine said. "Maruf and Shirin and Ahmed and everyone else *not* here. We should go back…"

"No one has turned over its location yet," Morgiana said uncertainly.

"Did you Street Rats really think you could talk to the genie, right under my nose, as it were? The genie whom I control? Oh, yes, Jasmine. I caught him coming back from your little tryst. He didn't want to tell me anything, not without me giving up my last wish for it, of course. It took me a while to convince him. Far longer, and with far more torture, than I expected."

Jasmine went pale. Aladdin put his arm around her waist as she swayed, sick with shock.

"But, in the end, he told me everything about your little plan. And with the help of some of my Branded Ones, I've learned about the location of your, and I use this term loosely, 'headquarters'.

"My scouts had already returned from Carcossa. Al Azif

is already in my possession. *This was just to lure you out…
leaving your hideout completely unprotected."*

"My father…" Duban said, eyes wide. "The children…"

"We have to go back," Morgiana said grimly.

Aladdin agreed. It was probably another trap, but what
choice did they have? They couldn't let Maruf and the
children perish. The four of them began to run.

Jafar's voice followed them mockingly.

*"You still don't understand, little Rats. True power is not
the will of the people. It is not brute force, or trickery, or stealth
or planning. All of this,* all of this, *can be overcome
with magic. Your people of Agrabah understand that.
Magic brought them gold, and bread, and police, and peace,
and prosperity. Magic brings pain and obedience. Magic is the
only way to change a corrupt, broken system. Magic is the only
true power in the world. And you have* none."

Aladdin didn't think he had ever moved so fast.
Morgiana, lighter and swifter than he, raced on ahead like
a gazelle. Then came Jasmine. Duban brought up the rear,
and as much as he huffed and puffed, the veteran thief
didn't weaken or slow his pace.

*"PEOPLE OF AGRABAH. Behold those who would
make life hard for you. They scurry like the very rats they call
themselves and escape into the filth and the diseased parts of your
beloved city. If you would see Agrabah at peace and prosperous,*

I would implore you to turn in any of these villainous wretches who are trying to tear it apart."

As the friends finally got close to the Quarter, a strange smell began to permeate the air. It didn't come and then fade, like when they passed a rubbish pile or an open sewer. It *stayed* as they ran... and grew stronger the closer they approached the hideout. The stench was terrible, like rotten meat, filth, decaying corpses, all mixed in the heat of the sun.

Aladdin shook his head and tried to focus on running. The four of them had to veer to the left quickly to avoid hitting a Peacekeeping Patrol head-on. The patrol turned to follow them but in the same ominous, constant-yet-slow pace they walked through the rest of the city.

Aladdin and Jasmine barged through the secret entrance of the hideout first, sliding down into the main room. The horrible smell was stronger here, almost overpowering in the close quarters.

Jasmine held her nose and hurried into her war room. Aladdin pulled his vest up over his face and followed close behind.

The map of Agrabah was gone.

It had been completely erased from the floor. The pebble buildings were strewn across the room like a giant wind had taken them. The Mark of Rajah on the wall was ominously blurred, like someone had tried to wipe it off.

Aladdin frowned, either someone from Jafar's camp had been there or the Street Rats had tried to destroy everything to keep anyone from seeing their plans. It was impossible to tell.

Morgiana and Duban entered their lair by other secret means and ran through the rooms at their end to meet up with Aladdin and Jasmine.

"It's empty," Duban announced, trying not to breathe.

"Everybody already godd oudd?" Jasmine suggested doubtfully through a pinched nose.

"What *is* that smell?" Morgiana asked, gasping.

Aladdin had no idea. But he didn't like the way things were adding up. Something was *off* about the whole place.

And still Jafar's voice echoed through the walls.

"I'm afraid… that until we have quelled this terrorist group, I will just have to keep a closer *eye on everyone. I've tried the carrot, and now it's time for the stick. And just in case you're wondering how serious I am about your safety, please come to the palace gates and see what's left of some Street Rat sympathisers we caught."*

Jasmine turned white. Duban looked sick. Morgiana spat in anger. Aladdin wondered how bad it was, if what he imagined was worse than what Jafar had actually done.

"We should gedd oudd of here," Aladdin said, choking on the stench.

They didn't even bother trying to keep their noises and movements small; the bad guys already knew where they were. The four friends burst out of the entrance with daggers drawn, ready for an attack.

Down the street, palace guards were heading towards them, rising up into the air.

"What the…" Duban said, rubbing his eyes.

"Is this more of Jafar's trickery?" Morgiana demanded.

The guards eerily hovered above the buildings, hands at the ready over their swords.

Without even seeming to try, they arranged themselves in military formation, two by three. Their uniforms were slightly different from those of the rest of the red-and-black guards; each wore thick, colourful cuffs on the ends of their sleeves that were strangely patterned for a military group.

"Oh, no," Aladdin said with horror, recognising the design.

"It's the magic carpet," Jasmine whispered.

"Jafar must have cut him, it, up." Aladdin felt sick with shame. Despite the carpet being just that, a carpet, magicked into being able to fly and having a rudimentary understanding of the world around it, Aladdin felt like he had betrayed a friend.

Abu chittered sympathetically on his shoulder.

Jafar had taken another mysterious, beautiful thing and destroyed it, twisting it for his own purposes. Everything he touched he desecrated.

And the guards *stank*. They were the source of the terrible smell. What was Jafar doing now, forbidding baths?

Jasmine pointed to the captain of the flying soldiers. He was large and manoeuvered silently into place at their lead.

"Ra-Rasoul," she stammered in disbelief. "He was *dead*. He died that day…"

Aladdin bit back a cry.

It *was* Rasoul leading the phalanx. His eyes were red. A dead black-red that somehow made them look smaller and infinitely deeper than they should have. His skin was white, like an insect larva or old nail clippings or the fat of a long-butchered sheep. His arms and legs hung, unmoving, by his sides.

"He is… risen from the dead," Morgiana said. For the first time perhaps ever, Aladdin heard fear creeping into her voice.

Aladdin had never meant to kill Rasoul. And the guard certainly didn't deserve *this*. To be turned into a ghoul. Was he in pain? Did he have any control over his actions? Did he just long to be at peace? Was he enraged at the living?

Whatever happened now was, in some ways, Aladdin's fault.

He straightened his shoulders and shook off the nausea. Guilt he would deal with later. Mistakes he would make up for later. Right now they had to survive.

The four Street Rats watched as, in the distance, more and more squadrons of slow-moving flying soldiers assembled themselves over the city.

"As I said, that foolish genie really doesn't know everything. I have completely broken one of the three laws of magic and learned how to bring back the dead. Permanently. Under my control. Every time one of my soldiers falls, he is replaced. Every time one of your Rats falls, he adds to my army. Death is my friend in the war for Agrabah."

Morgiana muttered something in the language of her mother.

"Street Rats. Jasmine." Jafar's voice became less playful and more businesslike. *"Even if you manage to avoid my army, you would still do well to turn yourselves in by dawn tomorrow."*

"Never!" Jasmine shouted to the sky. "We'd rather—"

But Aladdin touched her on the arm and pointed.

A great swirling cone of sand lifted up from the desert like a tornado. *Unlike* a tornado, it was broad and feathery at the edges. Sand danced around within the invisible wind in unnatural jerking motions. Suddenly, it made a picture: a giant hourglass, sand pouring slowly through it. In the bottom were Maruf, Shirin and Ahmed, desperately and silently slamming on the glass. Trying to get out.

Duban made a noise in his throat, a strangled cry.

"By sunrise tomorrow this little family of Street Rats will be dead. No great loss, I think. But if you actually bother to care about anyone besides your own worthless selves, you will turn yourselves in before the first light of day."

And then, without a word or noise or lingering echo, Jafar's voice just cut off. The sand that made up the image in the sky fell like rain.

"He has defeated us without drawing a single blade," Morgiana said bleakly. "Duban, we will turn ourselves in. We can't let them die this way."

"And then what?" Aladdin asked, turning on her. "Do you really think that will change anything? Do you think he will just let them go, like he promised? And if he did, forgetting for just a moment what he would do to us then, I'm thinking a quick execution and then four more ghouls for his army, what's going to happen to Agrabah? What's going to happen to everyone else? There won't be *anyone* left to fight him. The city will be his, one giant plaything for him to experiment on. And after that, who knows? The world?"

"I don't care about the world," Duban interrupted. "All I care about is my dad and my niece and my nephew."

Jasmine started to say something. Duban held up his hand.

"But you're right. Jafar has no reason to let them go. He has all the cards. And if they lived, I wouldn't want them to live in the sort of world he is building."

"But what do we do?" Morgiana demanded.

"What we should have done from the beginning," Aladdin said. "Grab the lamp. Rescue the family. Get the genie to undo all this and everyone lives happily ever after."

"Oh, is that all?" Morgiana rolled her eyes.

"Didn't you hear what he said?" Jasmine asked, eyes hardening as she thought about it. "He didn't call us *traitors* or *revolutionaries* or *insurrectionists*. He said, *'Death is my friend in the* war *for Agrabah.'* He thinks it's a fair fight. He thinks we're at *war*. As equals.

"Well, if it's war he wants… we'll give him one!"

Sympathies and Strategies

THE FOUR WALKED BACK through the streets of Agrabah in silence. Any initial enthusiasm they had felt from declaring war on Jafar ebbed away as the reality of the situation sank in. There wasn't a hint of the sorcerer's presence in the city as they went; he was silent now, his voice withdrawn back to the palace while he waited for them to make a decision. There was something anticlimactic about it.

Agrabah itself was full of tense and strange energy: although it was now fully evening and the Peacekeeping Patrols were active, people buzzed behind their closed doors or sometimes opened them a crack to trade opinions with a neighbour across the way, also behind a cracked door.

But no one could avoid noticing the corpses that were

occasionally sprawled in the alleys, left there as a warning.

Morgiana was holding Duban's hand, squeezing it and murmuring sympathetic and supportive words, but he didn't seem to notice. He just stared at the dirt or his own feet as he plodded along.

When they were back in Aladdin's hideout with the door safely shut, Morgiana was the first one to speak.

"Kidnapping *children?*" she said, dumbfounded. "And old men? I mean… you're the most powerful sorcerer in the world. Just… *why?*"

" 'Magic is only as great as the mind controlling it'," Jasmine said, quoting something she had read somewhere. She thought about the genie's story involving a previous master who had wanted a larger flock of goats. A happy man who was mostly happy with the life he already had. "Jafar is even sicker than I thought."

Duban silently collapsed onto the floor and covered his face with his hands.

"I'm so sorry," Aladdin said, kneeling down and putting his arm around his friend's shoulders. Duban looked up and gave a weak smile of appreciation but didn't meet Aladdin's gaze. "We'll get them back, I promise."

"And I'm sorry for not completely believing you, Jasmine," Morgiana added. "I really thought the whole thing about the army of undead was just… I don't know… a little…"

"You thought I exaggerated it to get you to help?" Jasmine asked, not unkindly.

"Well, come *on*... It's like a story some grandmother would tell you. But those... *ghouls*... in the *sky*... Rasoul himself..." The thief shuddered.

"We need to come up with a plan, a war strategy," Jasmine said, slamming one fist into another. "We need to *organise*..."

Duban finally spoke, his voice bitter: "It's all very well to declare war on Jafar. But what can we actually do? We're *thieves*, Jasmine. Not soldiers. You would need the greatest army Agrabah had ever seen to storm the palace and rescue my family."

Aladdin grew worried at the desolate tone of his friend's voice. There was no light in Duban's eyes, no hope at all.

"But that's what you and Morgiana gave me," Jasmine said. "A *Street Rat* army."

"They don't have swords! If they did, they wouldn't know how to use them. Most are just kids."

Morgiana stepped between the two. She had her back to Duban, but it was more like she was protecting than ignoring him.

"We *do* have an army," she said. "But it's an army skilled in moving silently, picking locks, *stealing* things. We could probably lift every magic book out of the palace right under

Jafar's nose, but I'm not sure that's going to help any more."

"I don't know what anyone can do against that monster now," Duban murmured. "He is the very incarnation of powerful, limitless evil."

"We *are* going to save your family," Jasmine promised. "We just need to figure out *how*. That's what we're doing right now."

"We don't have a lot of time to figure that out," Morgiana said, looking nervously out of the window at a sky that was already deepening from the grey of early twilight to the dark blue of early night.

Jasmine and Duban also turned to glance out of the window, breaking off from their escalating fight. Duban swore under his breath. Jasmine tried to look strong but couldn't hide the dismay in her eyes.

"Wait," Aladdin said suddenly, breaking the silence. "You're *both* right. And you're both looking at this backwards."

The three looked at him, confused.

He leaped up, the beginnings of a smile on his face.

"Jasmine, *you* said that magic is only as great as the mind that controls it. We've already seen that Jafar isn't thinking like a completely sane man, what with chasing you and taking the children as hostages. So we need to ask ourselves this: *what is Jafar expecting us to do?*"

"Go to war against him," Morgiana said, a little irritably.

"You heard him, Aladdin. We all did. And we're planning to. But we need more time. If we tried now…"

"We would do it pretty terribly, as Duban said. But proudly and energetically," he added quickly, before Jasmine could interrupt. "Now, what are we *actually* good at?"

"*Stealing things,*" Morgiana snapped. "Aladdin, are you an idiot? Haven't you been listening? What does…"

"So," Aladdin continued, putting a finger on her mouth to shut her up, "we wage war on Jafar, big, obvious, ugly war, while some of us *steal* Maruf and Shirin and Ahmed. And the lamp. And the book. And anything else that seems useful. *Right out from under his nose.*"

Everyone was silent for a moment.

Jasmine's eyes went from confused to clear as she thought about his plan. A smile began to form at the edges of her lips.

Even Morgiana seemed impressed.

"That's not half bad," she said grudgingly. "War is a pretty spectacular diversionary tactic. There's no way he could ignore it. Add some carefully set fires—"

"Maybe one in the palace itself," Duban said, unable to help himself. Strategising complicated heists was his speciality. "To add to the confusion."

"*Brilliant!*" Jasmine said, clapping her hands together. "This could work!"

"But what about Jafar himself, bright eyes?" Morgiana demanded. "We're going to come face-to-face with him at some point. I can't imagine he keeps that lamp or book out of reach, much less out of sight. What do we do to prepare for that?"

"All of his physical magic, offensive magic, seems to take time and concentration," Aladdin said, thinking back to the Square of the Sailor. "I'll bet in close combat he'll have a distinct disadvantage."

"You're betting your life on that," Morgiana said archly. "And what about knowing things about us and our plans? In advance? Can't sorcerers do that kind of thing?"

"The future is a realm... unavailable to him," Jasmine said uneasily. "The only time he managed to foresee anything, it involved complicated blood magic and the sacrifice of the one dearest to him."

"Who was Jafar close to?" Aladdin couldn't help asking. "He didn't love anyone."

"Oh, holy heavens," Morgiana said, suddenly getting it. "The *parrot*. His stupid parrot. That's why it's on all his coins and flags and everything. That was the one dearest to him. What a complete lunatic."

Aladdin shuddered. Before Jasmine, Abu was certainly the one closest to him... he could *almost* see it from Jafar's twisted perspective. Unlike Jafar, however, nothing in the world would induce him to kill Abu.

"Let's get back to the plan," he said quickly. "So if it comes to battle directly with the sorcerer, it will be ugly, and we will try to avoid that. The plan is to distract him and his undead troops and those still loyal to him with a direct assault on the palace itself, while the best thieves…"

"Us three," Morgiana interrupted.

"Four," Jasmine corrected.

"Three. You're not a thief," Aladdin pointed out. "We'll sneak in the back. Each of us will have a task… I'll grab the lamp."

"I'll grab the book. You'll free Maruf and the kids?" Morgiana asked Duban.

His face was unreadable.

"I think we should switch," he said slowly. "I'll… take the book. You free my family."

"Why?" Morgiana asked, confused. "Don't you want to be the one who saves them?"

"I… I won't be thinking clearly," Duban said. He clenched and unclenched his fists nervously. "It's bad tactics. I'd be a liability to the team, putting my family before the rest of our objectives. Besides, I trust you."

Morgiana gave a funny smile: it was surprise and sweetness and perhaps the revelation of something deeper.

Duban gave her not *quite* a smile back, but his face brightened a little.

"All right, this sounds like it's the beginnings of a strategy," Jasmine said. "But even though I'm not a thief, I could... be useful in distracting Jafar, or something..."

"Jasmine," Aladdin said, putting his hands on her shoulders. "Am I trying to keep you out of harm's way because I care about you? Absolutely. But your task is also just as important as ours. You're the *face* of the revolt. People, your leaders, your army, *your* people, need to see you. Need to know that *you* are the one telling them what to do. You need to stay here and organise the assault on the palace. Who else is going to do it?"

Jasmine didn't say anything. Her hands fluttered for just a moment.

"You're... right. This is my first job as sultana. I just... I'm worried about you guys. And I've *lived* in the palace. And dealt with Jafar. I want to be there and make sure everyone's all right. I just feel like I could have a greater role..."

Morgiana smiled and looked like she was almost going to touch Jasmine, squeeze her shoulder or something. "We'll be fine, Jasmine. We have to be."

She might have said other things, but Aladdin had noticed that once again a shadow had fallen over Duban's face. He had gone over to the broken terrace and was looking out at the sky and the palace.

"We *will* rescue them," Aladdin said quietly, coming up behind his old friend.

"Sure, Aladdin," Duban said. He didn't say it sarcastically or patronisingly, yet there was something not entirely honest about his tone.

"Duban..."

The thief shook his head.

"I thought Shirin and Ahmed would be safe once their father was gone. I thought they would be safe, if hungry, with my dad. I thought they would be safer still surrounded by thieves and... *tigers*. Aladdin," Duban suddenly turned to look at his friend, his eyes wide and searching. "We need to *end* this. This insanity that has taken over Agrabah. We need to end it now. By any means."

"Yes, Duban. I agree," Aladdin said slowly. There was something... *off* about the usually most level-headed of the Street Rats. "That's what we're going to do. Rescue your family and defeat Jafar."

Jasmine and Morgiana had finished their discussion and were quietly waiting for Aladdin and Duban. Jasmine raised an eyebrow at Aladdin. Aladdin shrugged, what could be said? The boy's father, niece and nephew were being held captive by a madman sworn to kill them.

Aloud Jasmine said: "All right, let's go over the plan one more time amongst ourselves. Morgiana's had a couple of brilliant ideas we should discuss. Then we'll summon the various faction leaders we can count on and have a war council. *Quickly.*"

"But not here," Morgiana said. "And not at our old HQ."

"The bread warehouse," Aladdin suggested. "The... *baguette* warehouse," he added, tossing a hopeful grin at Duban.

But his friend did not return it, only looked out over the city and put his hand on his dagger.

The Plan

OUTSIDE A DUSTY old bread warehouse, defying curfew, citizens from all walks of life waited for orders. They milled around anxiously, keeping an eye out for Peacekeeping Patrols. They spoke in low voices, polished their knives, and readied their torches.

Inside the warehouse, Duban, Morgiana, Jasmine and Aladdin stood on one side of a giant, crooked table, where dim lanterns barely illuminated the hastily drawn map of Agrabah.

On the other side of the table were the de facto captains of the Street Rat army.

Some of the faces were old and well known, but many were new. Many were not even originally Street Rats. Representing the jewellers and other high-end guilds was Amur. They supplied the resistance with beautiful but deadly weapons like gem-encrusted daggers. Representing the disaffected guards, soldiers and ex-military was the general Sohrab. Speaking for the different religious colleges was Khosrow, who brought wisdom, extraordinary intelligence and a hundred acolytes, furious that their studies had been suspended. Representing the Alchemaics was the scarred and one-eyed Kimiya, who despite her frightening appearance, greeted everyone with a friendly, lopsided smile. She brought incendiaries.

A surprising number of people came representing no one but themselves; angry young men and women upset with what Jafar had done to their city. They brought whatever they had: weapons, food, fists.

It was the most diverse crowd Aladdin had ever seen outside of a holiday market day.

"The basic plan is quite simple," Jasmine said. "Aladdin and a couple of hand-picked thieves will sneak into the palace not from the back, as Jafar might expect, but from the side, *here*, where it's easiest to get into the Princess Courtyard." She indicated the place with a tap of a stick. "It would *make sense* for Jafar to keep the genie's lamp, as well as the genie and the other prisoners, in his secret dungeon, *here*." She indicated the place Aladdin had 'escaped' from with another tap. "No doubt that place is now locked up and trapped like the devil's own treasure room. We don't think the lamp is there, anyway, the sand image in the sky yesterday had a few unintentional details in it, like the tail end of a tapestry that I know for a fact hangs in the throne room. Which makes sense. Jafar probably wants to keep Genie, the lamp, and Maruf and the children very close to him. And *Jafar* likes keeping very close to the throne room. It's important to him that he seem like a sultan, and he sits on the throne whenever he can.

"They free Maruf and the children, grab the book, grab the lamp and free the genie. We then overthrow Jafar by wishing all of his powers away."

"So that's it," a teenage thief said sarcastically. "You're just going to march up to the palace through a city filled with *ghouls*, sneak into the most heavily guarded room and steal something out from under the nose of the sorcerer."

"That is the *basic* plan," Jasmine said patiently. "You're going to help us with the *other* part. Given what he said yesterday, Jafar will be expecting us to do something warlike, probably a direct frontal assault on the palace itself. So we will give him that, using the siege to distract him while the thieves get done what they need to."

There were nods and murmurs of agreement at the cleverness of the plan.

"But the sorcerer is so powerful! He can summon bread and gold from the sky!" Hazan, the little Street Rat, piped up worriedly.

"Nope!" Aladdin countered with a grin. "Only the genie can do that. If any of you were at any of the parades or feasts, you'll have noticed that the genie was always there, waving his hands behind Jafar, while Jafar took credit for it. And the big question is, where has the genie been the last few days?"

"Tortured," Jasmine answered bleakly. "Imprisoned. Locked up. Out of service. Because he was helping us. So except for Jafar's last wish, I think we can count him out."

Aladdin saw the doubtful expressions on everyone in the crowd. "Look, I'll give you this: in a direct fight, in person, Jafar is a powerful enemy. But that's *my* worry. Apart from that, he is no more powerful than any other sultan."

"He's also no *smarter* or *wiser* since obtaining his nefarious new powers," Amur pointed out. "He still thinks like the old Jafar, and the old Jafar knew nothing about tactics or military manoeuvres. Keep that in mind."

"And speaking of fighting..." Jasmine said. "Duban?"

The stocky thief came forwards. Any overwhelming worry he had for his kidnapped family seemed to be set aside while he explained logistics. "As far as we can tell, there are about 500 Branded Ones and undead troops. Many of the merely 'enlisted' have deserted over the last few days. Those that remain are arranged in either Peacekeeping Patrol phalanxes of six or the usual cohort of ten. It can be assumed that at least a hundred of them will stay inside the palace walls for defence. So that leaves about 40 to 50 individual groups to keep busy and keep Jafar's attention on while Aladdin, Morgiana and I sneak in."

"And what about the *ghouls*?" someone else asked. "How are we to fight those already dead?"

"You could start by remaining alive," Sohrab said mildly. "Keep from adding your corpses to Jafar's numbers."

This was greeted by a worried silence.

"Remember, this is war, but it's also a distraction," Jasmine quickly pointed out. "To defeat the sorcerer we need to steal his book and lamp, not actually kill everyone in his command. Do not put yourself unnecessarily in harm's way."

"As for dealing with the ghouls you encounter," Khosrow said, a sad look in his ancient brown eyes, "the magic animating them is not as strong as you think. The body, as is natural, wants to remain dead. Sever the mind from the soul, the psyche from the heart, and they can rest. As God intended it."

"Cut their heads off," Sohrab translated. "Or slice through the spinal cord at their necks. That should do them."

"I am dividing you all into smaller troops and assigning quadrants of the city and jobs as appropriate,"

Duban continued. "After that, Sohrab will take over entirely while I help the others. Artemis here will be in charge of distributing weapons."

"How many of us are there at last count?" Jasmine asked.

"About 300," he admitted.

"That will not be enough," Sohrab said grimly. "We're going to need more men."

"Why are we only talking about *men*?"

The woman who said this was short and round and covered in robes. She pushed her way to the front. Aladdin was surprised to see the Widow Gulbahar shouldering the various faction leaders aside.

"I have all the mothers, grannies, widows and spinster aunts of Agrabah behind me. *You* want to take us on?"

"What can women do?" a man next to her asked disparagingly.

In answer, Gulbahar whipped out a wooden ladle and clocked him on the head. He yelped in pain and fell backwards.

"You want *more* of that? I've been laundering rugs for 50 years and got the arms to prove it."

"But what can you do against ghouls, Old Mother?" Amur asked, but not unkindly.

"I'll show you," she answered, tightening her lips. "Bring him forward."

Several older women shuffled around in their voluminous robes, manipulating something unseen, and soon the widow had a little boy by the shoulders. He was no more than nine. At first he looked normal, if a little subdued and sickly. Then Aladdin noticed the red glow around his eyes and the green tinge to his white flesh.

"My God," Jasmine said, putting her hand to her mouth. "He is… a *ghoul!*"

The crowd gasped when the widow turned the boy's head to the side so the flickering lights caught his sad, monstrous face.

"The poor lad," Aladdin murmured.

Gulbahar did all but spit. "He was killed when some of the soldiers were tearing apart the Eastern Marketplace, looking for traitors."

"*Any* person who dies becomes a ghoul," Khosrow said sadly.

"*You are the Princess Jasmine,*" the boy said, his dead eyes widening. "*I must take you to Jafar. I must kill the Street Rats.*"

He slowly lifted his arms to attack.

"Cut it out, Jalil," Gulbahar said promptly and sternly. She whacked his behind. The boy winced, a little, and drew his arms back. "How many times have I told you, *no fighting?*"

"*Sorry,*" the boy said tonelessly.

"He… listened to you," Jasmine said slowly. "He knows who you are. They *remember?*"

The widow nodded. "They *all* remember. A little."

"But how does that help us?" asked the man whose head had been struck. There was a sizeable lump forming on it.

"Every one of them out there is some mother's son," Gulbahar hissed. "A mother can bring her boy home. And failing that, she will fight like a tiger against anyone who tries to stop her."

Aladdin had thought that losing his parents was the worst thing that could happen to a person. He never thought about the reverse, when parents outlive their children. And then to have their children come *back*, but not the same, never the same…

"'There is no more powerful force on earth than a mother frightened for her children'," Khosrow murmured.

"Great, that's at least a couple of hundred more," Sohrab said, reducing the drama to numbers: he had more soldiers to work with now and didn't care about their gender or motivation. He nodded to Duban. "I'll talk to the women after to work out the details."

"We will need a… holding pen," Gulbahar said delicately. "The… *harmless* undead need to be kept from returning to Jafar."

Sohrab looked doubtful but didn't disagree. "We'll see what we can do."

"All right, back to battle plans," Duban said. "Rajah can take on a cohort or two of his own. We're having Navid the goatherd gather those who are loyal to us and blockade the Western Market area…"

"What about the flying horrors?" someone asked.

"We have archers, some of the best, thanks to Sanjar and his hunters, and some of the defected guards from the palace Sohrab has brought along. They will be positioned here, here, and here… and here." He pointed out certain broad rooftops in the middle-class part of town.

"And *we* have some things cooked up for them as well," Kimiya said gleefully. "A couple of hits from our shrapnel-loaded firebombs should take them apart. This is in addition to the incendiaries and bombs that we will set off at different times in seemingly random places… as well as very close to the palace walls to increase confusion."

"And speaking of fire," Jasmine said, pointing at the map again, "we will be lighting one at the top of Jafar's own Moon Tower, here in the palace, to further distract from Aladdin's heist. I suspect Jafar will be smart and use some of his aerial forces to contain it."

"And how will you know when to do this? When who should attack whom? When to let loose Rajah? Or the grannies?" a tall young woman demanded the leader of one of the student groups.

"Ah, that is also a good question, which we were getting to," Morgiana answered, stepping forward with relish. "Besides shooting down the flying ghouls, the archers will act as our messengers. Once Duban and I have divided you up into your separate teams, we will teach you the appropriate signal: how many arrows of fire means what."

"Any other questions?" Jasmine asked.

There was the shuffling of feet and little else.

"Any comments?" she asked, a little more gently. "Anything at all? If you have something to say, we want to hear it now."

Amur looked around and then cleared his throat.

"Down with Jafar!" he said in a voice unaccustomed to shouting.

"DOWN WITH JAFAR!" the crowd repeated, much more loudly.

"Hey, this might actually work," Aladdin said with a hopeful grin.

Jasmine put a finger on his lips.

"Don't jinx it."

A Pause Before the Dust Storm

AFTER THE MEETING had broken up, and Sohrab and Duban and the others set about dividing their army into logical groups, Aladdin finally had a moment to himself. He wandered outside and perched atop a crumbling wall, looking out at the dimmed lights of Agrabah. Even the palace seemed gloomier than usual, as if a strange extra helping of night had fallen over the city he loved.

He rubbed his hands into his eyes. His body wasn't tired, exactly, and he was certainly eager to *do* something. But first he had to say goodbye to Jasmine. The weeks had passed strangely, and the only thing he could ever be sure of was how much he wanted to be with her.

As if summoned by his thoughts like a wish granted by a genie, Jasmine came up behind him. She *thought* she was being silent; to a thief her footsteps were as loud as a horn flourish announcing her presence. She knocked on a piece of the wall.

"Come in," Aladdin said with a wry smile.

"I thought I'd find you here," she said, leaping up to sit near him and take in the view.

"So, Royal Princess, excuse me, *Sultana* Jasmine, coming to admire your soon-to-be kingdom?" he asked with a smile.

"Yes, I want to make some changes. I think it could use a few more lights," she said, finger to her chin in contemplation. "Torches there, there and there. And maybe a different shade of white this time. More 'eggshell' or 'moon'. Less 'sand'."

"*Definitely* less sand," Aladdin agreed. He put his arm around her and drew her close. She leaned her head on his shoulder. They were like two cats, he thought. Sitting on a fence together looking at the moon.

Except that they were looking at the palace. And in that palace terrible things were happening. He could feel her heart betraying her calm, joking exterior: it beat as nervously as his. Or maybe that was *his* heart he was feeling. It was getting hard to tell.

"We *have* to get Maruf and Ahmed and Shirin," she murmured. "The rest of it… if we fail, we can try again later. But we *cannot* fail them."

"I know," Aladdin said, his arm tightening around her.

"I keep seeing his face… and Shirin's and Ahmed's in the sand…" Jasmine said. "But…"

"But what?" Aladdin sat her up gently and turned her to face him.

"You're going to think what I have to say is stupid. And weird. And selfish," she said, blushing.

"Tell me," Aladdin urged quietly.

Jasmine sighed. "At least… at least they're in there *together*. The children have Maruf trying to help them. And Maruf has us trying to rescue them. If it was me, I'd be in there by myself. Before I met you, before I joined Morgiana and Duban and the Street Rats, I was completely alone. Before I ran away, my closest friend was a tiger."

Aladdin laughed softly. "Before I met *you*, my closest friend was a monkey." He kissed her on the forehead. "We're quite a pair."

Jasmine took his hands in hers. His were larger but somehow they felt smaller inside her fingers: covered, warm, protected. She looked up at him with eyes large and shaky.

"Aladdin," she whispered. "I *love* you."

He started to open his mouth. A month ago, a few

weeks ago, something glib and silly would have popped out to make the moment seem less serious.

"And I love you, Jasmine," he said instead.

He turned his palms over and squeezed her hands. "Whatever happens next, whether we save the city or it falls into a pit in the earth and is lost forever, I would never, ever change a moment of our time together. You are the best, the *only*, good thing that has happened in my life."

A half-asleep chitter came, annoyed, out of a shadow in the rocks.

"Except for you, Abu," Aladdin said, smiling.

Jasmine smiled, too. She leaned over and kissed him. Her lips made him warm all over, warmer than the hot desert night. He could no longer run his hands through her thick, long hair, it was now always up in the tight braid she wore. But her neck and back were soft and he stroked them with his fingertips while they embraced.

When they pulled apart, Jasmine rested her head on his shoulder again. "And now all of your friends are my friends, too. Suddenly, I have *friends*."

Aladdin snorted. "They didn't become my friends again until you came along. You kind of helped us... bury the hatchet. With, you know, all the unimportant stuff about saving the kingdom and feeding hungry people."

Jasmine smiled. "Yes, well, I wouldn't have known about

the hungry people if it wasn't for you and them. I'll bet there's a lot more about Agrabah I don't know. Once I am sultana, I'll rely on the Street Rats to keep me grounded."

"Really?"

"Absolutely. I need to know the people of my city to rule it properly. And one of the best things to have come out of all of this is the support network that the Street Rats have grown into. Maybe I can somehow use that on a greater scale."

Aladdin laughed. "That sounds like a great idea. And I'm *sure* Morgiana and Duban would like a piece of the future action in Agrabah. Even if it's *not* illegal."

"Oh, I can't wait until this all gets started!" Jasmine said, standing up impatiently. "I want to know how it all turns out. I want to *win*. When we rescue Maruf and get the lamp and the book, everything begins."

"Yes," Aladdin said cautiously. One of her words had jumped out at him. "But we're *burning* the book, right?"

Jasmine stopped her pacing and stared at him. "*No*, Aladdin. We talked about this. It's a valuable resource. We can use it to defeat Jafar."

"I do *not* need an evil book to defeat an evil sorcerer. That even *sounds* like a bad idea."

"*You* sound like one of the suspicious, anti-magic old folk," Jasmine pointed out. "Like everything that comes out of magic is bad."

"Can we talk about the genie for a moment?" Aladdin asked hotly. "He doesn't seem evil at all. But the moment he appears in our world, his powers are used to do terrible things. He's not bad and his magic isn't bad, but *other* people are."

"I'm not Jafar!"

"No, but you're *human*, Jasmine. What if someone managed to convince you that the people really *would* be safer and healthier if we kept the Peacekeeping Patrols going? What if a grieving mother begged you to bring her dead child back, even as a ghoul? Wouldn't you do it?"

They were very close, looking into each other's eyes. Jasmine had her hands on her hips. Aladdin had his hands clenched into knots.

Morgiana appeared below them. Her footsteps were, of course, silent. She saw the two, heard the silence and coughed nervously.

"Uh, I hate to interrupt you two... lovebirds? But it's time."

"We'll be right down," Jasmine said without taking her eyes off Aladdin. He didn't turn, either.

"Okay... but hurry. By the stars it looks like it's already past the third watch." Morgiana tiptoed back the way she came, as quickly as she could.

Aladdin shook his arms out and took a deep breath. "You know what? We can talk about this *after* we've rescued Maruf, Ahmed and Shirin, and stolen the lamp, and grabbed the book, and defeated Jafar, and come back out alive."

"Excellent point," Jasmine said. She put her hands on either side of his face and kissed him. "Let's not leave arguing."

"I'd rather not leave at all," he said, pulling her close one last time.

Seems Like Old Times

ONCE AGAIN Aladdin found himself sitting on a rooftop. This time it was a leather tannery to the north of the palace. He wondered vaguely if this would be his *last* time sitting on a rooftop.

Around him was the usual detritus one found on the roofs of Agrabah: mats for drying fruit, lines for hanging washing and rugs, a small chicken pen, the boards and ladders that had nowhere else to be stored. Also a goat, which stood there chewing and paying absolutely no attention to the strange humans who had invaded its penthouse.

With Aladdin were Morgiana and Duban, the two 'handpicked thieves', and Pareesa, whose speciality turned out to be arson. Jasmine was directing the siege of Agrabah with Sohrab back at the bread warehouse. She would order the signal for when they should set out. So now the four were just sitting under still skies, above the fear-darkened city, waiting.

Finally, after a quick look to make sure that Pareesa was trying to distract Duban with a pair of jacks and a game of nine squares, Morgiana broke the silence.

"You guys fighting?"

Aladdin took a deep breath. It was funny that he had come to this point with Morgiana; first they were close, and then he wrote her off… and now… and now? It was easy to talk to her. Almost like an old friend.

"We have very different ideas on what to do with the book *Al Azif* when we grab it."

"Oh, that's easy. I'd use it to wish for a giant mansion and hundreds of servants." Morgiana sighed, swinging her legs like a young giarl.

Aladdin shot her a look.

"*Kidding!* Sort of. My dreams of riches have been ruined by that lunatic Jafar. I don't know what I'd do with it. Maybe bury it in the desert."

Once again Aladdin thought back to the Cave of Wonders, the buried treasure, the buried lamp. History repeating itself…

"It's not like the lamp or the genie, Morgiana. It doesn't grant wishes. It's an ancient, dark tome of evil knowledge that raises the dead and kills people and breaks all the known laws of magic. It needs to be burned." He sighed, kicking his feet over the side of the building. "*She* thinks it could somehow be used for good."

Morgiana frowned, thinking. "That's tough. But if I were you, I'd give in to her."

Aladdin looked at the thief, surprised.

"My friend," she said gently, "Jasmine is the best thing that ever happened to you. You should do anything to keep her."

"*I* should? And what about you?" he asked with a thoughtful smile. "When was the last time you gave in to Duban?"

"We're not together," she answered promptly.

Aladdin raised an eyebrow at her.

"Officially," she added.

He waited.

"Oh, shut up. He gets his way enough," she said, hitting him in exasperation.

"I'm worried about him," Aladdin admitted, glancing at their friend, who was refusing Pareesa's game. "He usually manages to suck things up and deal with them in his own way. He's never been the broody type."

"I know," Morgiana said, frowning. "I'm worried about him, too. He's acting strangely, almost secretive. Pulled into himself. If I didn't know better... wait, look!"

She pointed. Arcing high into the sky from the Garden Quarter were four flaming arrows, tracing a giant tiger's claw across the night sky.

"That's the signal," Aladdin said, crawling over to the edge of the roof to get a better look at the city.

Somewhere in the distance a noisy, torch-carrying crowd was assembling to very obviously march on the palace. Uneasy patches of glowing red across the city reacted immediately, heading towards the disturbance. Like ants suddenly realising that their home was threatened. Overhead, the phalanxes of soldiers and ghouls patrolling the skies stopped their manoeuvres and headed in the same direction.

Aladdin found himself counting in his head. Just as he reached 20, an explosion lit up the Old Market. The aerial guards paused, unsure what to do. One scout broke away and made for the palace. Morgiana and Aladdin watched this one zoom impolitely over the walls and through a large mid-level window. Moments later, the shutters flew open on the Public Balcony and Jafar stormed out to see for himself what was going on in the city.

"Let's go!" Aladdin ordered.

The four thieves appeared to dive straight over the side of the warehouse.

But of course each of them grabbed a clothesline below.

They pulled themselves hand over hand across the street above the heads of some human soldiers running out into the night. On the other side they dropped onto a terrace. From there they leaped to the ground and made for the shadow of the palace wall. Morgiana, Duban and Pareesa clenched daggers in their teeth, but Aladdin held nothing as the four of them scurried up the old battlement which was made for keeping out armies and militias, not thieves. They were terribly exposed: four dark shapes against the expanse of white that fairly glowed, even under dim conditions. At any moment a guard pacing the top could look down and easily see them.

Aladdin just worked steadily at finding footholds and pulling himself up. He refused to look up or down to check his progress.

Finally, at the top, he flipped himself up and over and landed in a crouch, looking quickly both ways. The plan seemed to be working: there was no one else up there. The only guard left was running towards the main gate to help release the outer portcullis. Aladdin fixed a rope around a sturdy beam to prepare for shinning down the other side.

Morgiana's head popped up beside him, and then her body, light and fleet as a bird. She couldn't help taking a moment to survey the palace, laid out so perfectly below: the towers, the gardens, the hidden courtyards, the waterworks that supplied the baths. It looked like one of the old sultan's toy models from up there.

She shook her head and allowed herself a low whistle. Aladdin gave her a rueful, sympathetic grin.

Duban and Pareesa finally made it up. When they were settled, Aladdin pointed to the tallest tower in the palace.

"That's Jafar's? The Moon Tower?" Pareesa asked.

Morgiana nodded. "Good luck!"

The girl gave a wicked grin. "I don't need luck. All I need is flint and tinder."

Then she silently ran along the top of the wall. Despite her grace and speed, Aladdin still turned away as she made the leap to the tower. There was a vast expanse of night air between her and it, and he didn't want to see if she missed.

"All right," he whispered to his remaining team. "Let's go."

The three of them abseiled down the inner wall and landed silently on the soft, fragrant grass of the bailey. The palace had grown like a clump of mushrooms over the centuries, each new building like a single stalk. Aladdin counted carefully and picked out one of the shorter structures near the Moon Tower. It contained the library, which, at least before Jafar became sultan, was not a particularly well-guarded part of the compound, according to Jasmine. Aladdin waved Morgiana and Duban forwards and pointed at the lowest window that was wider than an arrow loop.

The three of them started to run across the short stretch of open field. Sensing something, Aladdin stopped short. He skidded to a halt just as a strange red light swept in front of his path. He looked up.

Hanging in the air above them, silent as death, was a pair of ghouls. As their dead eyes moved inhumanly across the landscape below, one of them slowly swung a strange black lantern with an intricate hood that directed the red beam.

The three thieves froze. Morgiana whispered an expletive.

Time also froze as the dead things made an agonisingly slow pass across the courtyard and then back. The sky behind them was black as sin. It was the darkest time of the night... which meant that dawn wasn't far off. Aladdin felt his heart thump furiously within his still body.

Eventually the beam continued past them on its steady path and kept going.

The ghouls moved on, soundlessly patrolling the night with their evil lamp.

Was it Aladdin's imagination? Or did the grass look drier after the light passed over it? Did it somehow look *less* than it had looked before?

The three thieves made a dash for the relative safety of the shadow of the tower.

"What terrible new magic is that?" Duban cried.

"There is a special place in hell reserved for Jafar," Morgiana muttered. *"And* his servants."

"I feel sorry for whoever those two once were," Aladdin said pointedly. Although, privately, he thought it might not have been such a *terrible* thing if the men had died a little more explosively and left no bodies behind to reanimate.

Morgiana pulled out a tiny-clawed grapple, one of her favourite tools, and, after swinging it on the end of its slim silken cord a few times, let it loose. With a neat *kkrrrlkt* it landed inside the window. She tugged and it held, digging its claws into the plaster. Duban motioned for the other two to go first while he held the cord steady. Morgiana and Aladdin scurried up it like monkeys and then he hurried up after them.

After he pulled his stocky body through the window, he paused and looked around in wonder. "Wow. Not what I'd want in my own castle... but impressive, nonetheless."

It was a giant room filled with shelves and cabinets and drawers. Occupying every nook and cranny were tiny statues of *everything*: people long dead and beasts that never were and buildings that seemed unlikely. The remaining space was taken up with books. There were piles of books on the floor, stacks on the tables, shelves stuffed with books lining all the walls. Dozens of urns held hundreds of rolled-up scrolls. Wax and clay tablets with ledgers in strange languages sat in open drawers. Maps of colourful oceans and strange countries lay unrolled on special slanted tables.

The room was dim, just as Jasmine had predicted; only two small lamps burned at the door, far away from any of the flammable parchments or precious scrolls. It was hard to tell just how big the library was or how much it held. Aladdin began to understand a little more about Jasmine. She had access to all of that knowledge, all the collected information and wisdom of the world, it seemed, and couldn't go out to see it for herself.

"Aladdin!" Duban suddenly hissed, interrupting his thoughts. He crept up to the doorway and listened. "Guards are coming! Two, I think."

"Already?" Morgiana cursed. "This mission is doomed."

"Quickly!" Aladdin gestured for her to move to the other side of the door.

There was nowhere for Aladdin to hide; the tables and desks were all tall with narrow, elegant, and very hard-to-hide-behind, legs. This seemed to be the one room in the palace without a divan or sofa.

Unable to think of anything else to do, Aladdin picked up a scroll and began to make a big show of studying it.

Two human guards appeared in the doorway to give the room a cursory check, and then saw Aladdin.

They scowled and drew their scimitars.

"Funny," Aladdin drawled, turning the scroll upside down and frowning. "I always thought the Hyperboreans lived in the *north*, not the south…"

The guard on the left recovered from his shock first and opened his mouth to order Aladdin to do something or other.

Before a single peep came out, Morgiana and Duban grabbed a couple of large bronze urns and brought them down on the guards' heads.

The guards slumped forwards immediately and the two thieves caught them, less for their safety than to keep the noise down.

Duban swore. "They'll be missed if they don't return to their watch!"

"We should kill them," Morgiana said promptly.

"And have them reanimate into undead soldiers who can't feel pain? *Not* a good idea," Aladdin whispered. "Come on. I think I have a plan."

Dawn Approaches

BACK AT THE WAREHOUSE, Jasmine was watching the skies and sending out orders to the various divisions of the Street Rat army with Sohrab by her side.

Even Khosrow, the old religious leader, had been surprisingly adept in helping organise their army. "I've had 50 years of teaching acolytes," he had told her with his gentle smile. "It's not war. But it has its similarities."

A runner came in, exhausted and breathless.

"Jasmine. The angry crowd with torches is working… they've shut down the Street of the Doves and the way by the old synagogue. Akin reports, and I've seen with my own eyes, that they took down about 15 armed guards and three ghouls."

"Excellent news!" Jasmine said, clapping her hands.

Though she wished there had been a few *more* guards and ghouls subdued.

"Also, they think 20 more guards, primarily ghouls, have been dispatched to deal with the fires now burning in the Old Market. Yahya witnessed several troops, some 20 men strong, fanning out through the Leather District towards them."

"Thank you for your report. Please refresh yourself with water and food and then come to me again for your next detail. Iza, Deni!" She called for two more runners. The two who presented themselves couldn't have been more than eight. "Go tell the archers to fire the second signal. It's time to send out Rajah."

The two little kids nodded and ran downstairs.

Jasmine clicked her tongue and the tiger bounded up to her. Sensing the excitement, he didn't lay at her feet like he usually did, but stood nearby, tense and watching. Now his tiger sinews and muscles expanded and contracted in delight. *On the hunt, finally.*

Jasmine threw her arms around his neck. Their cause needed all the soldiers it could muster, of course. But what real free will did a pet tiger have? Or two eight-year-olds desperate to please, for that matter? And here she was, sending them off into danger and, in Rajah's case, battle.

"Good luck, old friend," she whispered in his soft ear.

Then she took out the things obtained for this dark purpose: a turban, a sash, a boot… all belonging to guard captains. She commanded an army of thieves; *stealing* things was the easy part. Jasmine held them up for Rajah to smell. His giant nostrils expanded and contracted. He frowned as if taking the matter incredibly seriously.

"Go," she ordered when he was done. "Attack."

Rajah growled and leaped down the stairs, tail swishing.

Jasmine told herself she didn't have time to worry or mourn. People were sacrificing far more than she was in this. The poor boy Jalil. His parents. Rasoul.

Besides, Rajah could take care of himself. He was a *tiger.*

She shook her shoulders and turned back to the map on the table, updating it with the latest developments. An explosion rocked the hideout. She grabbed at the wall as bits of dried clay and wood and pebbles rained down.

"What was that?" she demanded. "Someone! That signal was too early!"

Sohrab came striding in, a grim look on his face. "That wasn't one of ours. Whatever it was hit near Duban and Morgiana's old lair. We need Hazan to come back and tell us what happened."

"*Jafar.*" Jasmine swore, looking towards the palace.

———

In the dim halls of the palace complex, Aladdin and Duban walked silently down the middle of the cool marble floors.

"Jasmine said the baths are this way," Aladdin whispered. "And the throne room is upstairs past them, on the way to the..."

Two guards turned the corner and moved towards them, blocking the end of the hall. They raised their scimitars.

The two thieves raised their stolen scimitars back, and gave the clacking salute that Aladdin had observed the last time he had broken into the palace.

"Sloppy, there," one of the guards remarked with an eye to Duban's technique. But the two real guards marched on.

Aladdin practically crumpled with relief when they were gone. Duban smoothed down the front of his shirt with injured pride; they were dressed in the uniforms of the guards they had tied up and stuffed in a wardrobe.

Morgiana ran up from behind them, where she had been hiding out of view.

"*Told* you I should have been the other guard," she hissed.

"The turban didn't fit you," Aladdin hissed back. "We *talked* about that."

A tremor ran through the floor under their feet like a

giant had stomped his foot or there was an earthquake in the desert. Not enough to make things fall but enough to make them dizzy.

"Was that inside the palace walls?" Duban asked, uneasy.

"No, I think it was farther away," Aladdin said. None of the explosives they had planned to use were that big. What was going on out there?

He shook his head. He just had to trust that Jasmine and the Street Rat army would distract Jafar and his legions until they could steal the lamp and the book and rescue Duban's family. His job was to concentrate on the task at hand.

It was a strange feeling, to have to rely on somebody else.

"This is ridiculous," Morgiana said, rolling her eyes.

"If you have a better plan, speak up," Aladdin suggested.

"I got nothing, kiddo," she said pleasantly.

"All right. Then let's stick to the current one. The fate of Agrabah, and Duban's family, rests on us."

So they pressed on.

"It's some sort of fiery cannonball or something," Hazan reported, out of breath. His eyebrows were singed. "It hit exactly where the old hideout is... was. It's all on fire. Purple and red."

"*Purple?*" Sohrab asked. "That sounds like magic... or the work of the Alchemaics."

"And we know *they're* not working with him," Jasmine said.

"But why hit the hideout?" the military man wondered with a frown. He pointed at the chalky map of Agrabah. "He already cleared that place out. Only an idiot would have gone back there after he grabbed his hostages. Why not hit here, here, or here, where he could do some *real* damage that would be visible to all?"

"Because he's just lashing out in anger," Jasmine said with grim triumph. "Like we said, he's not a brilliant tactician. He's a sorcerer and grand vizier. And he's never been in battle before. This is exactly what we wanted! He's distracted, and angry, and not able to see what's going on right under his nose. It may all be easier than we thought."

"*Jasmine!*"

A bloody young man came into the room, limping and straining under the weight of his burden. In his arms he carried an injured younger man. An ugly blue-and-black gash disfigured his forehead and his face was deathly pale. His eyes were rolled back, unseeing.

"Lay him down over here!" Jasmine said immediately, indicating a place on the floor with a few pillows and cloths on it. "We never thought to set up an infirmary... Hazan, before you go to refresh yourself, please speak to some of the older women and see if we can organise something."

"Absolutely, Jasmine," the boy said, bowing and trotting out.

Sohrab took one look at the wounds, and his face turned stony. He obviously had few doubts about the boy's chances.

"Some water," Jasmine ordered. "Bandages!"

He opened his mouth to say something and then thought better of it. "I'll send one of my men up. But Jasmine. If he dies…"

"We will lock him up. With the other ghouls."

Sohrab shook his head disapprovingly. "This is not some child, Jasmine. This is a nearly grown man who would be hard to defeat as a ghoul. It would be kinder to end it for him."

Jasmine closed her eyes, feeling the truth of the matter. "I know."

And the hideout rocked with another blast.

Aladdin and Duban creeped forwards, ready to spring back into military stances if they were caught. Morgiana followed silently behind. There was a not-quite-secret staircase in the back of the library building that led up to a balcony bordered by delicately arched windows. These looked out over a small courtyard lined with sour-orange trees. Across from this were the royal baths, which connected directly to the audience chamber, banquet hall and eventually the throne room itself. That had sounded strange until Jasmine explained to Aladdin that sultans often entertained foreign guests and consulted with top advisers while enjoying a pleasant mint-scented sweat in the steam rooms.

"Nice work if you can get it," he muttered.

A pair of guards passed through the courtyard. One took a lazy swipe at an orange branch as he passed; the razor-sharp blade of his scimitar neatly and silently cut an orange from its stem and it fell, with a quiet *thunk*, to the ground like a head after an execution.

Morgiana swallowed in nervousness.

"I just wanted to pick pockets for a living," she said. "Maybe get involved with some high-end jewellery theft. I'm going to lose my head over this little civil uprising."

"I'll take these guys over the ghouls *any* day," Duban shot back in a whisper. "Better to die at the hands of a man."

"Wait… we haven't seen *any* ghouls recently," Aladdin said slowly. "They're all *human* guards here inside the palace. Alive. Except for the ghouls outside in the air, with that lantern."

"They need guards who can actually think and act independently close to Jafar," Morgiana said, nodding. "Not just, you know, go, '*Ooogh, die!*'"

Two more human guards marched into view. The three thieves fell into silence.

"Forty-five heartbeats," Duban said when they were gone. "That's how much time between them we have."

Morgiana took her grappling hook and swung it round and round, estimating the distance between them and the opening across the way that led to the baths. She kept swinging until the next set of guards marched by below them... and then she immediately let the hook fly.

It missed.

She cursed as it hit the far wall and clattered to the floor.

Quietly as she could, Morgiana coiled the cord, hand over hand like a fisherman trying to draw in a line before the end got caught. When she pulled it up the wall, it dragged, making little scratchy noises.

Two more guards came into view.

Morgiana froze.

The hook hung there, obviously, in the middle of the white marble wall, at the end of a long, suspicious-looking rope.

The guards walked straight past it.

The three thieves let out breaths they didn't even know they were holding.

Morgiana swore again and yanked the hook in, then cast it back out immediately.

It grabbed hold of the opposite ledge, and this time it stayed.

They held their breath again when the next set of guards came past, but the rope hung high above them, unnoticed, as they passed underneath. As soon as they were gone, Morgiana lightly leaped up on it and ran across like it was a tightrope. Duban was next, more slowly, but just as surely. With a measured pace he made it to the other side and dived through the window just as the guards came by.

Finally, it was Aladdin's turn. *He* had braced the cord for the other two; now he had no one to do it for him. He grabbed a chair and pulled it close to the window, quickly looping the cord through its arm in a highwayman's hitch, a knot that would release easily when he was ready. Holding the extra cord in his hand, he waited until the next guards had gone and then leaped up onto the ledge and stepped onto the rope.

He was more than halfway across when the chair tipped.

The sudden slackening of the cord caused Aladdin to pitch forward. He swung his arms desperately, trying to regain his balance.

He didn't.

He fell…

…and the next pair of guards rounded the corner.

Casualties of War

THE DYING MAN BREATHED strangely. First it was quick shallow breaths. Then, gasping, deep, horrible noises, like all the air in the world couldn't help him now.

Jasmine kneeled over him, holding one of his hands with her left hand and nervously stroking his brow with her right. In addition to friends, babies and the rest of the world, the royal princess had also been isolated from sickness and death. She had no idea what she was doing. She was terrified in a way she hadn't been when her own parents had died. It took all of her energy just to keep the tears in check and her face calm.

Sohrab had tried to persuade her to let him... do what was necessary. But she had sent him away to continue giving orders in her name. "I am sultana. I cannot expect people to do for me what I cannot," she had said to the general.

"It will be all right," she murmured to the man, wondering how bad it was to lie to the dying.

But he didn't appear to be listening; his eyes were wide and focused on something beyond her.

A long, glittering, sharp knife lay on the floor next to him.

After endless moments of laboured breathing and silent staring he suddenly spasmed. His head lifted like he was looking for something.

Then he fell back and stopped moving.

His eyes were still open but there was nothing in them at all now.

Jasmine bit her lip in a furious attempt not to cry. She bowed her head and began to whisper the only prayer she knew that fit the circumstances.

Khosrow finally appeared at the door. He came over and made some gestures over the young man. He closed his eyes and began to pray with her.

The dead man also closed his eyes.

And then he opened them again.

Where his eyes had been were now pools of dark, evil red.

Khosrow's own eyes widened but he did not stop praying; he merely spoke the words more loudly.

Jasmine picked up the knife.

The ghoul sat up and made clicking noises in the back of its throat, the unlikely sound of clearing leftover, drying blood from it.

Jasmine gritted her teeth and brought the blade down across its exposed throat. She flinched but didn't hesitate as the edge hit sinew and bone.

The ghoul didn't scream.

It didn't thank her.

It gurgled and made some more sounds before growing still, lifeless again.

The guards were heading across the courtyard straight for Aladdin.

Aladdin flailed his arms as he fell, desperately trying to grab for the rope. At the very last second he managed to catch it.

"Quick!" Morgiana hissed, working the hook out of the wall. Together she and Duban wrapped the cord around their fists, trying to pull up Aladdin as he dipped precipitously towards the ground.

He bent his torso like a performer in the market, *slowly*, so as not to draw attention to himself. Straining his arms, he managed to pull his knees to his chest, his toes braced on the underside of the rope. He hung there upside down like a bat.

The guards kept marching forwards... *under* him.

The red feather on the turban of one tickled Aladdin's back as he passed under the thief. The guard unthinkingly reached up to stroke his feather back into place. And then they were gone.

Aladdin uncoiled himself slowly, feeling his stomach also uncoil in relief at the same time.

Hand over hand, he pulled himself towards Duban and Morgiana. Duban reached over and grabbed him; the knot on the chair loosed itself and the rope fell to the courtyard.

Aladdin quickly pulled it back up and wrapped it around his arm.

"That was close," Morgiana whispered.

"Aw, that was nothing," Aladdin said. "I've escaped worse with a bunch of stolen bananas."

"Hey, speaking of, where *is* Abu? He always comes on your little adventures."

Aladdin looked bleak. "I... left him back home. If things got bad, I wanted him to be free."

Silent and sober, the thieves pressed on.

When Sohrab came in, he clapped Jasmine sympathetically on her back and then resumed his duties, like a good soldier. He reported on what her various battalions were doing and what the score was. Some of the religious acolytes had taken the body away, but Jasmine still felt its presence.

"I'm sorry *how* many down?" she suddenly asked, realising she hadn't been paying attention.

"We don't know exactly who was caught in the second blast," Sohrab said, a little impatiently. "Honestly, I have no idea what our true numbers are. This is all a bit more sudden and disorganised than I'm used to."

" *Numbers?* These are *people*. And they are being *killed*. And raised from the dead. And added to his side, unless someone puts them to their permanent rest. This has to *stop*. We have to *stop people from being killed*. Now."

She said this last part shakily, barely in control of herself.

"Jasmine, this is war," Sohrab said calmly. "A strange, unholy war. You might have read about tactics and history and wars in the past, but this is reality. People get hurt. People get killed. Do you want to save Agrabah and Maruf and the children?"

"Of course," Jasmine said. She took a deep breath. "Of course."

She walked to the doorway and looked up at the sky; even with the dust she could see Hormozd, the large red planet, just beginning to sink behind the mountains. On the other side of the sky, the heavens were a shade lighter than they had been just a little while ago. The sun was preparing to rise. "I will do what needs to be done."

"Of course, Princess. You would... you would make the warriors of old proud."

Sohrab saluted and went back inside to give more orders.

The moment his back was turned, Jasmine ran out into the night.

She drew her robe close to obscure her face and body. She passed by the crowds of Street Rats running off on their missions, completely unnoticed. There was a strange excitement in the crowds incompletely illuminated by the scattered torches. People who would normally never have *talked* to each other were cursing and planning, arguing and preparing. Such teamwork as Jasmine had never been part of. Ever. She wished she could have stayed and joined them.

Well, hers was a different fate. It was up to *her* to save Agrabah now.

She walked alone into the darkness, leaving the Street Rat army behind her.

She kept to the back alleys, hiding whenever anyone came too close: frightened citizens, angry mobs, scimitar-wielding imperial guards. There was so much confusion in the streets she didn't worry about any of the aerial soldiers; all they would see, if they spotted her, was one scared, running woman with no torch or weapon. There were far more important things that night for them to deal with.

She passed a courtyard where smoke and fire blanketed everything in blurry light and shadow; despite this, she could see the dark outline of a large tiger pounding through the streets.

Jasmine smiled and waved, although he couldn't see her.

A *fsssst* caused her to look up: four more fiery arrows passed through the night sky, making a giant Mark of Rajah. Time for Pareesa to start her fire.

Everything was going according to plan. Without her. Good.

Eventually she found what she was looking for: a lone red-eyed ghoul standing in a pool of darkness, scimitar out. Waiting for orders. Blocking a street.

"Lower your weapon," Jasmine ordered, stepping forwards into its line of sight.

The ghoul slowly raised its head.

"Do you remember me? I am Princess Jasmine. The bride Jafar wants to marry. I am turning myself in. Take me to him."

Though they were sneaking silently through the shadows quite possibly to meet their doom, *still* Aladdin couldn't help thinking how great it would be to live in the palace.

The royal baths were larger than some of the more impressive mosques and synagogues in Agrabah. Vaulted ceilings soared overhead, tiled in white and blue squares that made patterns like waves on the ocean. Delicately latticed, impossibly thin stone screens separated the women's baths from the men's. A separate area for cooling off appeared to have its own kitchen and wine cellar. Golden taps controlled the water flow in sunken tubs while jewel-encrusted fountains splattered out perfect diamond-like drops, reflected by the ropes of actual diamonds that draped over tiny blue oil lamps.

Morgiana obviously had similar thoughts, albeit less from a *living in* than a *stealing from* perspective. "Duban, we should have hit this place ages ago."

"Pareesa should have finished her job by now," Aladdin said, glancing out of a window to look at the stars. "So this is the part where we cut through the audience chamber and then the banquet hall to get to the throne room. And *then* comes the hard part."

"Yeah. Stealing a lamp and a book and saving Duban's family out from under the nose of the world's most powerful sorcerer," Morgiana sighed. "My mother never warned me about things like this."

"Think of the stories you'll be able to tell! Think of the bragging rights!" Aladdin countered. "Think of the..."

As they went into the next large bathing room the three almost walked smack into two patrolling guards.

"Prisoner," Aladdin amended quickly. "Think of the prisoner, she could get away!"

Suddenly, Morgiana was much closer to Duban, who quickly had his arm around her shoulders like he was preventing her from escaping.

"What goes on here, soldiers?" the older guard demanded. The gem in his black turban was a strange, opalescent yellow. That must mean something in Jafar's crazy new reorganisation, like maybe he was captain or something similar.

"We caught this lady trying to make off with a… diamond soap dish," Aladdin said cheerfully. "She thought the chaos outside was a perfect time for a brazen theft of the palace."

"I put it back," Morgiana whimpered, cringing effectively. "Please let me go. Whip me if you have to. *Don't* take me to the sultan!"

The yellow-gemmed guard snorted with derision. "We would never bother His Highness with a Street Rat. Your *fellow* Rats are ganging up and trying to overthrow the government tonight, and you aren't even brave enough to join them? You really are a cowardly piece of filth."

Aladdin noticed the tone in the captain's voice, it

wasn't respect, exactly. But it wasn't outright condemnation of the insurrection.

"Hand her over to me. A few nights in the dungeon should teach her what's *really* worth fearing."

Morgiana looked at Aladdin in concern.

"Oh... I thought... we would take her down ourselves," he improvised. "I want the credit for having caught her single-handedly."

Duban coughed.

"With my partner, of course. Single-handedly *with* my partner."

"No, *you* should patrol and see if she had any partners of her own," the captain said, grabbing Morgiana's shoulder and pulling her. "All prisoners of the state must be handled by Branded Soldiers. *Right?*"

He narrowed his eyes and glared at Aladdin.

Aladdin felt his heart thumping hard in his chest.

And then Morgiana caught Aladdin's eye. Very, very slightly, she nodded her head. *Let me go,* she was saying. *Go on.*

"Of course, sir," Aladdin said, motioning for Duban to release her. "Just make sure I get the credit for the capture."

We'll come back for you, he mouthed as the guards dragged Morgiana off between them.

———

Jasmine tried not to show any emotion as the two ghouls carried her into the ominously lightening sky. Their arms locked through hers, round the elbows, and she stood on their feet; there was no fear of falling. She was just a little chilly in the high night air. But below her, Agrabah was burning.

The Moon Tower had been successfully set aflame; Jafar's personal rooms were at the top and bottom of the ancient observatory and no doubt there would be things, artefacts, personal mementos, books and scrolls, he would want to save. The plan seemed to be working: whatever he had been hurling at the resistance seemed to have abated for the moment.

The scary glow of ghoulish red dotted the city like a plague that was taking over an otherwise healthy body.

And dawn was not that far off.

To distract herself and keep from panicking, Jasmine sneaked a look at the thick, ornate cuffs the ghouls wore. Poor magic carpet. Another victim of Jafar's war on Agrabah. She wondered if what little sentience it had was still there somewhere in its ripped-up and resewn seams. She wished a silly, girlish wish: that she'd had a chance to *really* fly on the carpet when it was still a carpet. With Aladdin. Zooming through the night air like she was doing now, but with his warm arms to hold on to and the entire world at their feet. They could have gone anywhere they wanted. They would have been completely free.

They dropped down to land on the Public Balcony, the one where her father used to make speeches, the one where Jafar had murdered him. Now it was a landing pad for the undead soldiers of Jafar's terrible new army.

As skilled and ungraceful as large, ugly insects, the ghouls hit the floor hard. With wordless pushes from behind, they forced Jasmine before them into the antechamber of the throne room. The few people who remained from father's staff looked shocked when they saw her standing there, unresisting, chin held high. One chamberlain ran to find Jafar. The rest of them went back to whatever they were doing: drawing up lists, ticking off names against maps, and who knew what else. Bad things.

"Jasmine…?"

Jafar strode into the room, resplendent or ridiculous in his black-and-red cloaks, robes and sashes. He gripped his black cobra staff nonchalantly. But he looked, for once, uncertain.

"I turned myself in, Jafar," she said, keeping her voice steady. "There have been too many deaths already. I want peace.

"I will consent to marrying you."

The Final Wish

"THIS IS A TRICK," Jafar declared. He stepped forwards to look at her with his neck crooked, like a lizard examining possible prey. "This is a ruse."

"Oh, sure," Jasmine said. "Search me if you want, Jafar. I have no magical staffs, genies, rings, I don't even have a dagger or teeny, tiny crossbow. Or poison dart."

She opened up her robes in a way that could have been suggestive but was entirely *not*. She started to unhook her trousers.

"No, no, that won't be necessary," Jafar said quickly, holding up his hand and looking around to see if anyone else was watching. No one was. Or at least they had looked away quickly. "But I don't believe you've had a sudden change of heart, Princess."

"I *haven't*," Jasmine snapped. "I don't *want* to marry you. But this is tearing the city apart."

"*You* are tearing the city apart," Jafar snarled, leaning over her. "Everything was fine until your Street Rats began to get uppity. Everyone was safe. No one was starving. There was peace. My Agrabah was a far happier Agrabah than under anyone in *your* family."

"With people terrified in their homes, or wearing your brands like goats... no one allowed to go outside at night or speak against you, and your bands of flying undead patrolling everywhere? That's not *happy*. That's *enslaved* and *imprisoned*."

"I don't know if everyone would agree with you, Princess. But in any event, consider Agrabah as a test case... for the rest of the world. I'm still working out some of the finer points of my governance."

"We can talk about the rest of the world later. Half the reason you're doing all this to Agrabah is to get me back. Well, here I am. Please call off your armies."

"Hmmm," Jafar said.

He paced around her, examining her from all angles, like a cat with a mouse trapped on a chair.

Aladdin had told Jasmine what he had witnessed in the Square of the Sailor. She tried not to tense up, tried not to imagine the horrible things that could be done to her.

"Hmmm," Jafar said again.

The room was silent; even the scribbles of the secretaries had stopped.

"But I *want* you to love me," Jafar finally said with a terrifying mildness. "So what are we going to do about that, Jasmine?"

"We can… make everyone else *think* I love you?"

"Hmmm," Jafar said a third time. "Your honest discourse is refreshing, even if its content is not appealing. I shall consider your offer. In the meantime, I would like to give you a little demonstration of what happens to those who lie to me. Or otherwise try to plot against me."

He threw his arms open dramatically and used his staff to pull himself forwards into the throne room.

Jasmine gasped at the different scenes playing out in the space.

In one corner was the hourglass. It was the opposite of one of her father's models: instead of a large thing made tiny for play, it was a tiny thing made huge. In the bottom half were Maruf and the two children. He was tiredly, constantly moving: putting his terrified grandchildren on his shoulders, lifting them up every few moments so they could sit on top of the rapidly growing pile of sand, shifting to make everyone more comfortable.

Despite being used to the everyday horrors of poverty and a dangerous life in the streets, Ahmed and Shirin had faces that were now raw from weeping and the haggard look of exhausted terror.

In the top of the hourglass there was very little sand left.

The three of them saw Jasmine. Ahmed's and Shirin's faces lit up and they shouted with joy, or probably did; no sound transmitted through the glass.

Jasmine's first impulse was to cry out and run over to them. To pound on the hourglass. To try to get them out.

"And over here, in case you missed it..." Jafar pointed to the other side of the throne, throwing his arms open wide and letting his cape flutter behind him.

There was the genie.

Still larger than human, but pale and thinner somehow. He was tied down to a bed of nails, each point digging into his blue skin. The giant gold bracelets that covered his wrists were chained to a pair of boards crossed above his head. Everything glowed faintly purple.

"Hey, Princess," the genie said weakly.

"Are you all right?" she asked, and then immediately regretted it.

"Oh, sure. Never better. How's you?"

"Quiet, fool," Jafar snapped. He spun and stomped up to where the, *his*, throne was. He sat down and his cape flared out around him. He laid his staff across his knees. He reached out with one hand as if to stroke a dog or cat lying next to him. Instead, he petted the old, battered-looking oil lamp that sat on a delicate golden table there.

The lamp.

And next to it was a book with a blackened cover and what looked like a living human eye set in the leather. *Al Azif.*

"I don't take kindly to those who act against me," Jafar growled. "As you can plainly see. So let me ask you one last time, Princess. Do you *swear* you are here simply to declare your everlasting love and betrothal to me?"

"I cannot promise the love," she said as bravely as she could. "But I give you my word about the betrothal."

The horrible twitch of a real smile began to grow in the corners of Jafar's mouth.

The two thieves made it to the audience chamber without further incident. It was as impressive as the baths, in a smaller, understated way. A mosaic of Agrabah and the lands between the greater Western Desert and the Mountains of Atrazak covered the largest wall. A fresco, occasionally updated, it seemed, with fresher paint, on the other wall showed a reasonably up-to-date map of Agrabah itself, down to the small side streets. Aladdin wished he had more time to examine it closely.

"Ha," Duban whispered, pointing at the Quarter of the Street Rats. "This part's all wrong... that fountain hasn't been there since my mother's mother's time."

"Just as well," Aladdin whispered back. "But help me find the wandering dervish in the mosaic... he should be lost in the desert, like in the legend."

Duban looked confused but did as he was told, running his fingers over the design with Aladdin.

"Aha!" Aladdin said, the first one to find the image of the old man with a satchel over his shoulder, all made out of teeny, tiny brown tiles. He placed his fingers on their cracked surface and pushed.

There was a *click*, and a panel on one of the short walls slipped away to reveal a dark passage.

Aladdin grinned. "Jasmine told me her father was often late to meetings... so he had this installed to get from the banquet hall to here directly!"

Duban gave a low whistle.

They stepped through, carefully shutting the panel behind them. Tiny oil lamps flickered in the distance, just barely lighting a path.

"From here it's—"

"*Who goes there?*"

Duban and Aladdin stared at each other, agape. Jasmine had said this was a *secret* passage. He had assumed that meant it was only known to the sultan and his closest advisers.

Coming forwards out of the darkness was a pair of particularly burly guards, scimitars drawn.

"No one is authorised to patrol the secret passages except for me and Ali and our men," the man on the right growled.

"We just came back from Ali," Aladdin said quickly. "He had to bring a prisoner down to the dungeons and—"

"Liar. Jafar will hear of this! *Impostors!*"

Not burly *and dumb* guards, obviously.

The passage was too narrow for swordplay; as thieves, Duban and Aladdin weren't particularly good with scimitars anyway. They dropped the ones that were part of their stolen uniforms and drew their trusty daggers.

The guard on the left didn't hesitate: he immediately lunged with his scimitar, hoping to skewer Aladdin like a kebab. Aladdin bent over backwards, watching its deadly point slice just above his face, where his stomach had been a moment ago.

He snapped back upright before the guard could react and whirled his dagger so it danced over his thumb, then swept his arm out at the last second.

Besides being smarter, this guard was also *quicker* than most: his scimitar flicked down sideways and neatly turned aside Aladdin's blade.

It wasn't a strong enough blow to knock the dagger out of his hand. Aladdin recovered and jumped up, wedging his feet against the passageway's walls to hoist himself up and over and land two metres back. At least now he had a little breathing room.

He saw Duban and his own opponent sparring: his friend had two daggers, one in each hand. He used them like a skilled butcher to trap and grab the blade of the other man's scimitar whenever it came close to him.

Seeing that Duban was doing all right, Aladdin focused on his own battle and let his dagger fly with a neat flick of his wrist.

The guard saw this and tried to deflect the missile but moved just a second too slowly. The handle of his blade only caught the edge of the flying dagger, causing it to spin off target. It still got him on the side of the neck, though. It drew a ragged, bloody gash.

The guard barely reacted, flinching with more embarrassment than pain.

He spun his scimitar round and suddenly dived, lunging at Aladdin's legs.

Not expecting such a fast recovery and immediate attack, Aladdin leaped straight up in the air and then flipped, putting his hands on the guard's shoulders to vault over him.

The guard immediately spun round to try to face his

opponent in this new direction, blade flashing like the deadly fang of a cobra.

But Aladdin was faster and kicked him squarely in the backs of his knees.

The guard went down, hard.

Aladdin made it harder by delivering a roundhouse kick to the guard's side. As he fell, Aladdin put his hands together and delivered a final chop to the guard's neck.

By the time he hit the floor, the guard had stopped moving, his unconscious head lolled to the side.

Aladdin spun to help Duban. The other guard was also down.

But so was Duban.

He was lying on top of his opponent and clutching his side.

"Duban?" Aladdin carefully rolled his friend onto his back.

"I'm all right." Wincing with pain, but not letting himself groan, Duban pushed himself up. He hobbled forwards, holding his side with one arm.

"Let's go."

Aladdin wanted to argue with him, but couldn't. They *all* needed to work together if the plan was to succeed. Besides, it didn't look like anything would stop Duban from freeing his family.

They hobbled together to the end of the dark passageway. There they slid a panel aside and stepped out into a giant banquet room.

The ridiculously long wooden table that took up most of it was devoid of food or place settings; chairs were askew, no lamps were lit. Jafar was obviously not as intrigued by dinners as the previous sultan. The only light in the abandoned room came from an eerie red glow at the far end: the entrance to the throne room. After Aladdin's eyes adjusted for a moment, he realised the light was coming from the dead face of a man blocking the way.

It was Rasoul.

"We don't have much time," Jasmine urged Jafar. "In just a few minutes, the Street Rat army is going to launch an attack on your front door and take the palace down. Call off your assault on the city. Let's not lose any more lives over this."

Jafar started to laugh. Then he looked over at one of the guards waiting for orders, a captain. The guard didn't look so amused.

"There are hundreds of them, Your Highness. And the... *living* members of our army don't want to kill women and children. There's a lot of chaos in the city. Many of our legions are trying to put out the fires caused by their and your explosions."

"Let the city burn," Jafar growled, clenching his hands into fists.

"Who will be left to love you?" Jasmine asked, unable to keep the irony out of her voice.

Jafar narrowed his eyes. He turned to the guard.

"Get as many men as you can muster to the front of the palace. Blockade it while I work out what to do." He drummed his fingers on his knees and started to mutter, seemingly to himself. "So close… I am so close… I've already mastered the raising of the dead. It's only a matter of time before I learn how to break the other laws of magic. I just need more time. *GENIE!*" he called out suddenly.

"Yes, Master?" the genie asked tiredly.

"We need to put on a big show for the masses. The princess and I are to be married this instant."

The genie lifted his head weakly to look at Jasmine.

"Sorry, Princess," he said. "But if it means anything at all, I really respect what you're doing. You would have made, you'll *make* a great sultana."

"Yes, yes, wedding dress now, all that," Jafar said, impatient. "I'll summon some priest or mullah or something… it doesn't matter. On the balcony, where everyone can see."

The genie feebly waved his fingertips. Suddenly, Jasmine was wearing the dress he had made before, the one his own wife had worn. Flowers and streamers and banners appeared all over the room and, presumably, the outside of the palace.

She watched it all, torn between laughing and crying.

Jafar walked over to the balcony and raised his hands above his head. His magically enhanced voice rang out over the kingdom.

"PEOPLE OF AGRABAH! LAY DOWN YOUR WEAPONS. PRINCESS JASMINE AND I ARE IN AGREEMENT. WE ARE TO BE WED THIS VERY MOMENT. CEASE FIGHTING. COME TO THE PALACE TO BEAR WITNESS."

A guard came rushing into the room, pushing a confused-looking old man in religious robes in front of him.

"I'm sorry, my lord, we couldn't find Khosrow. This one will have to do…"

Jasmine took a deep breath and began to walk forwards.

"Stop," undead Rasoul said. *"Proceed no further."*

"Rasoul," Aladdin said, swallowing hard. "I'm… I'm sorry about what happened to you. I never intended, I never meant for you to be killed."

The ghoul looked at him impassively. Neither forgiveness nor anger showed in his bloody glowing eyes.

"Rasoul. *Please*," Aladdin begged softly. "You swore to protect Agrabah. Against thieves like me… against harm to the people. Your army is now attacking *children* and forcing families to turn each other over to Jafar. He makes people line up and get branded and turns them into ghouls like you! Is *this* what you want to protect?"

Still Rasoul said nothing.

"Look outside, Rasoul," Aladdin pleaded, pointing at the window. "Look. Agrabah is burning. *Your* city is burning."

Rasoul turned his head to look, moving nothing else. Faint orange light flickered over his deathly white skin. Some of the glow was from the rising sun, Aladdin realised with horror.

"They did not obey," Rasoul said slowly.

"Obey *what*? Obey *who*? Rasoul, don't you remember anything from your life? You swore to serve a sultan who, while he might not have been the best ruler, never launched an attack against his own people. Jafar is killing and torturing anyone who disagrees with him. And if he can't win, he'll destroy Agrabah so no one else can have it. Don't you see that?"

Rasoul remained silent, watching.

"Please," Aladdin whispered, glancing at the horizon out of the window again. "I know I'm the last person in the world to ask you for anything. I am truly, truly sorry for what happened to you. For what I did to you. But you know me, think back on all the years you have known me, Rasoul. I may be a thief,

but I am not evil. And I am not lying to you now. I saw a *nine-year-old boy*, undead like you. Do you want your fate to be shared by children?"

Rasoul turned his head back slowly to look at Aladdin. But there were no pupils to focus on, nothing beyond the dead red glow.

Aladdin began to despair.

Then Rasoul's scimitar clattered to the floor.

"End this, Street Rat."

His voice was just as dead and hollow as it was before. There was no indication of what thought processes had gone on in his monstrous head.

"Thank you," Aladdin whispered in relief. "I hope you find peace."

But Rasoul didn't respond or move to get out of the way.

Duban and Aladdin slunk behind him and out of the door. The ghoul continued to stare into nothing in the middle of the pitch-black hall.

"And Jasmine, royal princess and daughter of the sultan..." the old religious man trailed off, confused. "I am sorry, daughter. I don't remember all of your names. Rose of Agrabah? Twice Great-Granddaughter of Elisheba the Wise?"

"I think it *was* Elisheba," Jasmine said thoughtfully. She kept an eye on the dais behind them, in the throne room. An eye on the costly gold drapes that hung around the outside of the throne and fell from the ceiling.

"Hey," she suddenly said to the sorcerer. "What's *your* full name?"

Jafar blinked. "What?"

"Your full name," Jasmine said patiently. "For as long as I can remember, everyone has always just called you by your title, grand vizier, or Jafar. What's the rest of it?"

"That is my only name," Jafar snapped. "The only thing my parents gave me and the only name you should ever be concerned about. In public you shall address me as *'My Lord'*. Now *continue*, old man, before I set your lungs on fire."

Jasmine's eyes appeared to glaze over again as the poor religious man began to invoke the laws of Agrabah, etc., etc...

And then the curtains behind the throne shivered.

Relief flooded Jasmine's body like a plunge in a cold bath on a hot day. She tried not to let it show. Aladdin popped his head out and took a quick look around. When he saw her, he winked.

She nodded her head as slightly as she could at the table to the left of the throne, where the lamp and the book sat.

Aladdin gave her a smile and a thumbs-up. Then he dropped to the ground.

"Is something wrong?" Jafar asked, frowning at her.

"Just tearing up on my wedding day," Jasmine said sarcastically. "Or it's ash from the fires you've been setting all over the city."

"*They* started it," Jafar shot back. "Hurry up. Get to the part where she says 'I will'."

Aladdin was scuttling over to the table as silently as he could. One of the ministers looked up, eye drawn away from whatever terrible lists he was going over.

Jasmine sucked in her breath.

Whether he never actually saw Aladdin… or saw him and chose not to say anything, she would never be sure. He *did* turn to look at her for a moment and then went back to his work. As if nothing had interrupted him.

Jasmine let out her breath.

Aladdin slowly reached for the lamp.

"Under the indulgence of the Royal Sultan, most High and Exalted be he, I give you to each other now."

Suddenly, a high-pitched shriek filled the air. Like the noise from an angry falcon but much, much louder.

Strange beaked creatures grew from the shadows on the walls. They screamed and flapped their wings in Aladdin's face.

Jasmine did the only thing she could think of: she leaped forwards to kiss Jafar.

Jafar struggled away from her, turning his head and making little *pfft pfft* noises. When he finally managed to throw her off, he spun round to look, then laughed maniacally at what he saw.

Jasmine despaired.

Centimetres from the lamp, Aladdin's hands were caught up in what looked like golden vines that grew out of the painting on the table itself. The more he struggled, the more they tightened. The shadow gargoyles faded, their work of warning done.

"Oh, *nicely* played," Jafar said with the benevolence of someone who had just won. He strode towards Aladdin, his cape flaring out menacingly behind him. "I should have expected something like this. Oh, wait, I *did*. Thus the gargoyle alarms and the vines."

"Jafar…" Jasmine said, unsure what she could accomplish.

"It was *very* clever, my dear. Saying it was all for peace. If you had pretended to actually have fallen in love with me, I wouldn't have believed it for a second."

The calmness in his voice didn't fool anyone. Those ministers and servants who weren't actively running out of the room were very *casually* and quickly finding reasons to gather their stuff and leave.

"Aladdin," Jafar said, tapping his cobra-headed staff

on the floor once. "You are an exceptionally talented and relentless young man. I admire that. I really do. You remind me of myself in some ways. So I'll make you a deal.

"You join me. Jasmine marries me. You convince the Street Rats to give up and give in. We all live happily ever after in my new world, Agrabah Ascendant."

"*Never,*" Aladdin hissed, pulling at the golden tendrils around his wrists.

"I can bring back the dead now, boy," Jafar drawled. "*Really* bring them back. I can bring back anyone who has ever died. Even long ago.

"Even... your mother."

Aladdin stopped struggling.

How did Jafar even *know* about his mother?

"She would just be another one of your ghouls," Aladdin said uncertainly.

"No, my dear boy," Jafar said, leering. "My understanding of *Al Azif* has only deepened... all levels of life and death are being unlocked for me now. She could be returned in perfect health with whole body and mind."

Before he could stop himself, Aladdin began to think about what Jafar had said. His *mother.* She could come back. Healed of her disease. He could give her the life she deserved. He could treat her like a queen, give her a big house, all the food and fine things she had always wanted to give him.

He saw Jasmine bite her lip anxiously.

But she needn't have worried; these thoughts spun and died only a moment after he conceived them. Even if Jafar was telling the truth about his powers, Aladdin had seen Rasoul. He had seen the little boy. Who knew what his mother would really be like?

And even if she did come back alive and whole, he knew what she would have to say about it. Making an alliance with an evil sorcerer would only guarantee more deaths and more unhappiness.

"Not even for my mother," Aladdin whispered. "I will *never* ally with you."

"Oh, well, it doesn't really matter," Jafar said with an unsurprised shrug. "Once I crack the third law of magic, all of Agrabah will love me. *Jasmine* will love me. And you… well, no; I won't force you to love me as well. I shall leave you as the only sane man left in Agrabah. While everyone else around you worships me… you will be *completely alone.*"

"That's where you're wrong, Jafar," Aladdin said with a grin. "No Street Rat is *ever* alone."

Before Jafar could raise his eyebrows in a suitably nasty sneer, a scimitar flashed down out of the air, slicing the golden tendrils from Aladdin's wrists. Duban came out from behind the throne.

A moment later a tattered, flying mess of hair and trousers

came dashing into the room. Morgiana was only bleeding a little and carried a short sword in each hand, plus an extra scimitar in her right.

"Took you long enough," Aladdin said accusingly.

"You said 'no killing'," she said, shrugging. "Stuff like that takes time."

She turned and tossed the scimitar to Jasmine.

Jasmine caught it with a grin.

Jafar snarled. He snatched the lamp off the table and thrust it into his robes. Then he lifted his staff.

"I feel I should warn you," the genie said weakly. "The camel dung is about to hit the fan."

But the Street Rats weren't waiting around.

Aladdin leaped up onto the magicked table and aimed a roundhouse kick at the sorcerer's head. Duban made for *Al Azif*, reaching for it with his two daggers held like tweezers. Morgiana ran over to the deadly hourglass and began to slam it with the hilt of her sword.

Jafar swung his staff sideways and blocked Aladdin's blow.

"*INSOLENT FOOLS!*" he roared, eyes turning red. "*You dare defy the most powerful sorcerer in the WORLD?*"

He raised his hand.

A wall of fire sprang up between Duban and *Al Azif*. Elsewhere, furniture began to lift into the air and fly across the room. Sofas scraped along the floor. Vases spun out of control. An ottoman aimed itself at Aladdin's head.

Aladdin leaped down from the table, doing a flip and hitting the ottoman aside with his feet as he tumbled. Duban dived for the floor, avoiding a brass-and-gold hookah that was meant to connect with his face. Morgiana and Jasmine leaped around the smaller pieces of furniture meant for them.

Aladdin swept his foot round, spinning like a dervish. He connected with Jafar's ankles.

The sorcerer started to topple to the ground, then stopped midway.

With a nasty laugh, Jafar rose back upright in a thoroughly unnatural fashion.

He threw open his cape, revealing the robes he wore beneath. Aladdin saw to his horror that cinching them in the middle was the last piece of the carpet, the end with the tassels that he had always thought of as the poor thing's 'face'.

While Aladdin was transfixed, Jasmine took her scimitar and ran at Jafar, trying to bury it in Jafar's side. He easily turned the blow aside with his staff.

"*JASMINE!*" Aladdin cried. "What are you *doing*?"

"Distracting him," she said, ducking as the sorcerer tried to clock her in the head, too angry to remember to use his powers for a moment. "That was my job, remember?"

"Yes! And you did a great job. Now *get out of here* before you get killed!"

With obvious difficulty, Jafar mastered his rage and calmed himself. His eyes glowed red again.

Things around the room now began to explode into flames, things that normally *shouldn't* be flammable. Stone vases and metal bric-a-brac. The throne itself exploded, throwing Duban to the floor.

Shrapnel and debris went flying towards the back of Jasmine's head, streaked with fire and smoking as they went.

"Jasmine!" Aladdin cried.

The princess spun round but not quite fast enough to avoid the flaming missiles entirely. She screamed as they connected, covering her head with her arms. The air filled with the smell of burned hair and flesh. Angry red skin bubbled up and pulled apart in a fleshy split across her forehead.

Another vase lifted up and aimed at her.

Morgiana immediately abandoned her attack on the hourglass and threw herself in front of Jasmine.

Shirin and Ahmed howled silently as Morgiana seemed to abandon them, and the spider's web of cracks in the glass she had managed to start, but Maruf merely looked resigned, understanding what they needed to do. It was too painful to watch.

Using both of her swords, Morgiana swirled into a blur of movement, batting aside one flaming object after another as the sorcerer focused all of his rage on the princess. The faster the projectiles came, the faster Morgiana moved.

Jasmine reeled from the pain of her wound, stumbling around in her attempt to stay upright. She gritted her teeth and forced herself to stand firm. She raised her scimitar to defend herself.

"Morgiana! Forget me!" she ordered in a croak. "Go back and save the children!"

The thief looked unsure for only a moment, then nodded and went back to attacking the glass. Shirin and Ahmed wept in relief.

Duban began to crawl back to the table that had *Al Azif.*

Aladdin noticed that Jafar was frowning while things exploded and flew; he seemed to need to use all of his concentration for these multiple attacks.

The thief immediately acted on this and leaped at the sorcerer. But he fell on the floor instead, grasping nothing.

Jafar laughed maniacally, suddenly on the far side of the room.

He aimed a finger. Fiery bolts shot through the air.

Aladdin leaped from one foot to another, forwards and backwards, trying to avoid them and remain standing.

Jafar aimed his finger elsewhere this time.

Duban let out a tortured cry.

Aladdin spun round to look.

Standing between Duban and *Al Azif* was a figure made entirely of fire. A figure who looked exactly like Shirin. She even *stood* like Shirin: shyly, weight on her right foot while her left crossed over. But there was no expression on her red-and-yellow face.

Aladdin looked round quickly to see if Duban's niece was still in the hourglass. She was, watching with horror as Morgiana dealt with a new problem: she had made progress in shattering a small hole in the glass, but now it was in danger of being sealed up again. Flat, overlapping stones like snake scales had started growing up the sides of the glass, shielding it from her sword strikes.

Duban hesitantly went to reach around the fiery Shirin for the book.

Silently the effigy threw her hand out and burned a long, streaky black mark along his arm. Still her face was blank.

Duban hissed and pulled back.

Jafar smiled wickedly at Aladdin. "*You* don't seem to have anyone you love whom I could summon and kill you with."

Aladdin prayed the sorcerer didn't guess the truth about him and Jasmine.

"And *you* killed the only thing *you* ever loved," Aladdin spat back.

Jafar's face darkened with hate. His upper lip trembled in rage.

"There *is* someone you love, though, isn't there?" he growled.

Aladdin felt his heart stop.

"I cannot believe I *almost* missed it!" Jafar grinned, his gold-and-broken-toothed smile too wide to be human. He closed his eyes and clenched his fists.

Aladdin prepared himself.

A purple monkey made entirely of fire burned to life in the middle of the room.

Although Aladdin felt a huge burst of relief that it wasn't Jasmine, it also wasn't as funny as it could have been. It didn't look much like Abu, it was as if Jafar couldn't remember him properly and so couldn't summon his likeness. It was more like a large, angry *baboon*. The ape screamed and showed fiery, sharp fangs.

Aladdin slashed at it with his dagger. That only proved what he already suspected: the monkey was as insubstantial as the gargoyles had been. The blade cut through it and nothing happened except that the metal grip became too hot to hold.

Aladdin dropped his blade and quickly changed tactics.

He reached down and pulled up the edge of a rug like a magician about to do a trick. Praying the baboon would behave more like the fire than an actual animal, Aladdin threw himself on the thing, opening his arms out wide to engulf it in the carpet.

Searing hot air blasted from the sides as he crashed to the floor. The hair on his left arm singed off in a painful sizzle.

But when he looked down, the monkey appeared to be gone.

"Morgiana! Throw me a sword!" Duban cried, having seen the whole thing.

She paused her work and did so without hesitating. But in the space of the few seconds it took, the stone scales on the hourglass grew higher. They began to branch out like giant thorns.

With a pained expression on his face, Duban began to slice through the fire effigy with both swords. The fire-Shirin lunged at Duban, fingers splitting into long ropes of fire. He stepped back but increased his speed of attack, twirling his weapons furiously.

The edges of the demon began to blur, caught by the draught the blades were making.

Her mouth opened in a soundless scream. She lashed out with long whips of bloody red fire.

Duban evaded them as best he could but kept his swords going, whistling through the air.

Soon he was simply spinning the blades, deadly twin circles of metal.

The breeze was finally enough to disrupt the integrity of the fire itself. The effigy started to disappear, pulled into shreds. She howled silently as she tried to keep her coherence.

Soon she was nothing more than wisps of hot sparks rapidly dispersing into the air.

Duban collapsed to the ground, a hand to his wounded side and a sickened expression on his face.

"Aladdin! Duban! Help!" Morgiana cried desperately as the stone continued to form into jagged thorns. "We should—"

And then a stone branch broke through her right shoulder from behind. She was pinned to the stone tree.

She didn't move. She opened her mouth but didn't scream. Her face went white and tense with pain.

"Mia!" Duban shouted, but he could barely stand up himself after his exertions.

Slowly, and with obvious agony, Morgiana looked down and broke off the sharp, marble thorn with the pommel of her sword. Groaning with pain, she pulled herself off the stony tree.

No blood flowed; her wound was cauterised by whatever burning magic had created the thorn. Her arm hung limp.

Growling in fury, Jasmine leaped up and hurled herself at Jafar.

The sorcerer laughed at the sight of the angry princess and started to raise his staff to do something horrible.

That made Aladdin realise something. He was wasting his time trying to break through Jafar's defences to grab the lamp. He should have attacked Jafar's defences *directly*: the staff itself. Get rid of that and Jafar was mostly powerless.

Aladdin launched himself through the air, aiming feet first.

He crashed into Jafar's staff, but it didn't break. He tried to wrench it out of the sorcerer's hand. Jafar clung tightly, knuckles turning white. He closed his eyes, beginning to cast another spell.

Aladdin also closed his eyes and slammed Jafar in the head with his own head.

He might have been the world's mightiest sorcerer, but he had no experience with street fighting.

Stunned by the unexpected blow, Jafar opened his eyes in surprise. Blood coursed down his brow and poured out of his nose. He didn't drop the staff, but his fingers loosened slightly.

Aladdin grabbed the cobra staff and twisted, leaping over

it and pulling at the same time, like one of the demonic drummers from Jafar's parade.

Jafar clung to it like a cat, hovering in the air with the help of his piece of the magic carpet. His sudden lack of weight caused Aladdin to overextend himself and sent both of them flying to the floor.

Jasmine lost no time, throwing herself on top of Jafar and wrapping her arms around him. It was just enough extra weight and leverage to force him to the ground. Aladdin put all his effort into one final pull and wrenched the staff free.

Immediately, he felt his throat closing up as Jafar snarled and worked his other magic.

"Jasmine!" Aladdin croaked. As if they were in a simple game of catch, he quickly tossed the staff to her.

Surprised, she fumbled desperately but managed to catch it.

"BREAK IT!" Aladdin shouted as Jafar began to transfer his deadly magic to her.

Time seemed to stop as Jasmine looked down at the thing in her hands. Somewhere in a corner of the room Morgiana was shuddering in pain, trying to hold her remaining sword arm up. Maruf, Ahmed and Shirin were fighting against the sand. Duban was crawling towards the table and reaching for *Al Azif* with shaking arms. The genie weakly watched everything from where he was tied up.

Jasmine looked from the staff to Jafar. The man who murdered her father was *right there*. The man who held all of Agrabah in thrall. The man who brought nothing but suffering to everyone.

She raised the staff up over her knee and then... began to whisper.

"Ia, ia, shal-alyeah, a'hz'red abenna..."

She pointed the staff at Jafar and spoke louder.

"Ia, ia, shib-benathki alleppa ghoser!"

Jafar's eyes widened as he recognised the words. His face went white.

Then he crumpled over in pain.

Everyone else stopped what they were doing and watched, also in shock.

"Oh, yes, Jafar," Jasmine said with an angry smile. "I read those books you stole from all over the world. I picked up a few things I thought would be useful. Committed them to memory."

The stone scales growing over the room began to melt and drop away as Jafar gasped in agony.

"Jasmine...?" Aladdin said slowly.

She loomed over the sorcerer like a predator.

"And now, I think, I will put an end to all of this.

You will die. Powerless, in shame and completely alone. Just like my father."

"No, Jasmine, no…" Jafar winced and groaned under whatever magical torture she was putting him through. "Please. Anything. I wanted to marry you…"

"You wanted a princess. Any princess. You wanted to be sultan. You wanted all of the trappings of royalty. Well, guess what? You should have stayed grand vizier. Being *royal* is far more deadly. As my father found out. As *I* nearly found out. As you're about to."

"I've learned my lesson. I was foolish. Exile me. Imprison me. Don't…"

"Take out your dagger. *Now*," she ordered.

"Jasmine," Aladdin said cautiously, coming forwards.

Everyone in the room had reasons to hate Jafar, and yet everyone still looked away as the tears began to run down his face. With a shaking hand, the sorcerer reached inside his cape and pulled out a familiar, curvy black dagger.

Sobbing and sniffling, he pressed it to his own throat.

"*Jasmine*," Aladdin said loudly. "Don't do this. Not this way."

"What, you want me to let him go?" Jasmine asked. "*Imprison* him? He's… *Jafar*, Aladdin. He'll escape or bribe someone or magic his way out. No, if I kill him, it all ends. *Now.*"

"At what cost?" Aladdin asked. He pointed at the confused crowd beyond the balcony, still waiting to destroy a palace or watch a wedding. Beyond *them* the war for the city was still going on. "You said you wanted a new Agrabah. A *better* Agrabah. Where people are free and the laws are just and everyone takes care of each other and no one slips through the cracks. That means *everyone*, even him. If you want to execute him, fine. Have a trial first. A public trial where everyone can see the law being carried out in the light. Don't just murder him behind closed doors like this."

Jasmine didn't look at Aladdin. She kept her eyes on Jafar. He was still sobbing; the dagger pressed into his neck so hard that beads of dark blood began to appear.

"Please," Aladdin whispered.

Jasmine frowned.

"*Fine.*" She finally relented.

Angry, she swung the staff, smashing it against the hourglass.

The two magic items shattered together, sand and glass and wood and stone swirling around before disappearing.

All that was left were the cobra's two ruby eyes, spinning on the floor like marbles.

Shirin and Ahmed sprang from their grandfather's shoulders with exultant cries of relief. Maruf, a little unsteady on his feet, gave her a salute.

Jasmine took a deep breath. But the rage was gone.

She had almost killed a man in cold blood. Using black magic.

She gave Aladdin a look. She didn't have to *say* "you were right."

"I know how hard that was," he said, taking her hand and squeezing it. "But it was the right thing."

Jasmine shook her head, sighing. "I know. But we should—"

Whatever Jasmine was about to say next was cut off as a streak of lightning, black as death, cut across the room and surrounded Jafar.

"Jasmine may not have the heart to kill you, but *I* do!" Duban cried.

Everyone turned to look. He stood triumphantly, *Al Azif* clutched in his hand. Black wisps in the air whipped around him. A snarl of hatred was plastered on his face.

"This will finally put an end to your evil. *Die*, Jafar, the way you would have had my family die!"

A howling wind rose up. The eye on the book blinked and rolled.

Jafar began to choke.

He wheezed and coughed and grasped his throat, unable to make a sound. A trickle of blood and sand emerged from the side of his mouth.

Jasmine stepped away from him in horror, out of range of the magic. Aladdin and Morgiana watched Duban with shock and dismay.

"Just... *die* already!" he growled.

Shirin and Ahmed, so happy a moment ago, began to cry. The look on their uncle's face was terrifying.

But Jafar wasn't quite done yet.

He laughed a creaky, burbling laugh. Sprays of saliva and grains of sand and bubbles of blood flecked his black collar.

"I still have one wish left, you fools."

Jasmine shook her head and spoke softly. "Jafar, it's over. Try to find some peace. I'm not afraid of whatever it is you wish for. There will still be Street Rats left when you're done. Someone will be able to take the lamp and have the genie undo everything that you've done."

Jafar kept laughing, but this time silently, weakly. He coughed and cleared his throat one last time.

"Hear me, Genie. I wish... that when I die... *all magic dies with me.*"

The End — of Magic

JAFAR'S CLOTHES FADED and seemed to shrink back in on themselves. No longer in his magically created sultan's robes, he now lay in his old grand vizier uniform. Sand trickled around his body like it was already decaying in the desert.

His voice grew ragged and weak. "The world... will forever be ordinary now. Good luck fixing everything in Agrabah without *magic*. You need it for happy endings, you know..."

With one more shuddering breath, he was gone.

Before anyone could react to what had just happened, strange groans and horrible *thunking* noises came from the hallways.

At first Aladdin was confused by the sound. Then he

realised the truth: the ghouls were returning to their natural state. *Dead.* He closed his eyes, picturing Rasoul in the banquet hall. He wished he knew a proper prayer for all of them.

There were shouts of confusion and then triumph outside beyond the balcony.

"*NO!*" a strange voice shrieked.

Everyone in the room turned to look at the genie.

But he wasn't there. In his place stood an ordinary-sized man with ordinary flesh and hair, though his skin still had a faint bluish tinge. He was looking at his arms, splaying out his fingers, twitching his toes.

He snapped his fingers.

Nothing happened.

He pointed at a chair and murmured something.

Nothing.

A strangled cry came out of his throat.

"Genie. You're no longer... magical..." Jasmine said, her voice filled with pity. She came over and put her arms around him. He didn't resist.

"I never thought I'd be free again," he said hollowly. "And certainly not like this. I'm *human.* Ordinary. *Normal.*"

"Just because you don't have your powers..." Aladdin began.

"*THEY WEREN'T MY POWERS!*" the genie snapped.

"They were who I *was*. Who *all* djinn are. We can do these things the same way you monkeys can walk upright or read books. It's the way we are *born*.

"Sorry," he added quickly, running a hand over his head. "It's just a lot to take in."

"It's *all* a lot to take in," Aladdin said, looking around and finally resting his gaze on Duban. His old friend stood there, looking angry but confused. His eyes were red-rimmed and his face was pale.

Morgiana moved forward and put her hand on Duban's arm. It was hard to tell if it was out of solidarity, sympathy, or to pull him out of everyone's sight. Maybe it was a little of all three.

"Duban," she murmured.

Maruf approached his son slowly. He clapped an arm over his shoulder, unsure what to say or do.

"Son, I'm touched that you love me enough to... do... this. But..."

"I just..." Duban said, suddenly at a loss. "It's all I could think about... he deserved to die."

But he said it without much conviction.

"You planned this from the beginning," Aladdin said slowly. "That's why you wanted to switch with Morgiana and have her try to free the others. That's why you've been so... quiet and moody."

"I... *had* to!" Duban protested half-heartedly. "It *had* to be done. You *know* that. You all do. Jafar *had* to be killed. Nothing else would stop him or end his reign of terror. He *would* weasel out of whatever punishment you decided on. You *know* that..."

"What's done is done," Morgiana said. But she didn't sound convinced.

Duban looked at Shirin and Ahmed pleadingly, but they shrank back into the protection of Maruf's robe.

The old man took the children aside and whispered soothingly to them.

"They've just been through a lot," he said aloud, trying to sound reassuring.

But Duban was staring at the floor somewhere past the dead sorcerer, unseeing.

Jasmine surveyed the scene around the room and found that she didn't even have the energy to cry. Death, mess, sadness, confusion all around. Not a good place to start... She wandered over to the balcony and looked out.

"Too bad there's no way to make myself heard over that chaos," she said with a sigh. "Like magically."

"PEOPLE OF AGRABAH! YOU ARE FREE!" she shouted as loudly as she could, raising her arms. "We won," she added, a little weakly.

A few people noticed and cheered.

"You're going to have to get out there," Morgiana said to her, turning from Duban for a moment. "You're going to have to go down there into that mess and make sure *everyone* sees you and hears what the deal is."

"How is *any*one going to see me in all that chaos? I'm already a head shorter than everyone else. Even in my biggest crown."

"We'll carry you," Aladdin suggested as cheerfully as he could. "On our shoulders. In a triumphant procession."

"I could have *made* a triumphant procession," the genie muttered. "With horns and confetti and the whole bells and whistles."

And so the friends emerged from the palace in a hastily arranged parade. The palace guards were extremely pleased with the new situation; apparently they liked stability even more than they liked fighting. They raised the portcullis and provided an escort that preceded her, shouting that people should make way for *Sultana* Jasmine.

Jasmine balanced as gracefully as she could on Aladdin's and Duban's shoulders, a white silk bandage wrapping her forehead to cover her burn. Duban kept his head down, reduced to silence again. Maruf hobbled behind, along with the genie, who was having trouble picking up and putting his feet back down properly.

"This *walking* thing is the worst," he grumbled. "Is the gravity here always bad this time of year?"

Shirin and Ahmed ambled shyly behind them, exhausted but a little pleased to be part of the procession and the centre of attention.

Morgiana strode last of all, trying to grin but looking very uncomfortable, and it wasn't just because of her limp, bandaged arm. Thieves weren't *supposed* to be the centre of attention. She kept her good hand on her dagger.

The crowds closest to the palace weren't fighting any more; they were waiting to see what was happening with Jafar and Jasmine. News spread quickly when they saw her waving and smiling. Ragged cheers began in a wave. People raised whatever weapons they had in the air and shouted in triumph.

Then they joined in behind the parade, singing and dancing.

"You all right up there?" Aladdin asked as he shifted her weight on his shoulder.

"Absolutely. Head to the Street Rats' HQ, the new one!" she said with a grin. "Let's bring the party there!"

They began a slow winding route through the city, adding to their numbers with more revellers who joined in as they progressed.

But from her perch, Jasmine was able to see a smaller,

slower procession moving *away* from the noise: a family carrying the sadly familiar body of the undead boy Jalil, who was now at peace. Neither Agrabah nor its people remained entirely unchanged by what had happened. For some people, nothing would ever be the same again.

But a few streets farther on, an old friend came bounding out of the crowd and leaped up on the new sultana, practically knocking her down.

"*RAJAH!*" Jasmine cried, hugging him. The tiger had singed whiskers and still limped a little from when Jafar had injured him. Otherwise he seemed fine and licked her face like a puppy.

After that there was little need to stay on anyone's shoulders; Rajah drew more than enough attention to the sultana, and added to her mystique. She kept one demure hand on his back and waved with the other, looking every inch the sultana despite her bare feet and torn clothes.

By the time they finally made it back to the bread warehouse, it seemed like all of Agrabah was in the streets, partying.

Pareesa appeared out of the shadows and walked nonchalantly next to Morgiana and Duban as if she had always been there. She was smiling but smelled of smoke.

Little Hazan shouted with joy when he saw his friends Shirin and Ahmed safe and sound. He ran up to them, and the three happily danced around the feet of the grown-ups.

"Abu?" Aladdin called out, cupping his hands around his mouth.

He *wasn't* going to worry about his little friend. Abu would be fine wherever he was. If he had left for a free life somewhere in the jungles or at an oasis or something somewhere, so much the better. Aladdin was happy for him. "Abuuuuu?"

Angry monkey chitters rained down upon him from a fierce ball of brown and tan that leaped up and down on top of the warehouse.

Aladdin grinned from ear to ear. Abu crossed his arms, almost like a human, and didn't come down to greet him the way Rajah had Jasmine. He would, Aladdin knew, sulk for a while and keep his distance. Which was fine. As long as he was there.

The Street Rats at home were in full festival mode, pouring drinks into golden cups and handing them out to everyone. A small group of musicians had hastily formed a band and were playing out raucous dance music from a rooftop. Even Widow Gulbahar was lifting her skirts delicately and showing everyone how they *used* to dance in the old days, when music really was music.

But everyone stopped what they were doing and began

cheering wildly when they finally noticed Jasmine. She waved and the crowd only grew louder.

"Congratulations, Sultana," Sohrab said, coming forwards out of the chaos. He bowed his head and dropped to one knee. Amur and Khosrow and Kimiya quickly followed suit, as did Pareesa and Morgiana and the rest of the Street Rats. And then everyone else, side by side, together as one. "Agrabah is yours."

"No," Jasmine said, looking out at the sea of guild leaders, and the thieves, and the genie, and all the people of her city. "Agrabah is *ours.*"

Epilogue

AGRABAH WAS EXHAUSTED after its weeks of punishment, nights of siege, and then excessive partying. To celebrate their re-found freedom, people had stayed out in the streets until dawn, dancing and singing and chatting with old neighbours and new friends. The moon set on the festivities, and the sun rose on the sleepy aftermath.

Duban, Jasmine, Aladdin, the genie and Morgiana eventually made their way back to the palace in the rosy glow of the early sun. Maruf, Shirin and Ahmed, and what seemed like half the children of Agrabah were availing themselves of the old sultan's toys in the next room. Their happy noises contrasted with the thoughtful silence of the five people who had a kingdom to rebuild.

Duban desultorily kicked at *Al Azif*, now a smouldering,

almost unrecognisable heap of paper and ashes.

"There's the lamp," Aladdin suddenly noticed. It lay on the floor, battered and tarnished, the same old piece of brass it was when he had first found it.

What a long time ago that seemed.

Aladdin sighed. Everything he never thought possible had happened... and then everything had returned to normal. Back to the way it was before.

Well, except for the branding, the executions, and what happened to Duban and the entire city, of course. There was all that to deal with.

And *he* was certainly different.

He picked up the lamp and handed it to the genie, who took it with a sad smile.

"What a piece of junk," the genie said. "And *also* not very spacious. I can't believe I stayed there for 10,000 years, even if it *was* cheap rent..."

His voice drifted off, his heart not really in it.

"Yeah. I think I'm done here," he said finally. "Hey, Princess? Remember that thing I told you about travelling the world? Getting away from the place where my people were wiped out?"

"Yes," Jasmine said gently. She guessed what was coming next, even if she didn't like it.

"Think I'm gonna do it. I'm gonna go out and see the

world. Find some snow. Start a new life… as a human. Somehow."

She nodded sadly and took his hands in hers. She marvelled at how quickly she had grown used to someone who was blue… and now he no longer was.

"Thank you for everything. And… I'm so sorry. About everything." She stood on her tiptoes and kissed him on the cheek.

Aladdin came over and clasped his hand. "I'm sorry you're going. I wish we could've got to know each other better. You seem like one of the good guys."

The genie gave a weak smile.

"This is too much," Jasmine said with a sigh. "I… wish Jafar hadn't… I wish I had…"

Aladdin smiled and pushed a stray hair of hers back behind her ear. Like he had longed to from the beginning.

"Wishes are over," he whispered with a sad smile. "Maybe they never *were*, really."

"Genie," Duban suddenly called out. "I'll come with you."

"What?" the genie asked, surprised.

"I can't stay here," Duban said bitterly. "My dad was right. I shouldn't have killed Jafar like that. It… didn't need to be done that way. My own family can barely stand to look at me now."

"Duban, no," Morgiana pleaded. "They're kids! They'll get over it. Stay here. It's all right. We'll get through it together. It was just one mistake."

"It was… a pretty *big* mistake. No, I have to make amends. My own way. I'll come back one day," Duban promised with a sad smile. "When it feels right."

"Stubborn he-goat," Morgiana muttered, sniffing loudly. Duban laughed softly and came forwards, kissing her on the forehead.

"Well, all right then," the genie said cautiously, but sounding happier. "We'll travel the world, escaping our past. Penance buddies! Let's pack it up and go, shorty."

He looked lost for a moment. Perhaps he had tried to summon a rucksack or a suitcase. None appeared. A strange expression came over him… Aladdin recognised it after a moment; it was very much like when you're in a dream and know you're in a dream and feel like you *should* be able to do anything that you want… but you can't.

Finally, the genie just shook his head and headed for the door.

"Hate long goodbyes," he said. "Ten thousand years of watching you guys live and die will do that. So… bye."

"I hope you find peace," Jasmine whispered.

Duban gave Aladdin a little salute and bowed deeply to Jasmine.

"Sultana," he whispered. And then he followed the genie out.

And that was it. They were gone.

Morgiana watched them for a moment, trying not to sniffle.

"Those kids are tearing up *my* future office," she finally growled, stomping off to break the news to Maruf and the kids.

Jasmine sighed and walked to the balcony to look out over her city. The time for wishes might be over, but so was the time for tears.

Aladdin came over to stand next to her and put his hand on her shoulder.

Together they watched the crowds slowly disperse and the still-smouldering fires smoke.

"This is going to take a long time to fix," she said.

"Yes, but you're up to the task. You're going to be a great sultana. You understand better than anyone now that there are *two* cities in Agrabah. You've really seen poverty and understand it. You've experienced unlimited power and now know how to avoid its traps. And you have us... you have the Street Rats for when you forget."

"I'll make Agrabah the greatest city in the world," Jasmine said softly. "And the Street Rats and the guilds and the other community leaders will be as much a part of my council as the old ministers and viziers. Who it's time to replace anyway."

"Yeah, especially the grand vizier," Aladdin said, trying not to shiver. He shook himself. "All right. Agrabah day one. Let's start. So are *all* the Street Rats going to be on your council? Even Maruf?"

Jasmine laughed. "He might get an honourary, advisory role in thanks for his support in the rebellion. But I already told Morgiana I'm making her my grand vizier. She is one smart lady... I think she'll be able to handle it very well."

Aladdin wondered if his old friend would mature into someone who could resist the urge to stab anyone who disagreed with her.

"What about *me*?" He pouted. "I'm smart. I'm tough. And I've been with you from the beginning!"

"You're going to be too busy, darling," she said, patting his hand distractedly. "As prince you'll have other responsibilities and duties. But believe me, they will be just as important."

Aladdin opened his mouth to argue and then stopped.

"Wait... what did you say?"

Jasmine just kissed him.

Aladdin grinned and wrapped her in his arms. *Prince,* he could, at this point, take or leave.

The rest of his life with Jasmine, however... that was worth everything.

Twisted Tales

Unravel new twists in the tales that you already know and love in this series of thrilling novels.

Reflection

What if Mulan had to travel to the Underworld?

Still disguised as the soldier Ping, Mulan faces
a deadly battle in a mysterious world as she
tries to save the life of Captain Shang.

Part of Your World

What if Ariel had never defeated Ursula?

With evil Ursula ruling Prince Eric's kingdom on
land, it's up to Ariel – now the voiceless queen of
Atlantica – to overthrow the murderous villain.

As Old As Time

What if Belle's mother cursed the beast?

Belle makes an intriguing discovery about
her own mother as she starts to unravel the
secrets about the Beast's curse.

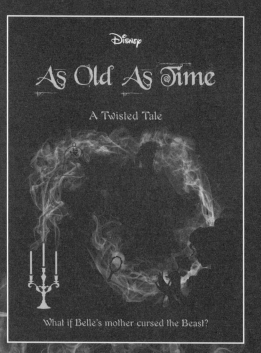

Mirror, Mirror

What if the Evil Queen poisoned the prince?

Can Snow defeat an enemy who will stop
at nothing to retain her power… including
going after the ones Snow loves?

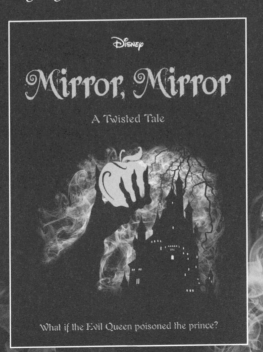

Let It Go

What if Anna and Elsa never knew each other?

When Elsa, Queen of Arendelle, remembers a girl from her past and mysterious powers reveal themselves, she embarks on a journey to find the missing princess.

Straight on Till Morning

What if Wendy went to Never Land with Captain Hook?

When Captain Hook reveals his sinister
plans for Never Land, can Wendy and Tinker Bell
save Peter Pan and the place he calls home?